This is the story of a magnificent horse-stealing raid led by Joe Cowbone: how it was planned; why it was planned; how it turned out.

It is also the story of a family split up in the turmoil of the Indian Wars: the Comanche mother, Little Brown Girl, and her pathetic faith in the strength of an old love; the elusive father, a white trader who had vanished many years before; and the son, rebellious Joe Cowbone.

It is, most of all, the story of Joe Cowbone's desire to become a man. The white man's way was alien and difficult. Yet it was no longer possible to take the Indian way. How Joe resolved his dilemma, and how he groped and finally fought his way to manhood, form the substance of this engrossing novel.

Benjamin Capps was born in Dundee, Texas, in 1922, and grew up on a ranch in west Texas, where he rode horseback to a one-teacher school. He graduated from high school at the age of fifteen and attended Texas Tech at Lubbock in 1938-39. After a hitch in the CCC's, he worked as a surveyor and truck driver in Colorado and Texas until entering the Army Air Force in 1942. He flew forty-one missions as navigator of a B-24 against such Japanese islands as Truk and Iwo Jima. After the war, he studied literature, psychology, and philosophy at the University of Texas, graduating Phi Beta Kappa, in 1948, and receiving his M.A. in 1949. After teaching two years at Northeastern State College in Oklahoma, he began working as a machinist and tool and die maker while writing fiction in his spare time. *The White Man's Road* is his sixth published novel.

Charter Westerns from Benjamin Capps

THE WHITE MAN'S ROAD

BENJAMIN CAPPS

C

CHARTER BOOKS, NEW YORK

THE WHITE MAN'S ROAD

A Charter Book / published by arrangement with
Harper & Row

PRINTING HISTORY
Harper & Row edition published 1969
Ace edition published 1972
Charter edition / April 1986

ISBN: 0-441-88549-7

Charter Books are published by The Berkley Publishing Group,
200 Madison Avenue, New York, New York 10016.
PRINTED IN THE UNITED STATES OF AMERICA

CONTENTS

1

GREAT EAGLE'S BIG FEAST

JOE COWBONE and Slow Tom Armstedt were thinking about going to Great Eagle's feast. Joe was dubious. It did not exactly seem like a good idea. But then a feast is a feast. At least you get fed. Or so he thought.

Great Eagle was known as a man who hung around the white soldiers too much, not dangerous particularly, also not to be taken seriously; though rumor had it that he had been known to steal bows and shields and holy things and sell them to the soldiers for souvenirs. The man's wife had recently run away and left him, and the feast seemed to have some uncertain connection with her departure. It was not clear whether Great Eagle expected the celebration to entice her back or whether he expected it to demonstrate that he was glad to be free. He was supposed to have acquired some sheep from the Caddoes, these to be the food of the feast.

They were talking about it at the Red Store, and one of the loungers asked another one, "Were you invited too?"

"Of course I was," the other one said. "Hell! Everyone is invited. No exceptions. Bring your dogs." But he was laughing.

Joe Cowbone walked out of the store with Slow Tom. To the west, the sun hung low over the Mountains of the Wichitas, those peaks which were the center and the heart of the reservation. Joe considered whether his own personal appearance was suitable to attend a gathering—in silence, since a Comanche man shouldn't appear to worry about his looks; if he had some fancy dress or ornament, all right, but if not, he should show himself above it by ignoring it. He had combed his braids that morning and replaited them; they hung down either side of his chest to his waist, their ends bound with twine. He wore a dark cloth vest, but no shirt. His arms looked clean. His dark-gray trousers did not appear particularly soiled. His moccasins were not badly worn. Actually, had he been trying to dress up, he would have added little; perhaps his silver belt buckle and some colored cloth instead of twine on his braids.

He thought that his friend probably was not concerned, even in silence, with appearance. Slow Tom wore white man's shirt and trousers and hard shoes and, topping his braided hair, a black felt hat, which he always wore level.

Joe said, "Maybe there would be a bunch of people milling around and gabbing. We could look things over, then leave if we wanted to."

Slow Tom said, "We could get my old lady to fix us up a big feed." He meant his mother, Mrs. Armstedt.

They sauntered along the wide road and Joe mulled it over. Slow Tom was leaving it up to him, but he was undecided, reluctant. He had lately become accustomed to facing a certain long-time vague dissatisfaction with himself and saying that he should do this or that. Only a few days before, he had told himself that he should visit more, make friends with more kinds of people. The trouble with his advice to himself was that when he tried to follow it he usually found himself in an embarrassing or awkward position. Great Eagle's reputation was bad. The feast would probably turn out to be a fiasco. But he was irritated at his own reluctance. Slow Tom would never make such an issue of it. And they could always leave. Finally he said casually, "Aw, let's walk up to Great Eagle's. He might have a crowd by this time."

Slow Tom shrugged and grinned. They headed north across the sandy flats. Great Eagle's lodge was past Caddo Crossing about a mile from the fort, sitting by itself on a slight knoll overlooking Beef Creek. The dwelling consisted of a large piece of canvas tied over an irregular arrangement of poles. Behind it stood an old wagon with two wheels missing, its front end down on the ground like a cow trying to rise, and it seemed to serve as a storage of sorts, for under it were thrown various tools, tangles of wire, pieces of harness, some barrel staves and other items. Over all this grew a pecan tree, and another one in front of the dwelling.

As they came up they saw little evidence of a celebration. Great Eagle sat on the ground with an Indian couple named Odum. A large cook fire blazed. Around in the back, tied to one of the wagon wheels by a rope on its neck, lay a large sheep. It rested placidly on the dusty ground, its head erect, its feet folded under. But as they came within speaking distance, they saw an interesting object in Great Eagle's hand: a bottle.

Great Eagle sprang up toward them. "Hey!" he cried. "Come for the feast, did you? We're getting ready." He was a man of medium build with rounding shoulders, wearing bulky shirt and trousers that did not fit. He wore his hair hacked off like an Apache and had a habit of grinning widely and staring intently at a person as if his grin demanded an answer. Now he seemed unsteady on his feet. He held the bottle by its neck, like a short club.

"What you got there?" Joe asked him.

He flourished it on high and said the English words: "Doctor Smith's Amazing Tonic!" Then he said, "Good for what ails you!"

It was a clear round bottle with a label, two-thirds full of amber liquid.

"Let's have a snort," Slow Tom suggested.

Great Eagle looked hurt. "After we eat," he said. "We're going to have a big dance after the big feast."

The Odums looked up meekly and did not rise. They were a poorly dressed man and woman, who sat on the ground with their arms hugging their knees.

Great Eagle yelled toward the trees along the creek a hundred paces away. "Wood! Hey, wood! Hurry up, you lazy devils!" He staggered back under the pecan tree and said to them, "Kids! What are they good for? They're all lazy. Good to eat you out of house and home. Good to squat right in the path instead of in the bushes. That's what."

With a wave of the hand out in the general direction west and south, he said, "They think they'll hurt my feelings and stay away from my feast. I know it. I'm not blind. I know what they say about me. It's all right. I don't claim to be something big up on a stick. I know my place. But I've got friends. I could have white soldiers at this feast if I wanted to. Black and white. I've got more soldier friends than any damned Indian on this reservation. They can get on their high horse and see if I care. Isn't that right?" he demanded, grinning.

Joe smiled a little at him, and inwardly at himself for having given thought to his appearance. It was true as he had thought that he and Slow Tom could leave whenever they wanted to. We should go right now, he thought. Vaguely he anticipated some unpleasantness or indecency from their host. The hope of a taste of liquor did not make it worth it. But he could put his finger on no good reason.

Three boys came out of the trees dragging wood up toward the fire. Great Eagle yelled at them, "Hurry! Don't take all day! Here are all these people hungry waiting for the feast. On the fire! On the fire! It won't burn out there on the ground. Break it up a little!

"Listen, you kids! I want a big fire. Get busy and stop playing around! Wood! More wood! Lots of wood!"

To the Odums he said, "Kids are all alike. That boy of mine is just like those of yours. If you was to ask me to pick out which one was mine, I couldn't tell you. They got no gratitude about them. They like my wife. Got no gratitude.

"She packs up and takes the girls and takes off. I ask her what's she doing and what's got into her. You know what she says? She grunts. Grunts! Would you believe it? I'm her husband and I'm asking her a plain question, and she grunts like a pig. I say to her, Grunt. Don't talk. What do I care? I say to her, I'll give you a kick in the butt to help you on your way. He! He!"

He looked at his visitors, frowning with a sudden wave of sadness. "Do I ask any consideration? I know I'm low down. I'm lower than a mangy dog. I'm lower down than a snake belly. I'm a Snake Indian for sure. I don't deny it. What's wrong with that? I was born that way. At least I'm good-natured." He turned and moved with uncertain but deliberate steps to the front of his irregular tipi, shrugged aside the flap and disappeared inside.

To Joe it was ludicrous. He told himself that it was nothing else and that he was foolish to feel involved or feel the need to escape. He exchanged with Slow Tom glances of amusement and asked, "You think he'll give us a drink?"

"Well, he talked like he would. You ever have any of that? That Doctor Smith's Amazing Tonic?"

"No. I guess it's crazy water, all right. But it looks suspicious."

"I wouldn't mind trying it though," Slow Tom said.

Great Eagle came out of his dwelling with the bottle still in his hand. From the way he was working his mouth, it appeared that he had retired a moment to take a drink in private. "Enjoy life!" he said. "Now's the time for jokes and fun! We don't live forever, do we? Today we're going to enjoy ourselves. Listen, folks, I'm going to tell you the funniest story you ever heard. He! He! I mean it! It's true too. He! He!"

He thrust out his empty hand toward Joe and asked, "Do you smell something? Do I smell funny any way to you?" He waved the hand in front of the faces of the Odums. "Do you think I smell funny? Do you detect anything?" They shook their heads in solemn perplexity.

"Well, listen. I'll tell you the story about that. He! He! You'll die! I know the joke's on me, but a joke's a joke. Isn't it?

"One time I was helping the soldiers from the guard-house chop weeds, see. They have this big hole out there full of water and all kinds of nasty stuff. Those white men are smart. They do those things on purpose. They have all these little tunnels like prairie dogs been digging under there, and all that putrid stuff runs out from those little tunnels into that big hole. We took the cover off so we could get the weeds around the edge better. Now, watch out! There's a place for a man to be careful! He! He! He'll catch it if he's not careful. But I didn't want them to think I was scared, so I paid no attention. You guessed it! That's it! I fell in the hole.

"He! He!" He gestured wildly and laughed, shaking all over, his chopped-off hair flying in disarray.

12

"I went under and got it in my eyes and ears. And in my mouth when I tried to talk. The sides were too slick to catch hold of, you see. My fingers just slipped. All those soldiers teased me about leaving me in. I smelled too bad! I was ruined anyway! He! He! They've got a great sense of humor. I told them it wasn't so bad down in there as they might think.

"And that's the truth. You'd think you couldn't stand it, the stink and all, but once you're in it and gone plumb under once, you're surprised. You can stand it. I remember when I first hit with a big splash thinking that was all, brother, I was ruined. But no. After you get soaked in it, it can't get any worse. Even the smell. The smell wasn't half as bad at first as you would imagine just thinking about it. Not strong. Only it was strange. Not strong, only unusual.

"I laughed and they laughed. I don't mind soldiers having fun. They said, What will you give us? He! He! We've got to go to the barracks, they said. We'll be seeing you, Great Eagle! You talk about a sense of humor!

"I couldn't scramble out. Finally a soldier, a buffalo soldier, stuck a hoe handle down there for me to get hold of. Some of them pulled and I got out. They all ran off holding their noses.

"I went down to the creek and got in deep water and soaked out my ears and hair and everything. Then I went out and rolled in the hot sand, and went back in the deep water and soaked good again. That's when I began to see that strange smell had staying power. Not real strong, but unusual, and if you ever smelled it, you couldn't forget it. Just funny, you know. I would run around and get sweaty and try to sweat it out of my pores, then jump in the creek. But I couldn't get rid of it. Sometimes I wake up in the middle of the night and I can smell it. I don't know if it was caused by vomit or what. Not strong, just peculiar. Like you started with puke, you know, and it changed once, it soured; then it changed again, not sour, but rancid like, something that wouldn't go away. I don't know."

He was solemn a moment, then remembered that it was a joke and began his "He! He!" louder than necessary either to express mirth or communicate it to his guests.

Joe's interest in the bottle had diminished on account of his reaction to the man, who seemed both fascinating and repulsive. For some reason it reminded him of a time he had watched a chicken snake trying to swallow a horned frog; the snake had tried eagerly to swallow it one minute, had tried violently to cast it from his throat the next. Why he should be reminded of such a comparison he did not know, and he did not want to figure it out.

Great Eagle turned again to the boys and the fire. "Big fire, kids! Put it all on! Lay it on there! Say, break that up a little! Don't you know how to build a fire?" The fire was now raging. They could feel the heat fifteen paces away.

Great Eagle started back to his dwelling and Slow Tom, moving fast for him, followed and took his arm. "Let us have a taste of that."

Great Eagle started to object.

"Just a taste," Slow Tom said. "Have you got any more?"

The man studied the two younger men, pulled the cork out with a *thunk* and offered it, not releasing his own hold. "Just a sip," he said. "Remember the big dance. That's enough."

Joe filled his mouth and tasted it suspiciously. It was sweet and hot with pepper. When he swallowed he could feel it all the way down. It seemed filthy, more so than any strong drink he had tasted before.

Great Eagle retired into the privacy of his dwelling to take his drink, and when he reappeared he began to yell at the boys. "Come on! Get away from that fire! Come on here!" He made his way around to the broken wagon, squatted down and began to fumble among the junk under it. He clumsily brought out a single-bit ax, one of his hands being of no use to him since it was occupied by gripping the neck of his bottle.

He went directly to the sheep tied at the wheel and began to strike at its head with the butt of the ax. He missed twice, for the weapon was heavy to use in one hand, then he hit the beast a glancing blow on the nose. It became excited, jerking against the rope and trying to rise. Great Eagle cried, "Hold still, you devil! Why don't you kids hold this sheep still? Get hold there!" He struck wildly. It seemed that he would surely harm one of the boys or cut his own foot off. "Hold him still! Grab him!" By luck he landed a blow at the top of the neck and the animal was stunned, sinking and twitching. Great Eagle methodically beat in the top of its head with the blunt end of the ax.

He chopped the rope in two against the wheel rim, dropped the ax, and began to tug on the rope to drag the carcass. "Grab hold, kids!" he said. "Pull! The legs! The legs! Come on! What's the matter with you? Scared a dead sheep will bite you? Get hold and pull! Come on!"

The Odums had risen but they stood in uncertainty. Joe and Slow Tom were willing to help but saw little opportunity. With much tugging, grunting, waving of his bottle, cursing and staggering, Great Eagle maneuvered the carcass around to the fire. "Onto the fire!" he screamed. "Pull! Get it on the fire! Push! Fire won't hurt you! On there! Push! On!" With great effort they tumbled the dead sheep rump over head into the fire. The coals were scattered, but the sheep lay in the middle.

"Hey! Let's skin it," Joe said.

Great Eagle almost fell as he retreated from the blaze. "Don't want the juices to get out."

"Aren't you going to gut it?"

"Gut it?"

Slow Tom said, "That's going to be burnt all over and ruined."

"It's the old-timey way," Great Eagle assured them. "Old-timey. I'll show you. Wait and see. You peel it off when the fire goes down and all that good meat inside. It's old-timey."

The Odums sat back down and gazed with suspicion at the proceedings. They had not said a word.

The fire had diminished slightly as the bulk of the sheep was thrown on it. Then the white smoke began to billow out of it in all directions, bringing an acrid stench. One of the boys came flailing out of the smoke, coughing and crying. "Get out of it!" Great Eagle told him. "Look at him! What's the matter with you? Use a little sense!"

Flames raced over the wool of the sheep, darkening it. Alternately the flames leaped up and the smoke puffed out to hide it. From where he stood, Joe could see that the sun had fallen below the Mountains of the Wichitas. They stood out stark and stern with the sunlight behind them. The smoke built erratically to a pier, higher and higher, thrusting up between him and the mountains, until at last the light of the falling sun struck it, turning it pink.

"I like to see that smoke," Great Eagle asserted. "And that smell too. I'll guess they'll all know they're missing the feast. They think it hurts me; it hurts them. No feast! They can go hungry! What do I care? I hope my wife sees that and she can think whatever she wants to. Let her go away! Go away, you bitch! What do you think?"

He took another large drink from the bottle, now oblivious to the impoliteness of not offering it to his guests.

"Enjoy life! Let's have fun, boys! Joke! Laugh and fun!" He seemed insistent that they should shout and tell loud stories and laugh and he seemed desperate to find a way to make them do it.

He is not like the snake and the horned frog, Joe thought, but like a mad snake who has turned back on a part of himself and has attacked himself and struggles to escape and pursue at the same time. He was on the verge of saying to Slow Tom, Let's go; we can find something better to do than watch this fool.

But his eyes were drawn to a sight of which Great Eagle was not aware, the smoke from the ruining meat rising to mingle with the sun. The tops of the mountains molded the fingers of the sun. The name, the Wichita Mountains, carried no connotation of ownership; if the Comanches had anything left of the wide earth, they owned these mountains. And the mountains owned them. A man might forget the pervasive nature of the Earth Mother, but there in the granite peaks she asserted herself. Her heights were stark and forceful in the red evening sky. She accepted the sun and hid him, and at the edge of their mingling the light came out eastward and touched the smoke. It seemed to Joe that the rising column did not merely reach the sun, rather that it purposely found the sun, for at that point it billowed and spread into a drifting bank.

Great Eagle was addressing first one then another. "Jokes! Time for jokes and fun! Come on! I tell you one on my wife. Not on me. Jokes are on other people besides me! On everybody, that's who!

"I've always had my white friends for soldiers. For friends. Whites are great soldiers. They have money. They have riches. They know all about important things. Those people out there, they think they're smart and they look down on me, but do they have white friends like me? Nobody!

"So one time my white brother and me, we made trades and drank together, and he says, 'I need a woman.' So I says, 'There's my wife up there asleep in my tipi. Go on up there.' He! He! He says, 'What does she say about it?' I says, 'She's asleep. Just go on in and make yourself at home.' He! He! He! 'Don't say anything; just go ahead and try it.' So he did."

Great Eagle was caught by such a gust of laughter that he lost his balance first one way, then another, stumbled over his own feet, and fell to his knees. He struggled up, pushed the hair out of his face, carefully gripping the bottle, and went on. The small boys were watching him with their round dark eyes, and Joe thought, I wish he would fall down and hit his head on a rock.

"Did she know the difference? No! A week later I did it again and she didn't guess! Didn't know! Three times! Four times! All four different times! It was some of my soldier brothers instead of me! The joke was on her!"

The carcass of the sheep had made many hissing and oozing sounds. It was a black heap lying on the coals, enveloped in flames. The only part Joe could recognize was one hoof thrust out.

Little smoke rose now. The bottom reaches of the bank of smoke far up the sky were dark, and only hints of the sun's touch showed through.

Great Eagle downed all the remainder of the liquor in large gulps, but held onto the bottle. "I says to her, 'Shut up your moaning and wailing, I tell you!' She says, 'But I thought it was you!' Thought it was me! Get that! Thought it was me! What a sap! Kept on saying, 'But I thought it was you.' I says, 'Shut up your pissing and moaning or I'll give you something to piss and moan about!' "

His voice rose with a strident tone and Joe listened with resentment and dread, staring down at the trees along the creek, now become indistinct in the darkness, avoiding the shameful sight of the man and the faces of the other listeners.

"Sleeping in the brush! I says, 'I won't have it!' Made her do what I say! Taking the girls off and sleeping in the brush! I'll bring my brothers any time I get ready day or night! That's what I'll do! I says, 'Get these kids out of here! My friends don't want kids hanging around.' I says, 'Be nice to my friend and I'll be back after while.' 'I'll go with you,' she says. 'Are you crazy, woman?' I says. 'Lay down!' 'I don't know him! I don't even know him!' 'Take your clothes off and lay down,' I says, 'or you're going to catch it!' She says, 'Right now? Let us wait till dark. I'll do it in the dark.' 'If you don't get your clothes off, I'll take your hide off! Lay down on your back!' 'Stay here,' she says. 'Are you crazy, woman? He don't want me here! All I ask for is a little pleasure and comfort for my friend. If you don't do exactly right, you wait and see! Just shut up! Don't moan! Don't say anything! Just do what he wants!' Hardheaded, stubborn bitch of a woman!"

He became less coherent in his speech and did not laugh, nor even seem to be speaking to his guests.

"That's the way! They don't care! Where would we be without the benefits? Whereabouts? Rations! Clothes!

Where would she be? All they can say what they want to say. Who has the road? There all of them talk about me!"

He stumbled a moment, then sat down with great deliberation. For a minute he spoke clearly and carefully. "I think it was the unusual smell. Very strange. It always came back. Can't make it go away. A thing like that gets on you, and you have it all your life. I think she noticed it. Got to sniffing it. Then she looked down on me. A very out-of-the-way smell. Peculiar. Peculiar."

Suddenly Slow Tom asked, "Where's the Odums?"

They had gone without a word, and two of the boys. The other boy was squatting beside the flap of the irregular tipi.

Joe walked over to the dying fire and kicked at the one hoof that was thrust out. It broke off. What had been the carcass of the sheep was now a black cinder. Great Eagle had fallen back on the ground and lay sprawled motionless.

Joe approached the boy and asked, "Do you know where your mother is?"

The boy said nothing. It was too dark to see clearly, but he could sense the suspicion and mistrust in the small figure. He asked, "Can you go to your mother if you want to?"

"Yes." The boy's voice was surprisingly clear and assured, and contained a kind of independent integrity.

Joe walked with Slow Tom down toward Caddo Crossing in the darkness. How he hated the unconscious man back there and felt sorry for him! The frustrating thing about it was that it should be merely funny. Why should he care? Sure, a white man might accept Great Eagle's friendship, and use him with contempt, and say, "There's an Indian." But a white man that stupid deserved contempt himself. He was too sensitive about it, he knew. Great Eagle was one man and nothing more.

Finally Slow Tom said, "That was quite a feast, wasn't it?" His words seemed tentative and noncommittal.

Joe replied in kind. "Yeah, and that big dance afterwards. Wasn't that something?" He knew that behind their cynical words they were trying to decide whether they had anything to resolve between them.

"You know," Slow Tom said, "I think I really could smell him, that funny smell he was talking about."

He couldn't tell how he meant it. He said, "That was the sheep burning you smelled."

They both got to laughing. The remark had not been so funny, but they laughed at all of it, including themselves, without explanation, slapping each other on the shoulder. Joe thought that someone listening to them would have thought them drunk or hysterical. After a minute they became quiet. It was a relief to have a good laugh with a fellow like Slow Tom. They walked through the darkness back toward the Armstedts'.

Slow Tom asked, "What do you say to going over on Blue Beaver Creek tomorrow?"

"I'd just as soon," he said.

2

IMPOSSIBLE NEWS OF
WHITE BUFFALO

IN A CAMP beside Blue Beaver Creek in the southern edge of the mountains Joe Cowbone was playing poker with Bill Nappy, Spike Chanakut and Slow Tom Armstedt. They sat cross-legged on a canvas tarp that was stamped USA, and were shaded from the midmorning sun by a thick layer of cut brush supported by crooked posts. It was the place where Mrs. Longwater cut up meat and tanned hides. The canvas had spots from grease and blood. Large green flies lighted on it and walked about tasting the canvas, searching for a place to lay eggs.

The cards, owned by Bill Nappy, were worn, some with corners missing, and with many marks on their backs. The players covered them with their hands as they were dealt and looked at them secretively. The queen of diamonds was missing, but they all knew it, and what was fair for one was fair for all. They had no idea what a queen is, nor what a diamond is—even Joe Cowbone, who could speak English—but the place of the card in the deck, its power and limits, they knew well. The pictures on the cards had no white man's meanings and were now only designs of faded color.

They played with plum pits and kept strict account, for though none of them had any money, they had expectations. First, there was a vague scheme of long standing to make friends with some of the Carlisle boys and entice them to gamble, then cheat them out of their money. Someday, when they did this, they would first divide all the earnings equally, then pay off the honest gambling debts they owed each other. Then, as a more immediate expectation, Slow Tom Armstedt had an uncle who knew some white cattlemen who hired men to build fences. They paid good wages and might need one man or two men. This was becoming an interesting possibility, for Spike Chanakut was into Slow Tom for a total of nineteen dollars.

"What you got to know to work on fences?" Bill Nappy asked.

Slow Tom said, "Nothing. They say you've got to be seventeen years old. That's all." He was stolid and casual as usual. "I told them I'm twenty-eight, and I've got this friend named Joe Cowbone who is seventeen, and he would make a good fence worker."

"Yes, you bastard, you're ancient," Joe said. "It's like that freighting job we had that time; you're scared to work for them unless you've got me along to do the talking."

Slow Tom went on, "I told them I know another fellow named Nappy, but he is only fourteen."

Bill Nappy said, "Well, I'm better off than Spike. He can't count. He may be fourteen or he may be twenty-seven for all he knows."

"Get in the frigging pot," Spike said. "Maybe I can't count, but nobody cheats me at gambling. Looks to me like soon as I get a streak going, all you want to do is sit around and joke."

It was a worn-out taunt they had, to accuse one another of being younger than they were, not particularly funny, Joe thought. They were all about the same age. Not that it made any difference, as long as it stayed between the four of them. If others were around, it could become exasperating, for it created the problem of keeping it a joke and making clear that it made no difference and still not leaving a false idea of one's age. Why should a man have to say, "I'm twenty-seven," as if he was afraid someone would think he was ten years younger?

Spike Chanakut was a skinny young man with a big beak of a nose. He never wore anything but a breechclout and moccasins, except in the coldest weather, and his lack of clothes looked comfortable on this hot day. The others wore white man's trousers, and Slow Tom wore also, as usual, a shirt buttoned up to the top and his black hat exactly square on his head. Now Spike was getting excited. When he found himself with the winning hand, he would rear forward on his bony knees and slap it down before them.

Bill Nappy had to keep saying, "Be careful with my cards. Don't mash flies with my cards."

Joe watched them with amusement. Slow Tom Armstedt was not dull-witted, as some people thought, but took his own good time in whatever he did. When Slow Tom dealt, Spike Chanakut would say, "Come on, deal! Let's have them while they're hot!" Spike was becoming even more careful in concealing the backs of his marvelous hands. Slow Tom, the loser, was not as concerned as he might have been. Joe realized that the man had a kind of an ace in the hole: he might see about the fencing job or he might not, and if he didn't, the plum pits might turn out to be nothing but plum pits.

Slow Tom Armstedt stopped his leisurely dealing and asked Joe, "Is that your mother down yonder?"

Joe followed the man's gaze down to where some children were playing under the elms on the bank of the creek and saw, with surprise, his mother standing, beckoning. "No," he said. "My old lady never comes down here."

"Looks like her to me," Slow Tom said.

"Deal the cards! Deal the cards!" Spike Chanakut said.

He could not imagine why his mother had come. She had no business with these people. His impulse was to get up and go to her, out of curiosity, but he did not want to appear too much concerned. It was not that he was ashamed of his mother or worried about the opinions of his friends, but only that a man ought to show that his business is important and not run too quickly to find out what a woman has to say.

Slow Tom Armstedt said, "That's her, all right, Joe. I guess she wants to see you."

"Are you going to deal the damned cards, you ass hole?" Spike Chanakut asked.

Joe looked around and saw that his mother was sending one of the boys running toward him. The boy was already yelling, "Joe! Hey, Joe!" He began to study his hand, hiding the backs of the cards from the others.

The boy, panting behind him, began to pat on his shoulder. "Joe? Joe Cowbone! Hey, Joe Cowbone!"

He said, "Boy, you want me to cut your ears off?"

"But, Joe Cowbone! She wants you!"

"You want me to cut your hair off and make a rope out of it?"

The boy was grinning widely and pointing.

He said, "Deal me out." He got up and grabbed the giggling, nearly naked boy and carried him under his arm a few steps, then set him down to scurry off.

His mother, her sturdy form erect, her shoulders back, her head held proudly, waited for him. As he came near, he saw that she had an unusual expression on her face, a kind of beaming serenity. Her broad cheeks were lifted in a suppressed smile, and she did not move her shining eyes, but seemed to devour him with them.

"What is it?" he asked. Any reluctance or irritation had gone out of him because of her appearance. It was clear that she was brimming with some great thing that pleased her.

"Joe! Oh, Joe!" she said.

He came directly in front of her and repeated, "What is it?"

"We must go home now," she said. "A big thing has happened. A very big thing." Her voice was lower than usual and it wavered, as if she were going to laugh or cry.

She gave no more explanation and, seeing that the children were near, he took it for granted that it was a thing she could not explain in front of others, but a private matter. And she would not have come this far for a small matter.

"I'll be ready in a minute," he said.

He went back to the brush arbor and told them, "I've decided to go home. I'll see you in a couple of days."

"What's the matter?" Bill Nappy asked. "Have you got to do what your mother says?"

He swung his foot and made Bill duck. He said, "She brought me a message. I have to see about some important business."

"You owe me two bits," Spike Chanakut said.

"Keep account of it," he said. "I'll be seeing you."

His mother had already begun walking back up the trail beside Blue Beaver Creek. He went after her, walking easily as if he were in no hurry to catch her. His curiosity was strongly aroused. He could not remember even having seen her looking exactly as she had this day, nor could he conceive of anything that could have brought it about.

His feelings for her were such that she had infinite power over him. In her presence his thinking was different, as if he were indeed only seventeen. She had been a standard of beauty, of loyalty, of mercy, of generosity. His feelings for her he might forget, as he had a thousand times, for she was as easy to forget as the earth, but as patient in her waiting, as pervasive, as unforgettable.

It seemed that she was one of the unchangeable things, that she had never changed in any way and never would. In all his years of existence, he had not seen her change. It was only in a rational sense that he knew she must have grown older, and he had once said to himself, surprised at the conclusion: "Back then, when I first remember her, she must have been a young woman! No older than I am now!" That was a startling truth about her, and there were others, but they did not alter her essential nature.

In later years he had seen occasionally that she could be petty, that she could argue in a childish way with another woman over a side of rancid bacon or over who got the sack when a sack of flour was divided. She could speak foolishly without thinking, could gossip with small-minded women who loved scandal, could be troubled lest the same women were talking about her behind her back. But the most important thing that could be said about these glimpses of her was that they were not like her. She was not that way at all.

For years he had found differences with her because she wanted to rule him. He should do this or that. He should make friends with this influential man. He ought to work more. He ought not to go around with wild young men, or gamble, or drink. He should tell her where he is going. He ought not to stay out all night. She might tell him not to go out, then after he had gone out, paying her no attention, she might forget it or she might fuss at him about it. He never knew what she might do. But behind every sharp word was the certainty that she would forgive him. Behind any difference was the knowledge that she would give her life for him. He might disobey her or neglect her or see at one moment that she was small and human, but altogether she was as far beyond disobedience or neglect as the earth is, and as little subject to blame.

She had two faces, one open and quickly responsive to the people around her. She could sing or joke or answer teasing with a flash of her eyes, and she could be disagreeing, and she could be eagerly working, saying, "Come on, let's do so and so." "Isn't it going well?" "What shall we do next?" When she wore this face she was speaking, answering, quite alive. The other face was closed and secret, sullen. The bulk of her features would be set and immovable, like a stone outcrop on a hill, darkening under a cloud. She would stare a long time at the horizon. She might answer a question briefly or not at all. Sometimes she would look down into her cupped hands, saying nothing, her face inscrutable. When he was younger, when he lived by her mood from minute to minute, it had been sad to see his mother look that way. It had been worse than any harsh word. He didn't know whether she fell into that impassive silence less in recent years, or whether he only noticed it less.

But he had never seen her look quite as she had this day. It was as if she had too much inside her to speak. She appeared as he imagined a person might after seeing a great vision.

The creek beside which they walked had pools of water scattered up and down its sandy bed. It was shaded by pecan and elm trees, and the still air was humid and hot. A smell of damp decaying wood came from the creek bottom. The path, winding in the edge of the trees, had rank dry grass and weeds of summer along it, so that when he caught up to her he had no room to walk beside her. She walked fast. He knew that she was aware that he was behind her. Finally he asked, "What is it, Mother?"

She stopped and the strange look was still on her face. "Joe," she said, "my little boy!"

He frowned at her and waited.

"If you could have anything you wanted—the very best thing you can think of—what would you wish for?"

She was so sincere that he laughed and said, "A hundred dollars."

She beamed and closed her eyes and shook her head, like a small girl playing games.

"The fastest race horse in the world?"

She shook her head.

"Why did you come after me if you're not going to tell me? I don't think it's anything."

Tears glistened in her eyes when she opened them. "Son, what little things you ask for! He's come back, Joe! He's come back! White Buffalo has come back to us!"

What in the name of heaven could the woman be talking about? It was impossible. The name White Buffalo raised varying and contradictory impressions. First, he thought of him as a man out of the far past, the long ago free time. All the men of middle age or older, whom he knew, were also of that time, but because he knew them now and could see that they were ordinary men, they did not have that legendary quality. White Buffalo was one he had heard stories about when he was a child. Since that time he had been surprised now and then that a person had never heard of White Buffalo, and he understood that it was not only the fact that Comanches had been scattered in separate bands, but also that the man was not so famous as he imagined. Still the aura of legend remained. It was as if his mother had said, "Old Man Coyote has come to live with us." Also within this same first impression was a mixture of white man's thinking, like some of the foolishness the Carlisle boys told children about a Mother Goose.

It could not possibly be true, and he said to his mother, "I don't understand."

"There's nothing to understand," she said. "It's true. You father has come back to us."

"White Buffalo?"

"Yes."

He had an impression out of the misty era of first memory. He knew it because he remembered it clearly and not because anyone had told him. He was sitting on the knees of a large man. The man was playing, bouncing him, jerking his knees apart and pretending to drop him. He himself laughed and clung to the knees. It was fun. The man spoke in a deep voice to him and laughed. How the man was dressed, or where they were, or what the man's name was—these were not a part of the memory. Beyond the play and the large warm laughing person lay only one general truth: the man was his father. He knew that this had been his understanding in that moment, and he believed it was his earliest memory.

Then, beyond the aura of legend and the one unsupported memory, were other more reasonable things he had heard about a man White Buffalo, incomprehensibly a white man, a Comanche by choice. He had come as a trader and had stayed as a brother, fellow warrior against the Utes and Jicarillas. He had been a crack shot, a good rider, a good hunter, a favorite because of his good humor. A white man, no less! Yet not at all in the same sense as the white men who now came among them on the reservation. More like a Mexican is a Mexican. They said of Bill Nappy's mother that she was a Mexican, but she was clearly a Comanche.

He was trying to make sense of his mother's outrageous announcement. Not a joke. It couldn't be that. Maybe a serious game of some kind. A vision. But all of that was no good.

Her broad face was shiny and beaded with perspiration, and tears moved down her brown cheeks and gathered the beads of moisture and ran together under her chin and dripped. She turned her back on him and gathered up the bottom of her faded purple skirt to wipe her face and eyes. When she straightened up toward him she said, "All our troubles are over, Joe. I knew he would come back to us someday. I knew he would. It's hard to believe it; my husband is back. I never gave up. It's been a long time, but I knew he would come back to us someday."

"Do you mean he's at our lodge?"

"No. He's the new trader. Isn't that funny; he's a trader again. You know the new store and the new house they are making up on the north agency road? It's his. I remember the first time I ever saw him when we were out on the Cimarron, and everyone had been talking about the trader who was coming. I was just a girl. But now he's a trader again. It's just like it was a long time ago."

He was still dubious and felt that there must be some error in this news. He asked, "Have you seen him? Are you sure it's him?"

"I'm sure," she said with perfect confidence. "Blue

Flower saw him with the agent at Fort Sill. And she asked the interpreter too. There's no doubt."

"But has he come to us?"

She saw his meaning and her eyes seemed to melt upon him. "Joe, Joe! You don't understand! You don't know how it was with us!"

"Will we wait for him to come to our lodge?"

"We'll rush to him as fast as our legs will carry us! As soon as we get dressed up and ready! We want to look our best." She turned abruptly. "Here we stand talking, wasting time. Let's go."

It was some ten miles home, up through the heart of the mountains, the peaks of which loomed to either side and ahead of them. They were mountains that dominated the scene, rising sharply out of the prairie, visible from almost all over the reservation from the Washita River to the Red. From a distance they looked misty blue, light or dark as the sun struck them, but always hazy. As one approached a peak it changed imperceptibly in color until its sides were mottled with clumps of dark oak and long clear slopes, gray-tan in color and apparently covered with summer grass. But on nearer approach the clear slopes broke down and they were seen to be not soil and grass, but granite boulders with delicate moss splotching their massive contours.

He followed behind her plodding figure until they turned away from Blue Beaver Creek and out across the high prairies between the peaks. He walked beside her in silence. There was no path. The grass was dry and thin on the yellow soil, fine needle grass and scattered bunches of bluestem and buffalo grass. In front of their feet grasshoppers shied up and sailed, their wings popping, forty feet ahead, to land and gather themselves in a scant shade, ready to fly again.

His mother was a natural walker, not intimidated by

any distance. In this she was a contrast to most of the people, who were a horse-riding people. Those middle-aged or older were squat of form, with strong bandy legs, suitable to grip the sides of a horse. Those younger were taller and had straighter legs, but none of them cared much for travel unless he could go by horse or wagon. The awkening of memories about White Buffalo stirred another when, as a small child, he and his mother had taken a long walking journey from some vague place on the wide earth to an equally vague destination; he only remembered that they had walked for many days, so long that he had believed that walking over the earth is a way of life.

She did not pause again until they came across the high prairies between the peaks and down to Medicine Bluff Creek. She stood a moment under the full shade of a pecan tree and said to him, "It's been such a long time. Sometimes I thought he would never come back to us. I thought he would and then I thought he wouldn't. Over and over. It's been a long time. It's been an awful long time." The look of victorious expectation remained, but it had gone deeper into her.

They turned up the creek toward their camp. He mulled over what she had said: "All our troubles are over." As for this startling appearance of a man out of the far past—that was confusing, a tantalizing perplexity; he was not as certain as she seemed to be that it was a sure blessing. But there was an implication in her statement "All our troubles . . ." that he should be able to judge as well as she. Did they have these things, an uncertain number of them, which had been with them a long time? Which waited upon them in a body to plague them again and again? Were the good times, the feasts, the horse races, the laughter with others only bits of time stolen from a troubled condition? He had never thought about it in that general way before, but here was a kind of truth. Something was wrong. An emptiness or a contradiction, a long-time thing. These mountains among which they lived were involved in it, as if they, in their age and grandeur, supplied a part of a whole, of which man should supply the other part; but that other part was lacking, unsatisfactory, unfulfilled or forgotten.

He thought briefly about Lottie Manybirds. Things were not right between him and her. Whatever success he had had with her was one of those bits stolen from a vaguely unsuccessful condition. He could not name the trouble. He felt a flush of jealousy, then pushed her from his mind.

They passed among the canvas tipis scattered along the running stream and by the square model house. This area had the bare earth and the worn paths of a permanent camp. Over it hung the smell of a place where people live, the dull odor of the toilet place, of smoldering wood, of decaying meat scraps, to which the nose becomes accustomed. Here and there a dog sprawled in the shade. One woman washed clothes down on the rocks. It was quiet in the heat of the day, and they passed through without greeting anyone, and out among the oaks to the tipi which was their lodge.

He soon discovered that his mother intended a great amount of preparation and that they would not make the long trip to the new trader's place until the next morning. It was a relief. He started to go up to wash at the swimming hole, but came back to ask her, "Do you want me to bring the mule?"

"No!" she said quickly. "No, it's better to walk than ride the mule."

He knew where the store was being built, several miles north of the fort, though he had not seen it. It was fourteen or sixteen miles away. He suggested, "We could ride him most of the way if you want to. Then stake him out and walk."

She was suddenly thoughtful. The clothes she had been looking at fell out of her hands and back into the rawhide case. "Joe," she said, "wouldn't it be wonderful if we had two fine horses?"

"I guess so."

"Why shouldn't Old Man Iron Lance let us use two good horses?"

"I don't think he would."

"I don't mean good horses. I mean his best. The red pinto. The big one. And the dark pinto. Not any others. The *ehkasunaro* and the *duuhtsunaro*."

He laughed. Old Man Iron Lance sometimes rode those two horses, he and his favorite wife, when they went visiting, or, less often, when he went hunting with important Indian leaders. Whenever he wore his best clothes and his feather headdress.

"I mean it! They owe me favors. I want you to tell him I want them. Those two. Just for one day or maybe two."

"I don't like to beg for anything, Mother."

"Don't beg! Who's begging? Three days ago I gave his family a whole beef's liver. It was supposed to be mine and you were away, so I gave it to them. Last year I cut the canvas for their big tipi. And lots of things. Today I'm calling back all my favors. Don't tell him why we want them. And don't beg, Joe. Just tell him what I want."

Still somewhat dubious, he started to leave and she said, "Be respectful, Joe."

"I'm not disrespectful to old men like him."

"Some young people are. Don't wake him up if he's asleep. But we want the two big pintos."

He left on the errand, thinking about how she, evidently under the inspiration of her great new expectation, was less humble and more demanding than he had ever known her. This camp was known as Old Man Iron Lance's Camp. Some people considered him a chief.

He forded the creek on the steppingstones and went to the old man's lodge, without much hope of getting the horses, but determined not to be apologetic. The old man sat cross-legged on a hide at the door of his tipi while his two wives padded about fixing food.

Joe went directly to him and asked if he might sit down. Then he forced himself to state his request in detail without hesitation. The old man's dark eyes strayed around the scene a minute. The lips of his wide mouth pulled down at the corners in an expression of permanent dignity. He grunted, "Where you going?"

He explained with as much gravity as he could muster that his mother's need for the horses was a private matter that she didn't wish to reveal, but that since she had never made such a request before and never expected to again and since she often did favors for other people, she thought it was reasonable. The horses would be well cared for.

The old man gave some directions to his women about the piece of meat sputtering over the fire, dreamed awhile, and finally said, "I have one little black mare you can use, I guess."

He patiently explained that it was necessary to have the two big pintos, that there was a good reason for this necessity, though he couldn't tell it. That he knew the horses' value and how to take care of them. He said, "I used to ride Quanah's race horses, you know, when I was lighter." He was amazed at himself, at his own audacity, that he could sit here calmly and insist.

The old man seemed to be covering up his curiosity,

or perplexity, by a show of casual deliberation. He seemed about to speak several times. "The meat's burning," he said slowly to the women. Then to Joe he said, as if it were of little consequence, "All right."

"Thank you, Mr. Iron Lance," he said. "May I take two saddles for them?"

"Go ahead. Don't run the horses on the rocks. They're not shod."

"No, sir, I won't. Thank you."

He walked away feeling confidence because he had succeeded and because of the manner in which he had done it. It struck him that if he had asked for only one ugly horse, or had explained, or had apologized, he likely would have got "no" for an answer. Could it be that somehow, as his mother surely believed, a new day was dawning? That the magic power owned by such a one as White Buffalo was already working for him?

He went into the model house to get two ropes. The two-room building, put up by the carpenter teacher from the agency, provided communal storage for the camp. The walls were hung with harness and saddles; the floor stacked with various supplies. The place smelled of leather and axle grease and of a musty, rancid bearskin tacked to the inside of the front door. He found a rope which belonged to him and another owned by Old Man Iron Lance. Then he went up the creek valley a half mile and caught the two beautiful horses. It was late afternoon when he staked them among the trees behind his mother's lodge.

When he came in she was standing with hands on her hips, staring at her clothes which were scattered about. He told her, "I got them."

"I'm glad," she said, but if she smiled it was only for an instant. She seemed not angry nor sad, but annoyed.

"What's the matter?" he asked.

She sighed and said sharply, but with resignation, "I'm fat!"

He laughed. "Why, Mother, you're not."

Yes, I am!"

"Fat? Of course you're not."

"You just say that to please me. I'm a fat old woman."

"You are not fat. You're just healthy. And you're certainly not old."

"I can see what I am. I might as well admit it."

"Mother, you shouldn't say that! Mrs. Willie is fat, and Slow Tom's sister. They're fat. You're not that way. You know it!"

It seemed that he had said the right thing to encourage her. In a minute she said, "I'm going to wear my doeskin dress with the fringe. It's the way he'll remember me best." After a moment's thought, she said, "I'm not the girl I once was, but everyone changes a little as they get older."

"I'm hungry," he said. "Are we going to eat today?"

She chipped up some dried beef to soften by boiling and made some large cakes out of cornmeal. They ate as darkness came on.

The same thoughts had evidently stayed in her mind for some time. She said, "We all change a little as the years pass. He will be a little older. We mustn't expect him to be exactly the same, Joe. But some things never change. The years pass, but some things stay exactly the way they always were."

He had a platform beside the tipi, upon which he slept during the summer. As he stretched out on the blankets, looking up into the deep sky, he thought of her words: "We mustn't expect him to be exactly the same. . . ." She knew what White Buffalo had been and could not understand that he did not know, but had only vague, contradictory impressions. As well as he knew and understood his mother, she was like the other older ones, holding secrets they did not even know they held, thinking that such as he knew about it, when such as he could not even guess the important parts of it. Old Man Iron Lance! What was in his memory? What was that long ago free time? Ages ago, which the older ones thought was only yesterday? Of which this White Buffalo had been a part? Or was it only yesterday?

Questions led him nowhere. He looked forward eagerly to the next day, then, noting the eagerness, he mixed it with skepticism and faint resentment.

3

THE WIFE OF THE NEW HOUSE

THEY ATE what remained of the corn cakes as the first light of day came on. He brought two saddles from the model house, one a stock saddle such as the white men ride, one an Indian saddle covered with hard rawhide and decorated with woven black and white horsehair. She chose the Indian saddle. When he had saddled the horses, she said, "Bring your rifle."

"I've got no shells."

"Well, you are so proud of it, I thought you would want to bring it."

It was a Winchester, of which he had indeed been proud at one time. The shells were expensive; he was almost always out. He got it and carried it across his saddle.

They rode east among the trees in the valley of Medicine Bluff Creek. In the low flats where oaks mingled with the other trees it was still dark. The horses were fresh and skittish in the cool air. They let them pick their way in the half-light.

The trail took a shortcut over a bare ridge away from the creek and they could see the sun rising, large and red, straight ahead. The mountains to their right were lighted on their rocky tops and had behind them long dark morning shadows; they were like giant spirits rising to the new day and wearing black robes that hid their lower portions. Out to their left rose the bare foothills, which some called the Ugly Mountains, massive and dry and inhospitable, now molded strongly by the angled sunlight.

All this land covered by the Mountains of the Wichitas spoke in a thousand moods. Its timeless face never left it, but now he thought it suggested new things, a beginning.

His mother looked beautiful on the horse, like the favorite daughter of a rich chief. She rode proudly. He thought she was worthy of any good thing that might be coming to her. He had a sudden start of suspicion and told himself, "If that white man says she's fat, I won't stand for it!" But that was foolishness. It was not a white man like that, but White Buffalo. White Buffalo! Could it really be?

They rode for an hour and a half, to where the creek turns south, and they left it to go straight east across the rolling plains. The grassland was cut at intervals by small creeks, their beds dry, sometimes shaded by a few cottonwoods, choked here and there by patches of willows. They followed no road, but found crossings worn deep in the soil, made by buffalo, some people said, now grown up with weeds. In low places sunflowers grew. Half their blooms were dried up, but the others were full and stiff and stubbornly yellow.

The morning grew hotter. They crossed a half dozen dry creeks and came in the middle of the day to a rise overlooking East Cache Creek, a larger stream with heavy timber along it. They could see at some points the beaten road which followed the stream and which connected the fort and agency in the north with the fort and agency in the south. Having come cross-country, they did not know their exact location. They rode forward to a hill where they could see better.

They could see the new store beside the road a mile downstream. Its unpainted lumber looked bright against the dark-green foliage. Behind it, toward the creek, stood another new building, barely visible through the trees.

She looked intently at their destination, then led off down the hill, not toward the store, but straight toward the road. They crossed the road and went among the trees, then turned downstream. They were still some little distance from the new building when she reined up. He could see that she was nervous and undecided. She dismounted.

In a minute she said, "Joe, I want you to do something for me, please."

He dismounted and looked at her.

"Do I look all right?" she asked.

"You look wonderful."

"I want you to walk to the store and see him first, will you?"

"See him?"

"Yes, just see him and speak to him. It's harder for me than I thought. Speak English to him." She added quickly, as if grabbing at a good thought, "He speaks Comanche better than we do, but he'll be very proud of you that you speak English so well."

He had not been able to picture the confrontation that was about to take place, but he had thought of himself as an observer rather than a participant. He certainly did not want to do what she was asking. He asked, feeling as if he had a sudden insight, "Mother, could this all be a big mistake?"

"No!" she protested. "It's all right."

"But I won't even know him when I see him."

"Of course you will! He's a big man. Strong. Good-looking."

"I don't think I should go first. I don't know what to say."

She laughed nervously. "Someone might be in his store to buy something. I want to see him alone. You see? I want him to watch me ride up. Tell him a woman he used to know is coming. Go ahead. It will be all right."

She was agitated and seemed to have her mind set. He was impatient of his own reluctance. What could he do but agree? He tied his horse and leaned his rifle against a tree, then, as he started away, she said, "If you bring him outside and I come riding up . . . when I come to him, walk away a minute and leave us alone. Just a little minute."

What disgusting and pitiful eagerness! His own excitement and uncertainty were growing because of her attitude. He would not know what to say, but it was clear that she was in no condition to understand and help him. He walked out to the road and down it to the new store.

The building's end faced the road, and in this end were a door and two windows. A hitching rail of freshly peeled poles stood between it and the road. Everything was quiet. He stood a minute, trying to hear something, then went to one of the windows and looked, but could not see inside, only his own reflection in the glass. He stood in front of the door and coughed. He said, "Hey!"

Any footsteps on the wooden floor would sound loud, but he heard nothing. He turned the knob and pushed on the door. It opened. The large room inside was empty, no goods, no groceries, nothing. It smelled strongly of fresh lumber and sawdust. There was a counter and a partition. He looked in the back room. Nothing. His movements sounded loud in the emptiness.

Outside, he looked toward the house down by the creek. He saw no horses or buggies or wagons, and heard no sounds. No smoke came from the chimney. He felt disappointment and relief. He went back to his mother and told her what he had found.

"He's in his house," she said.

"No, I didn't see any horse or anything there."

"He's asleep in his house."

"I don't think anyone is around at all."

She thought about it a moment and then began to instruct him to scout around the house. He could tell that she was not using good judgment, but simply did not know what to do next. What was the woman trying to do? She was trying to use him as if he were a child, when it was she who was anxious and uncertain.

"I looked at the house," he said. "You won't believe me, no matter what I say."

After a minute she said, "Well, come with me if you want to."

They left the horses. He considered wryly how they had brought the horses to make a good showing and now left them tied in the bushes in order to sneak up on foot.

They came through the trees toward the side of the house, and a hundred steps from it his mother paused to look. The house was not large, but seemed to be fitted into its spot like a nesting ground bird. At its rear and side rose two large cottonwood trees. The grass and weeds had been trampled down around it, and the ground carried some marks of hoofs and wagon wheels, but there was no sign of life. She suddenly walked forward as if she had found some source of confidence. He followed.

When she stopped on the porch in front of the door, he had the impression that she hardly knew he was near. She called softly, *"Tosakura?"* Then louder, but still tenderly, *"Tosakura?"*

She opened the door and they went in.

Like the store, the house seemed full of emptiness, but stacked about on the floor were boxes and rolls and crates. The fireplace had not been used. At the rear were two rooms, one empty and one which seemed fitted out for storing and cooking food. He went into this latter room and opened the back door, letting in more light than was provided by the two windows, which had pieces of cloth over them.

She had been walking about softly, studying it all, and when she came into the rear room, he could see that she had pride and confidence, even some of the serenity she had shown the day before, mixed into her nervousness. She touched the table and chairs lovingly. She felt of the cloth at the windows; it was white cloth with small blue and green flowers painted on it. She passed her hand along the shelves that were built on the wall. "This room is called a *kitchen*," she said, saying the word in English. "It's just like Saint Louis. Nearly." She was halfway with him, explaining, halfway by herself, loving the kind of things which she remembered.

"Saint Louis" was one of the words she had used before sometimes and had never been willing to explain, nor willing to accept that he did not understand. It was one of those distant mysteries. He could imagine a thousand model houses lined up in straight rows; whites like things to be lined up straight. But that left much unexplained, for somewhere in the large white world they did things such as make iron, and even more mysterious things such as make books. The information he possessed came from inadequate clues such as the statement she had made one time: "Great boats always came to Saint Louis." And she would explain no further. The word "Saint Louis" was connected with sadness, with long sullen moods without talking.

"Maybe I should clean this place up," she said. It was ridiculous, because it was already spotlessly clean. She was bustling about with little movements, doing nothing, but moving things slightly here and there as if she were hungry to possess them all at one time.

"I think I should cook something," she said. "I know how to use all these cooking things."

She had begun to work with the cookstove, opening the doors, lifting the round iron plates from the top of it. He heard a sound which was hidden under her clatter. "Wait," he said. "What's that?"

As she straightened up, they heard the unmistakable jingle of harness and a voice, or voices, out in front. For a moment they stared at one another as if in sudden recognition. Then they moved cautiously into the front room, far enough to see out one front window.

They saw a vehicle with four horses to it, the kind that army officers ride around in, and which they call an ambulance. Beside its open door stood a black-skinned white soldier.

But already footsteps were on the porch. And the strange voices of white women.

As they were retreating toward the kitchen, as the light steps rattled on the wooden porch, as the door was opening, in those hurried instants, the high-pitched voices told a startling and horrible truth. They did not pause to understand the English. If one had not been speaking English recently, he must tune his mind to it, saying, This is English; now what does it mean? The same as in speaking, when one must think of what he means and then think of the English way of putting it.

There was no time for that. But the voices told it. There is a tone in the voice of the woman of a lodge, and when she has something new the tone changes a little, and when she brings women friends to look it changes a little more. The voice is loud and any boastfulness in it is hidden under friendliness, and the woman is chatty and gay.

The louder of the voices belonged to the wife of this house. It was as blatant as if it had been explained to him for an hour. And he knew that his mother knew it.

They had retreated as far as the door into the kitchen when the crowd of white women penetrated into the room, seeming like a great number, though they were only three or four. The one in front, a skinny woman with yellow hair, wearing a blue straw hat with cloth flowers on it, stopped her speech and her mouth stayed open. Her blue eyes were wide. She screamed immediately, piercingly.

"Ee . . . ee . . . ee . . . ee!" The cry was full of fear and outrage. It belonged as much to his mother and himself as to the strange woman, expressing the panic they were too stricken to express.

The sound moved him, as if he had been bound there and the scream had cut the ropes away. He scrambled with his mother past the kitchen chairs and out the back kitchen door. She missed the step below the door and nearly fell; he took her arm and they fled together into the safety of the trees and on. They thought only to get away, and when the creek loomed before them, they turned up it, crashing through the high grass and brush, oblivious of any trail.

As they slowed he looked back and could now and then see the house through the trees. The black-skinned white soldier had left the ambulance and was standing out some distance from the house, shouting, "Halt!"

The shout sounded distant and unconvincing. The man had no gun and was merely shouting into the trees, "Halt!"

They slowed to a walk. His mother was panting, and her breast was rising in great trembling heaves. He was surprised to see that, though they had not chosen a direction, they had come back to the area where the beautiful spotted horses were tied. His mother looked at the horses, and stopped, and sank down onto the dry grass. He sat down beside her.

They were in the edge of a patch of milkweeds, now blooming profusely in this dry autumn time. The flowers were tiny and white, but the leaves at the tops of the plants had turned creamy, like large flowers themselves, false flowers to draw the insects. He stared at the milkweeds dully, contemplating them to take his attention off his mother.

She sat leaning forward. Her whole body still heaved, but slowly. She covered her face and eyes in her hands.

He said, "I'm going to kill him, Mother." He thought she would probably assent by staying silent.

But she said, "No, you're not."

He had a strong feeling about it that seemed to be swelling up from his guts, up through his chest and head. Connected with the feeling was an idea, a cool little stream of wisdom, about the rightness of it. An act might appear cruel, heartless, and yet be really best in the long run. He said, "Yes, I'm going to."

"No, you're not," she said.

She straightened up and took her hands away from her face. It was haggard and splotched, but she was not crying. She looked and said, "Joe." Her voice was shaky, but her manner was as if nothing had happened, as if she had merely been running and got out of breath. "My little boy!"

He felt as if she had struck him. He said fiercely, "Don't call me that!"

"Why not? You are my little boy, Joe."

"Because it's an insult to me! I want you to stop it!" He thought she was trying to change the subject, to take her mind off her disappointment, turning her bossy, motherly, smothering attitude on him.

"You shouldn't talk that way to your mother, Joe."

"Why not? I say what I mean."

"Because it's disrespectful and disobedient."

"You are disrespectful to me."

Now, he thought, they were both quibbling, trying to stay off the subject, but he wanted to prove that she was wrong. "Listen," he said, "you came after me yesterday, and I came along like you asked. Didn't I? I got the horses from Old Man Iron Lance. Didn't I? I came with you and did what you wanted. Didn't I? I'm not disrespectful and disobedient. But I want you to stop calling me what you did. I don't like it. Just stop it."

She did not answer, and he thought that he might be getting through to her. That maybe she was finished with the nonsense and ready to think about what they were doing here. Then she looked at him with tenderness and her voice was broken as she said, "You're right. Men your age have been chiefs."

She seemed to stop to calm herself and then be unable to find what else to say. Finally she said, "It's all a big mess. I don't know what's wrong."

He felt determined to stop all the quibbling. "I'll tell you what's wrong. That damned devil ran off and left you and now he has married a bitch of a white woman. That's what's wrong."

"No," she said. "You don't understand."

"That's another thing I wish you'd stop saying! If I don't understand, why not? I'm not stupid! I can understand anything if I know what it is I'm trying to understand." He felt bitter toward her and also felt remose at his own tone of voice. She was crushed.

She said nothing, but began staring down into her cupped hands, not as if she was thinking about a problem, rather as if she was lost in some gloomy other world.

He had an impulse to flee from her, run a long distance away from her haggard stoic face, do something different, a thing of his own, unencumbered. He picked up a piece of dead limb and began to slash at the milkweeds near him, causing them to bleed their white sap. They were a plant with a kind of perfection in their thick leaves and a kind of success in their nature which allowed them to stand up stiff and green and even to bloom in this hot, dry autumn. He took a futile revenge in wounding them. Out of the side of his eye, he saw his mother paying no attention to him, but sitting stolidly as if she meant to sit there in the sunshine forever. She was sitting awkwardly, clumsily in her doeskin dress with the fringe on it.

He asked, "What are you going to do about it?"

She had evidently given thought to it. "I'm going to get Duncan Bull to make some medicine against her." She was speaking of Old Man Iron Lance's brother, a *puhakut*, a man of religious power.

"To kill her?"

"To make her get away from here and stay away and go back where she belongs!"

He had little faith in Duncan Bull's powers, especially against a white person. Some said white people had more kinds of medicine than any Indian had ever had, and some said the whites had ruined all medicine so that none of it had any power anymore. But he saw no point in repeating these ideas to her now.

She began to rise to her feet and said, "Let's get the horses."

"I'm not going home with you," he said. He felt urgently the need to go somewhere. A certain place. Do something. A definite thing. But his mind would not name it clearly.

"Why not?"

"I'm just not."

"What are you going to do, Joe?"

"I don't know. Nothing especially. I'm not going to do anything."

"Then why don't you come on home? Where are you going?"

"Down to the agency. I might go to the Armstedts'." Strictly speaking, there was no longer an agency down south past the fort; there were the stores and the school and the white doctor's office and the house of the farming teacher and the place to draw rations. They still called it the agency.

"I wish you would stay away from those wild boys like Slow Tom Armstedt. I'm afraid they'll get you into trouble, drinking whiskey or something."

"Where would they get whiskey? I may get a fencing job with Slow Tom."

"Joe?"

He was surprised at the tone of her voice. It sounded as if she were asking his permission for something.

"I'm afraid sometimes about what you might do."

Not caring to cooperate in her fussing, he did not answer.

"I'm afraid sometimes you might do what George Longwater did."

"What in the world has that got to do with me? It's nonsense! What do you know about George Longwater?"

"I know he killed himself."

"What nonsense! What has that got to do with me? Nothing!"

"He ran around all the time. He stayed away from home. He drank whiskey one time. His mother said so. He ran around with Slow Tom Armstedt and those Blue Beaver boys."

"What in the world has that got to do with it? He ran around with me too, as far as that goes. I don't know where you get these crazy ideas! You know nothing about him! You want me to get a job one minute and you want me to stay home the next minute!"

She seemed to ponder her own inconsistency, then turned away, saying, "I hope you come home soon."

He got his rifle and watched her ride west across the road, leading the horse he had ridden, and out toward the ridge. He was irritated with her, over it all, over the foolish hope she had held and more so over what she had roused in him. Over the ridiculous position she had put them in, and over her petty attitude. Her motherly fussing was hardly bearable and it became worse when she mixed it with more serious matters. He could think of a dozen reasons to criticize her, but as she grew smaller in the distance, he also felt a deep aching pity for her in his throat and heart.

There was no reason why he should not take the road, but he was reluctant, lest he meet someone. He went down the bank of East Cache Creek to a crossing where it was only knee deep, waded through the clear cool water, and walked downstream in the edge of the trees on the eastern side. His wet trousers were cool on his legs. He went out on a white sand bar, doused his face and head with water, then walked on.

He didn't know whether he would decide to kill the man or not. In any case, he would have given it careful thought before he did anything. She seemed to think that he was hasty, hotheaded. That was really almost the exact opposite of the truth. He pondered over things that were important to him at great length, even too long, and he thought that if he failed in his thinking, it was because there were so many things he could not find any true information about. As for killing the man, if he decided to do it, he was sure that it would be a wiser thing to do than listen to every piece of advice of his mother's.

After an hour's walking he could see the course of Beef Creek converging toward the creek he followed and out on a slight knoll the dilapidated dwelling of Great Eagle. It seemed a year since the aborted feast, but it had only been three days. He mumbled a few curses and turned his attention away from it.

He was coming into the region where farms were scattered along the broad flats on either side of the creek. The fields were enclosed with rail fences or barbed-wire fences, and they had been planted mostly in corn, the dry stalks now broken over by the wagons which had been used to gather the crop. There had also been melons. A few yellow pumpkins could still be seen lying around on dead vines. Some of the people living here kept milk cows, and a few even lived in plank houses or log cabins, though the most common dwellings were tipis covered with weather-bleached canvas, these scattered in bunches near the creek. The people who lived down this way were those who had been willing to live nearer the agent and his helpers and the missionaries.

A mile away, out across the creek, he could see the light-gray limestone buildings of the fort, squat and solid, and the great wooden water tank on a tower. All ironically peaceful, for it represented coercion, a threat, and in a good-natured way as if everything was right and acceptable in the world. He did not know why he felt such a pang of anger as he looked at it.

Below the fort he crossed on the bridge and, passing the commissary and the stone quarry, he faced the question of where he was going. realizing at once that more than anything else he wanted to see his sweetheart, Lottie Manybirds. He had argued with her when he had been here with his mother on the last issue day. He had been pushing her from his mind, but now, after the ridiculous farce he had played out with his mother, he needed to make up with the girl, talk to her, gain her good opinion, court her, make love to her. He told himself that she was actually more desirable than he had assumed that last time, worth more persistence, and if he persisted, she would surely love him.

But he needed food and a blanket for the night. He headed for the hospitable lodge of the Armstedts, at the mouth of Sitting Bear Creek.

4

HOW MANY COUPS
AND HORSES . . . ?

THEY HAD a good breakfast, and Joe said to Slow Tom, "Let's walk down toward the church."

"The church! I thought we might go hunting or go see about the fencing job."

"We can do that later."

"The church? What's down there? Let's go hunting. Have you got any shells?"

"No. I'll go see about the fencing job with you tomorrow or the next day. I want to go down yonder."

"What the hell's down yonder? Why don't you say what you mean?" Slow Tom's broad face was solemn and innocent. "If you feel a need to go see the missionary, just say so."

"Well, for one thing, Mr. Frank Manybirds lives down that way."

"I thought so. What do you want me along for? I believe you're afraid of that man. If I was stuck on his daughter, I'd walk right up to him and say, 'I've come to court your daughter.'"

"Yeah, I notice how you do things like that. About the first time you said that he would sic his dogs on you, and that would end your love affair. All I mean to do is just walk down that way; you don't have to come along if you don't want to."

"Did he sic the dogs on you the last time you came around?"

"No, he just called her and said she had chores to do and quit trifling around. You don't have to come along if you don't want to."

Slow Tom said, "All right, I guess I'll walk partway with you."

He carried the rifle, for no reason unless it was that if he did not carry it he would be empty-handed. They walked down the broad flats beside the meandering stream, past the old agency offices and the Red Store and the church. It was a fine autumn morning.

He had not told Slow Tom anything about the experience with his mother. It seemed a private thing, a shamefully sentimental thing. He was trying to keep it out of his own mind. They came to the north side of Frank Manybirds' field and crawled over the crooked rail fence. Down at the other end, a quarter of a mile, could be seen the canvas tipis of a camp and a model house and Frank Manybirds' plank barn.

But they were surprised to see over at the edge of the field the flashing movement of bright red and blue cloth. Lottie and her sister Annie were gathering wood and throwing it over the fence into the field. The younger girl's laughter rang out shrill and clear.

The girls saw them and stood looking, shielding their eyes with their hands. Then Lottie began tucking in strands of hair and retying the red handkerchief that was over her head, and the younger girl came skipping toward them through the broken cornstalks.

Her tangled hair was flying and her white teeth were flashing. "Are you going hunting?" she asked, out of breath.

Joe told her, "We're just messing around."

The girl skipped around them as they walked, crashing through the dry stalks, giggling.

Lottie smiled when they came up, and answered their greetings. She was glad to see him. She showed no trace of remembering their disagreement. He was conscious of her clear eyes, the mellow brown skin of her face and arms, the shapeliness of her body. He had been taking her too much for granted. Once he had told himself that she was like a young wild mare, not that she kicked up her heels, but that she was able to, and that she was strong at the same time that she was all woman. She had been very warm toward him, and responsive, and he had forgotten how she looked, for a man standing off and looking at her. Now, seeing her standing in her long red dress on the other side of the fence, doubting how attainable she was, he was smartly conscious of her desirability.

"Need some help?" he asked.

"I guess so."

"I need help," Annie said. To Slow Tom she said, "Slow-poke, will you be my horse?"

"Go play," Lottie said. "They don't want you around here teasing."

"Yes, they do." She kept jumping around and giggling.

The top rail of the fence had been lifted down. He sat on the second rail, and Lottie climbed up to sit a little distance from him, not hindered by her long red skirt. They said things: "What have you been doing?" "Nothing much." "Where have you been?" "Oh, around." Meaningless things, while they explored with their eyes and listened to the tone of each other's voice.

He said, half joking, "Those little dry limbs are no good. They'll burn up like grass."

"We have to get some green wood too."

"How?"

"We have an ax right down there by the fence."

"Now if you could just find somebody to do the chopping you'd be all fixed up."

She wrinkled her nose and briefly stuck her tongue out at him, in the contagious spirit of her little sister. "If I think of somebody I'll call him."

"How will you get it home when you get it chopped?"

"Put a rope around it and get a horse and drag it."

He reached over and took hold of her upper arm as if testing her muscle. "I believe you could chop it, all right."

Slow Tom slumped against the fence. The little girl was begging to wear his black felt hat and he was making faces at her. Joe said, "Go ahead, if you want to. I may stick around here awhile and chop some wood for these gals."

"Go ahead where?"

"Oh, walking around or wherever you were going. I think I'll stick around here and—"

"I know, you may stick around and chop some wood. Well, if you come back to our place, I may not be there. They saw a big bunch of turkeys out this side of Arbuckle Hill, and I may go out there and get some."

"All right, buddy. I'll see you. Maybe we'll go over on the Blue Beaver tomorrow or see about the fencing job."

"Yeah," Slow Tom said as he started walking away. He was too good-natured to take offense simply because he had been dismissed from a place where there was good reason for his not being wanted.

Annie followed behind him a ways, chunking clods at his back. Slow Tom turned, picked up a clod and threw it hard at her bare feet. She jumped into the air and ran back screaming as if she were terrified.

Joe moved over against Lottie and put his arm around her, caressing her waist and stomach with his hand. She took his hand in her own and held it.

"I've been thinking about you and dreaming about you," he said. "Can't get you out of my mind."

"Boy, what a line," she said.

"It's no line, honey."

"How many other girls did you tell that?"

"Other girls? It doesn't seem like there are any other girls." He looked at her face. She appeared to be teasing, yet, strangely, a little embarrassed.

He said, "We're still lovers, aren't we?"

"I don't know."

"You don't know? Why not? What's the matter?"

"All right."

"What do you mean, all right? Are you my girl or not?"

"Yes."

"And my lover?"

"I don't know."

He tugged at her waist with his arm. "Let's get rid of that little nuisance and go walking down by the creek."

She was silent a moment, then said, "I can't."

"Why not? Don't you want to be alone with me?"

At that moment the younger girl started hitting him in the back with a cornstalk. He said, "I don't see how you put up with that little devil."

"Annie, stop it! Right now. Do you want everybody to hate you? Go play."

"Joe Cowbone! Say, Joe Cowbone, can I see your rifle?"

"If you get dirt in the barrel I'll skin you alive."

Lottie said, "Are you ready to start chopping green wood?"

"What's the hurry about the wood?" He could see that she was smiling, kidding, flirting, but it was only a front, to avoid his question about being alone.

"Well, you said you would help us."

"I will, but we can get wood any time. Why don't you send the kid away?"

"Reverend Fairchild says that men should help the women on hard work."

"What does a white man know?"

"He's a preacher."

"That's worse. Lottie, I'll get you a mountain of wood. I'll chop down all the trees on this creek and make it a bare prairie if you want me to."

She laughed and asked, "Is that rifle loaded?"

"No. Why don't you send her away? We can't even talk."

"Is that all you want, to talk?"

"I want to be alone with you."

"I can't."

"You can't? What's changed?"

"I just can't."

"If I go away and come back to see you in a week, will it be like it used to be with us?"

She busied herself by smoothing the handkerchief on her head and tucking in imaginary strands of hair with her free hand, then said, "No."

"Don't you like me anymore?"

"Yes."

How much of it was play and how much serious he could not tell. He thought of acting angry to see what she would do. "Send the kid away," he insisted.

She searched his face with her lucid brown eyes for

a moment, then said, "Start cutting a tree, so if anyone asks her, she will say you are cutting wood."

He got the ax and began chopping at the base of a young pecan tree a few steps from where she sat on the fence. She called, "Go down to the barn, Annie, and get the horse. Put the rifle back where you got it." The girl started to argue, but then seemed to decide that going after the horse alone was an interesting adventure.

The white chips flew from the ax blows. He pushed the tree with one hand and it fell. Seeing that the child was skipping away, he sank the edge of the ax in the stump and went back to where Lottie sat on the rail, watching him. He walked up to her and put his head in her lap and his hands around her hips. which felt fuller and warmer than one could imagine from looking at the red dress. She combed at his hair a little with her fingers.

"Let's go down toward the creek," he said.

"I'm sorry, Joe, but I can't." She would not allow him to put his hand under her dress.

"Why do you keep saying that? You can if you want to."

"I don't mean to do that anymore."

"What is it, Lottie? Here I am. Here you are. I'm crazy about you. You say you like me. You say you're my lover."

"Seems like that's all you think of."

"What's wrong with that? I'm crazy about you. Can you blame me for that? Come go with me and then we'll think about whatever you want to. Didn't I say I'd cut you a mountain of wood if you wanted me to?"

"I don't care if you cut wood or not."

"Why did you send Annie away?"

"Because you kept saying to. And I want you to

understand. I want to see you, but I don't want to do that anymore."

"You don't want to?"

"I mustn't."

He backed away from her. "Who in the hell have you been talking to? Here I am. Here you are. Alone. Just ourselves. Whose business is it what we do? We should do what we want. Who have you been talking to?"

"Nobody. But it is their business. I don't want to be a loose woman."

"You're not a loose woman. Who says you're a loose woman?"

"Nobody."

"Who is 'they'? Whose business is it?"

"All of them. I want people to respect me and not think I'm a loose woman."

"What ideas! Is it that Fairchild? Is he putting crazy ideas in your head?"

"No."

"Is it your father?"

"No. It's everybody."

"Lottie, I didn't ask you to go running around and being a loose woman. I'm the only man you've got, and you're the only woman I've got. I swear it. We're going to be married and live all our lives together."

"When we are, it will be all right."

"So that's it! You're in a big hurry to get married. All right, if that's all the trouble is, let's do it. I'm ready. How will we get married?"

"I don't know. I want to."

"Suppose we just say to each other we're married. I'll love you and keep you all your life. It's nobody else's business."

"That's the trouble. It is their business."

"Whose? That's what I want to know! I want to know

who 'they' is! And what do they say we've got to do?"

"I don't know, Joe."

He became so exasperated that he turned his back on her, then walked over and worked the ax loose and swung it as hard as he could, sinking it twice as deep into the green stump. He looked back at her. She seemed quite solemn, even forlorn. She was standing by the fence as if she didn't know what to do. He returned to her, feeling contrite, but when he put his arms around her and pressed her against him, he felt the surging awareness of her desirability.

"Lottie, we are by ourselves. If you love me, what else matters? No one will know what we do."

"That's just what the white soldier said."

"What!" It was like the burn of a quirt on bare skin, so sudden that it was hard to grasp.

"That no one would know."

"Who?" In heaven's name, what was she saying so calmly?

"The soldier who comes to help Reverend Fairchild at the church."

"What happened? What did you do?" He was gripping her two shoulders.

"I didn't do anything. That's what I'm trying to tell you. I'm not a loose woman."

"What did he say to you? Tell me! Tell me!"

"I don't understand everything in English. He said something about going walking and be sweet to him, and I know he said no one would know."

"What did you say? What did you do?"

"Nothing. I went away from him and went home."

Suddenly in rage he slapped her cheek as hard as he could.

She was knocked to the side, but caught her balance

and stood still, stooping a little, her head bowed. Her hand moved slowly to her face, to touch it.

He was amazed at himself. His hand tingled. His first thought was that he should work the ax out of the stump and cut his hand off. Why had he done such a thing? He thought that she was stunned and that in a moment, when she was over it, she would turn her back on him and go home; but she made no move except to straighten her head scarf. She kept her head bowed.

Why had he done such a thing? He had no doubt that she had told the whole truth. Or had she? What right did she have to assume that he would be sure she was faithful? How could she act so innocent about it, so casual, beyond reproach, when she must have known how it would bother him? But he had no excuse. He was like a cruel boy stepping on bird eggs.

Amidst his chagrin, he was still angry, at himself, at it all. What could he say to her? The familiarity between them was gone. He started to say he was sorry, became flustered, then flung out stupidly at her, "I think you like the white soldier more than me!"

It seemed as if she should turn away from him, but she didn't, so he turned himself and went back to the chopping work. She said something like, "I didn't do anything," and he pretended not to hear. He trimmed the fallen tree, slashing the side limbs off, each with a single blow. Then he went along the trunk at intervals of a long step, cutting deep notches. He kicked the log over on the other side, hardly pausing in his vicious chopping. When he had cut it into lengths, he left the pieces scattered around and attacked another standing tree.

He thought that she was trying to act as if she were gentle and reasonable about it all—maybe she even believed that she was. He was a stupid brute, but that

wasn't all of it. It was also true that her stubborn head
had been filled with this ridiculous new idea that it was
other people's business. He had heard suggestions or
rumors of Indians getting married by white man's meth-
ods. Some of the white men evidently thought it was
their business; they had tried to tell even Quanah that
he had to get rid of some of his wives. What white man's
marriage would amount to, the ceremony or afterward,
he had no idea, though it seemed to include preachers,
and it might include army people, and who knew what?
In any case, it was an alien and unwelcome thing. What
right did white people have to meddle in things between himself and her? As for the old kind of marriage,
it included a valuable gift to the father, horses if possible, to show friendliness and generosity and the worth
of the girl, but more than that it meant living together in the midst of the band and having everyone
know you were man and wife, and having certain ways
of acting, she toward his kin and he toward her kin.
But now the bands, the Nawkoni, the Kutsueka, the
Tanima, the Yamparika, the Kwahadi, they were all
split up and scattered and strung out and mixed. Even
the old women, those experts on proper marriage, disagreed now on what it was. Could a husband speak to
his wife's mother? Was he a part of his wife's father's
family? Who knew? She couldn't tell him who the "they"
was whose business it was because it was nobody. She
was a traitor to him and to herself, looking around to
get some "they" mixed up in it, and closing her thoughts
against anything he could say. But why had he been
such a fool as to ruin things between them by hitting
her?

How could she manage to look so small and sad
standing there in her red dress? He knew that she did
it on purpose, to affect him. She had a stem of dry grass

in her hand, her head bent looking at it as if it were important, doing nothing but wrapping it around her finger and smoothing it out, over and over. It was maddening that he could not keep from being aware of her stillness and the way she stood. And maddening that he could not find a way to apologize to her.

As he was felling another tree he got a glimpse of the little devil Annie leading a gray horse up the field. He swung the hardest blow yet, not watching carefully what he did, and struck beyond the trunk, breaking the ax handle in two.

Lottie came over to where he stood with his hands on his hips. She said, "It's all right. It was old and maybe it was cracked. I'll tell my father I did it."

He was too much out of breath to speak to her.

"This is plenty of green wood," she said. "I'll tell my father I broke it. He won't mind."

She saw Annie coming with the horse and began throwing the wood over the rail fence. The mark of his hand was barely visible on her cheek. He watched the two of them work with the wood until they began to try to tie it with the rope and were doing a clumsy job of it, then he went to help. He stacked the wood and drew it tight with the rope, puting a loop that would not slip on the horse's neck, and leaving an end long enough for a half hitch on the horse's nose so that he could be led. To Annie, who had evidently decided the project was fun, he said, "Don't make him pull too fast. It will hurt his neck."

Lottie said, "Aren't you coming with us?"

"Coming with you?" It seemed that she was going to try to pretend that it had never happened.

"Coming to visit us."

"I don't think your old man wants me around there."

"Sure he does."

"It doesn't seem like it."

He could see that she wanted to deny it and felt good toward her that she hesitated, that she did not say the easy thing and leave him stuck with the problem of the awkwardness. Of course, a visitor was a visitor, and if he went straightforwardly as a visitor, Frank Manybirds would not tell him to leave. But it could be an uncomfortable situation.

She said in a rush of words, "Couldn't you kill a turkey, Joe, and bring it? If you brought something like that and just said you were out hunting and got it and thought maybe my father could use a little fresh meat . . ."

"I haven't got any shells."

"We have some. I know we have some that will fit."

She supported her idea so anxiously that he was able to override his mixture of chagrin and embarrassment and anger. He asked, "Could you bring me some?"

"Sure, how many?"

"How many turkeys do you want?"

"I'll bring six. All right?"

"One will be enough," he said, certain that she was too anxious to bring only one.

She got the broken ax and ran after her little sister and the crudely laboring horse. He felt a rush of gentleness toward her because she was trying to forgive him, and at the same time observed himself, so much involved in what she did and in what was between them. Girls! he thought. She's got me roped up like Annie has that old horse, pulling a load sideways and plowing up the ground and about to cut his fool neck off. He was not sure that he had any more to gain from his efforts than did the horse, but he followed the figure in the red dress with his eyes until she disappeared in the trees at the other end of the field. He crossed the fence and walked down it in the same direction.

She was back into the field in a few minutes. He whistled and she came to where he was. She dropped one shell into his hand and said, "I hope you have good luck." She smiled at him uncertaintly a moment and produced another shell from her other hand and said, "Just to make sure."

Then she hurried away, as if she had urgent duties back at the Manybirds lodge, and he could not guess whether that was it, or whether she didn't want to stay alone with him even a minute, or whether she was in a hurry for him to go hunting. Or about the two cartridges, which were pitifully few: did she know how few they were and was she taking revenge on him, or did she trust what he had said and really believe that the second one would "make sure"? Who could tell what was in her mind?

He headed out east of East Cache Creek into the bare rolling hills, came to a dry wash called Whiskey Creek, and followed its course. After an hour's walking he climbed to a high rise and sat down to scan the country in all directions. He could see no movement. Hunting a turkey in this way took a lot of luck. At least he could see no other hunter, and he hoped that if a flock of the birds was in the area, he would have no competition. For an hour he sat still under the midday sun doing nothing but look. He could see Arbuckle Hill, with the abandoned stagecoach road leading over it, but thought it would be better to go farther north following the course of the wash, for there were seeping springs along it, and water holes large enough for birds to water. He walked on toward the northeast.

The autumn land was gray and barren, peaceful and lonely. He rambled, sometimes interrupting his musing to look across the distance before him. Finally he turned south along one of the sandy gullies that drained the higher ground he had been skirting. He saw a movement up on the sloping prairie nearly a mile ahead and stopped to study it. The air was dry and clear, but the heat played tricks with it along the ground; and yet there was movement in that one place as if the dim and indistinct details of the soil and the dry plants and the stones and the noon shadows shifted and flicked about. Suddenly he felt like a hunter. He dropped into the gully, put the two shells in the magazine of the Winchester, cocked it, throwing one shell into the chamber, and went forward bending low.

When he came to a convenient place to look again, he saw a flock of turkeys, the separate brownish birds clearly distinguishable. They were scattered over three or four acres of ground, feeding.

He moved toward them until the gully was no more than knee deep, then looked cautiously. The flock was still a quarter mile away, the birds threading this way and that, pecking, dawdling, scurrying after grasshoppers. They were gradually moving his way. The breeze was from the south; he could smell the faintly sour reek of their droppings. It was a matter of patiently waiting for them.

He sat in the warm sand and thought about Lottie. He thought that she wanted their lovemaking as much as he. But now all this confusion about marriage. And she had no more idea what marriage is than he did. He could remember her being as playful, as devilish as her little sister had become, and it seemed a pity that now she had turned serious and solemn and worried about others' opinions. His mind drifted to his mother. He could see her shining face when she had come to him— her great glad heart shone out of her face—when she brought the news to him, and then he could see her splotched face when she sat in the weeds, humiliated. He wished fiercely for her that whatever medicine thing she was now trying to do—destroy a white woman, level Fort Sill or turn a mountain on its tip, whatever, that it might somehow come true for her in spite of all reason.

And sitting there waiting in the lonely immensity, he wondered, finally, how it is that a man is caught by them, tied to them, wrapped up in them, subject to the whims and the deep twistings and imaginings and involvements of their female minds.

He could hear the turkeys talking. *Clark-clerk . . . Top . . . Chit . . . Clerk . . . Tit-clerk . . . Sot . . . Clark-clerk.* He could see that some of them were as near as two hundred steps, and among those in the van was a huge gobbler.

He crawled on elbows and knees to a place where the low bank sloped and was guarded at the top by a scrub chaparral. He poked the barrel of the rifle slowly through the bush and settled himself. If the big one came close enough, he would try first for a head shot, then jump up quickly and aim for the middle of the body. He waited, taking slow deep breaths, forcing himself to relax. He knew their motions. The big head would dart up high, suspicious, hold a second, jerk aside, cock, hold a second, alert to sight and sound. He would have only an instant.

His aim was just above the big one, and out of the sides of his eyes he could see some hens and younger cocks beginning to gawk, suspicious. No longer feeding. The big head bobbed up, questioning. He caught the round eye on his bead almost as soon as it stopped moving and squeezed immediately, deliberately.

The boom rocked the silence. He was aware of nothing for a moment as he quickly jerked the lever, throw-

ing in the second round, scrambled to his feet at the
top of the low slope and put the rifle back to his cheek.

The birds skittered in every direction away from him,
their necks stretched low, their wings spread and beating the air. They bumped one another in their desperation to escape, but moved fast for their apparent clumsi-
ness. The gobbler was down with his head in the ground,
tossing himself in a great circle with one leg, while the
other kicked in the air. Coming near, he saw that he
had blown the big head nearly off. He had been lucky,
but felt a surge of pride.

When the bird stopped kicking, he gathered its two
rough, scaly legs and hoisted it to his shoulder. It was
as heavy as any he had seen. He headed west toward
the Manybirds farm. Half of the afternoon was gone.
Blood was dripping onto his heels, and soon he needed
to rest, so he put down his burden and waited for the
blood to thicken. He rested several times and it was
late afternoon when he reached his destination.

Frank Manybirds' lodge was at the end of a string
of dwellings which were scattered among the tres. He
owned two canvas tipis, a plank barn, corrals, a log shed
with tin roof, a wagon, a buggy, a plow, a cultivator, a
milk cow and a dozen horses and mules.

Joe was welcomed by a squealing Annie, who came
running. Lottie followed her. He stood his rifle against
a tree and spread out one of the massive wings to show
its size. Mrs. Manybirds came and Frank came from
the shed.

Joe said his planned speech in a casual way: "I was
out hunting and got this turkey, so I thought about you
folks. I thought you could use a little fresh meat."

Frank Manybirds was a small man, hawklike in the
face. His shirt and trousers and hat always seemed too
big for his body, but he had the strength and vitality

to match even bigger clothing. He, like any Comanche, admired a good piece of game. He said, "Say, that's a good one!"

The man squatted on his heels and poked at the bird. "A good one! Where did you hit him?"

"The head. I got in a lucky shot."

"Beautiful!" the man said.

While they were poking at it, he found a chance to slip the unused cartridge into Lottie's hand. He knew that she was pleased and he thought that he could see that the relationship between them could become as easy as it had been before he struck her.

Frank gave directions for Mrs. Manybirds to take the turkey down to the creek and skin it and clean it. The girls evidently had evening chores to do. In the clearing before the tipis the hard-packed ground had been swept clean except for the space occupied by the fire and a small pile of wood. The man puttered around the fire and chatted with Joe in a friendly manner, but rarely gave him a chance to say more than "Yes, sir" or "I think so."

When the fire was going to suit him, the man brought a single cane-bottomed chair from the shed, seated himself and began to roll a cigarette as white men do. "You know," he said, "I like to see a young man that's good at hunting. A man could go out three or four times a week, if he would work at it, and he could put quite a lot of meat on the fire. The younger generation, they don't work at a thing like that hard enough. Oh, they may bring in something fit to eat once a year, just sporting around. Sometimes I think the younger generation is just going to the dogs." He chuckled to indicate that he was not being overly fussy.

"You take me," he went on. "I got two daughters. Now, say some young fellow was to come to me and ask about them. The first thing I say to him is 'How many coups have you got?' That's the old question. A fair question. Then I say, 'Did you mean to give her father a couple of good horses or maybe a few fine wool blankets or what?' That's another fair question, I would say." He chuckled. "Just supposing, of course, but that would get some of this younger generation to stop and think. Then maybe I say this: 'Are you a good steady hunter? Not did you ever make a lucky shot, but can you put plenty of meat on the fire?' Then trapping for skins. There are varmints on that creek there, down a way, that die of old age—coons, polecats, possum, badgers, coyotes. A man can make good money. They tell me they don't like farming, but I think it's keeping their nose to the grindstone, as the white man says, they don't like. If a man don't have good property how can he have a good name? And if he don't have good deeds and honesty how can he have a good name? And if he don't fix things up around him and work to get money how can he have a good living and the good things of life?"

The man stirred himself to help his wife mount the skinned turkey on a pole over the fire. It looked even larger naked of feathers, enough for two families. Then the man settled back in his chair, looking peculiar in his baggy clothes, but by his manner clearly the lord of his lodge. He laced his fingers together across his middle.

"Well, we were talking about the younger generation. I'll tell you my thinking. A man can be a good Indian. He can learn the old ways and stay by them. He can hunt and trap and raise horses and make things in the old ways. Or he can be a good man on the white road, a good Christian, a good farmer. Or he can even be both at the same time. But the trouble with young people nowadays, what they want to do is lay around and roam around and gamble and play and be nothing but bums."

The sun had gone down and it was growing dark. Lottie, Annie and Mrs. Manybirds stood by the fire. The bird began to make sizzling sounds. Mrs. Manybirds turned it frequently and she dipped into a can of water a rag bound onto a stick and patted the meat to dampen it. Annie was less boisterous in front of her parents, or perhaps it was that she had spent her energy during the day.

Frank Manybirds spoke on and on, now pompous, now friendly. To Joe the voice became like the drone of a bee. Lottie was more than beautiful standing and moving in the firelight. Her eyes seemed darker, more sparkling, her lips as luscious as a piece of fruit. Her hair was darker than the night, eloquently and simply and maddeningly framing her face and neck. The way she stood and the way she moved were mysterious. How had he dared slap her? He stared at the details of her face and body and it seemed almost as if he didn't know her. It seemed impossible that he had known the secrets of her body and had been her lover. She seemed as distant and unknowable as a star.

"If I was a young man," Frank Manybirds said, "I would go to work for the ranchers building fence. They have plenty of work and plenty of money." He went on talking.

The browning turkey dripped grease into the fire, sending up little flares of flame and delicious-smelling puffs of white smoke. Joe realized that he was hungry. He began to think he could eat half of it by himself. It was tantalizing to squat by the fire with the four of them, anticipating the good food, and strange too with the droning voice and the beautiful, silent girl moving before him.

After what seemed an interminable time, they ate, slicing off chunks and sprinkling them with salt from a box Mrs. Manybirds had set on the ground by the fire. They held the meat on knife points and exclaimed about how good it was and blew on burned fingers. Being hot, so that they had to eat it slowly and with difficulty, made it seem better. They chattered and it was an enjoyable feast for a time. When Frank had taken the edge off his appetite, he took one of the huge legs, sat back down in his chair, and began to talk again.

"What do you think about the allotments?" he asked.

"I don't know much about it," Joe said.

"Well, that's the way most of them are. They don't know much about it. Some of them are for it, some against it. Real strong, real sure. Ready to fight about it if you don't agree. Get all worked up. When they really don't know much about it.

"I say it's coming. It's coming. We'll get a hundred and sixty acres like a white man, and money for the rest. We might as well get the money while we can, I say. You know it's only seven years till the issues will stop? That's right. They better think about that. They better come in out of those hills and find them a good little piece of land on a creek."

He talked on about Indian politics, while the turkey steadily diminished. Mrs. Manybirds took the long neck, several clean bones and a piece of back she pulled loose to two old dogs that skulked out in the shadows, watching and waiting. The coals of the fire glowed dimly under their thickening cover of ashes. They picked smaller pieces of meat from the bones. Finally Frank stood up and stretched and said, "That was sure fine. Glad you came. Come to see us again sometime."

He found his rifle, and Lottie said, "Come back to see us again, Joe."

He walked out into the darkness, hardly thinking about the direction he was going. He came to the rail fence of Frank Manybirds' field, climbed over it and walked slowly along on the sandy earth. A small moon hung low in the west. Of all the things Frank Many-birds had said, two things he had said toward the first had stuck in his mind and had almost blocked out all the rest: How many coups have you got? And: Did you mean to give her father a couple of good horses? The crack about the coups was a good one to put any younger man in his place, whether the older man had ever earned any himself or not. The second question was some of the same kind of crap. Where would he get horses? Steal them? Work for them?

He would not have hesitated to go back to the Arm-stedts' at this time of night, even though Slow Tom was probably asleep, except that they had a shrill little spotted feist which liked to bark at the slightest excuse and wake up everybody in the neighborhood. He could see the darkness of the trees ahead of him beyond the fence and thought of sleeping on the dry grass·under the trees, but then thought of the danger of a snake crawling over him and decided it was better to stay in the field, where there was less ground cover. He sat down. The air was getting cool but the sandy soil was warm.

He arranged a few cornstalks to lay his gun on to keep it out of the dirt. Then, sitting cross-legged on the earth with the pale night around him, he thought awhile, or allowed his feelings their play. An idea with a cold and determined mien crept into his awareness. It was vague, but stern. Hard to see. It came in a devious way from his mother's exclamation: "My little boy!" He started to protest her words to himself, but stopped, and for a while felt sorry for himself. Then he felt the sternness of it. It was a cold and solemn idea that he faced. He must turn his back on them; that was it. In spirit. His mother and Lottie. He could be friendly on the outside, but inside he must say "no" to them. He had to find out what he must do and then do it, smiling at them with his heart closed up, and if he was lonely because of it, then he must be lonely. Above all he must do what he must do. He wished suddenly for a hundred coups which he could tell that old man in the baggy clothes, and it would take all night to tell them, and the man's ears would hear so much that they would swell up as big as his head and get so tired of listening they would droop down like a hound's.

He felt around on the ground for grass burs, then lay cheek down with his arm for a pillow. For a time before he fell asleep he thought about how easy it would be to sneak back to Frank Manybirds' corral and steal every horse he had.

5

MAKING POSTHOLES
AND SCHEMING

JOE AND SLOW TOM rode southwest mounted bareback
on two brown ponies of the Armstedts'. They had a job
helping build fence for a cattleman. It had been arranged by Slow Tom's uncle, who had been working as
a cowhand and had agreed to meet them on Pecan
Creek. Being poor at speaking English, Slow Tom had
been anxious for Joe to go and work with him. Joe himself was dubious about the prospect, uncertain about
everything he could think of at this time, but he had
an urge to see things he had not seen and do things he
had not done. The farther away from Lottie and his
mother, the better. If Lottie heard about it and imagined
that he intended to earn some horses to buy her hand
in marriage from her stupid father, she could think
again. As for building fence, if he didn't enjoy it he
would quit.

It was afternoon. They stopped at Snake Creek to let
the ponies drink, and slipped to the ground to ease
their legs by standing awhile.

Joe asked him, "You ever think about stealing some
horses?"

"Sure. Why?"

"I mean really make a big raid. You know. I don't mean just fooling around."

"You mean steal a couple of Frank Manybirds' old nags, for instance?"

"No, I'm serious."

"There's an old man that stays out hunting all the time, about half crazy. That Kwahadi. What's his name? If we could track him down, we could steal his pack mule."

"Hell, no, Slow Tom, I'm serious. I'm talking about a big horse-stealing raid. Like they used to go on."

"Well, I can't say that I've had it on my mind too much." Slow Tom's face was spread in a broad grin. "What kind of big plan have you got?"

"I haven't got a plan. And I'm not thinking about it especially. I'm just talking, see. But I'm serious. What's to keep us from doing something like that? We would get Spike Chanakut and Bill Nappy to throw in with us. Spike would go in a minute."

"What would we do it for?"

"Just for the hell of it. But do it up right. I don't mean pull a prank. You know the kind of stuff Bill Nappy would want to do—catch old preacher Fairchild's horse and cut his tail off. I don't mean that. We could get some real good horses."

"Whereabouts?"

"Down in Texas, for instance."

"We can't cross Red River. That's out of the reservation."

"We can't? Do you mean to tell me, Slow Tom, that you and I can't cross Red River? What is it? Some kind of a high wall we just can't climb over? You think we'll get stuck in the quicksand?"

Slow Tom laughed. "You know what I mean. You got to have a pass."

"Boy, you're sure some kind of a horse thief! Got to have a pass! Got to have a pass to steal horses? Let's say you've got to kill somebody to get away with the horses; do you have to have a pass for that too? Man, I can't seem to get it through your head what I'm talking about."

"Oh, I see. Yeah. I've got it now. I think Texas is out that way. Let's go, boy! Have you got plenty of shells for your rifle?"

"I told you I was just talking."

"Yeah, you're serious about talking, but not about doing."

"Well, buddy, I'll tell you what I really think. What the hell do we do all the time? Go around in circles! That's all. Why don't we *do* something? That's worth doing! Plan it, you know. Not rush into it, but give it a lot of thought. Then do it!"

They mounted, rode across the gully at the end of the water hole and proceeded at a leisurely pace. Finally Slow Tom said, "It sounds kind of like our scheme to gamble with the Carlisle boys that we've had for a couple of years."

"Maybe it does. But I'll tell you something." He rode along in silence a minute, trying to find a way to express himself, realizing that he had been insisting that it was serious, but also only talk, then said, "This isn't the same, Slow Tom. I have a feeling that we are really going to do it."

The land in this direction was nearly flat. It was rich sandy brown, with grass so lush in places that people cut it and sold it to the army for hay. The grass was cured now, from the heat and dryness, drab in color. The scattered prickly pears looked nearly the same, dusty gray-green. In patches and clumps across the distant flatness in every direction grew two plants that did not seem to know the time of year: tumbleweeds, surprisingly green, and broom weeds, yellow-green with tiny yellow flowers. They both carried a resinous oil in their leaves, and it lent a faint spicy scent to the autumn air. Their green color sketched random patterns across the stretches of flat land. Locusts were singing in the grass and fat grasshoppers flew before their horses hoofs.

Pecan Creek had little timber on it. They could see the cow camp, made of a covered wagon and one tent, two miles before they came to it. As they approached, a group of five riders came from the opposite direction, and Slow Tom saw his uncle among them. They went to him and, though he was not a talkative man, it was comfortable to have another Comanche to help them become familiar with the place.

Of those at the camp, Joe was most impressed with a white man named Mr. Powell, who was in charge of the fencing work. Mr. Powell drove up in a wagon with two Chickasaw boys, and Slow Tom's uncle took Joe and Slow Tom and introduced them to the man who would be their boss.

Mr. Powell shook hands with them.

Slow Tom grunted and nodded. Joe said in English, "Glad to meet you."

Mr. Powell did not act surprised about the grunt or the good English, but grinned and said to Joe, "Glad to see you fellows. I'll put you to work tomorrow."

He was a large man with a suntanned skin and, under his broad hat, a shock of steel-gray hair. The features of his face were rough and he had a stubble of gray beard. He spoke in a loud voice, but he was usually grinning, as if he wanted to be liked and expected to be, a man who was good at getting along with others.

They turned the two Armstedt ponies loose with the

unsaddled and unbridled horses of the other riders, and the bunch moved off together. Most of the horses that had carried saddles found a spot they liked and rolled on the ground. They crossed the creek and wandered out toward a band of some twenty horses that were grazing in the distance. Mr. Powell watered his team of mules and fed them some grain in a small corral made of poles and rope.

The ground around the camp was bare and cut up with horse tracks. The men lounged about waiting for their supper, the cooking of which had been sending a wonderful smell into the air. The man who was cooking suddenly yelled, "Yeah! Come after it!" and they began to gather at the table on the end of the big wagon and at the cook fire. There were piles of knives and forks and tin plates. Each man took what he wanted of the steak and red beans and biscuits and coffee.

Joe and Slow Tom watched the others, then filled plates and went over to a grassy spot beside a tree to sit down and eat.

In a minute Mr. Powell came with his plate and squatted in front of them. He asked Joe, "Do your people do the Ghost Dance?"

"No, sir. A few of them, but not many."

"I guess they don't believe in it."

"No, sir."

"But some of the Kiowas do, don't they?"

"Yes, sir. Some of the Comanches do too, but it's a certain band that lives up close to the north agency." He would ordinarily have felt reluctant or even suspicious to discuss such a thing with a white man, but Mr. Powell seemed so casual and agreeable that he did not mind.

"What do your people think about dividing up the reservation? Do they talk about it?"

"Yes, sir. Some are in favor and some against."

"How can they be in favor? Don't they want the land?"

"Well, they would get allotments of land, they say, and also some money."

"But the allotments would be for farms," Mr. Powell said. "They should raise cattle. This is good grazing country." He took a big bite of steak, chewed it for a while, then said, "They could do better ranching than farming. It would suit them better."

He made some further remarks along the same line and, when he stood up to leave them, said, "We got blankets right there in the front of the big wagon. Bed down wherever you can find a soft piece of ground."

The next morning they had eaten breakfast before clear daylight, and they went with Mr. Powell and the two Chickasaw boys in the wagon. After a short ride they came to the line for a new fence. The Chickasaw boys had evidently been working at the job for some time, but they spoke only a little poor English. Mr. Powell set about showing what must be done, speaking mostly to Joe.

First he gave the two new workers each a pair of work gloves made of leather and cloth. Then he showed how to step off ten steps from the last posthole, line up on the stakes ahead and dig a hole with the posthole diggers. A notch on one of the handles of the diggers showed how deep the hole must be. Mr. Powell did all this casually, but making it clear what he was doing. As he took the ten steps, he counted aloud and also on his fingers. As he lined up with the stakes out ahead, it was clear what he was doing by his act as well as his word. As he checked the depth of the hole, he put his thumbnail in the notch on the handle.

Joe was amused at the instruction process and interested in its meaning. The Chickasaw boys not only spoke poor English, but they were younger than he and Slow Tom; perhaps it was also significant that they were a different people. Teaching brings with it some opportunity for bossing. Mr. Powell had avoided making the younger men from a strange tribe into teachers. Then there were no insulting questions. How smart are you? Can you count to ten? Do you know that a fence must run straight? The man might have counted on his fingers because that was the way he always counted, for all anyone could tell. No one could misunderstand and no one was called stupid. It was a contrast to what some white men did. Sometimes a clerk at the store would weigh out sugar and pass over a handful of change and never say that the price of sugar per pound had gone up or down; you could figure it out if you could. Another might explain and explain an obvious matter, speaking English baby talk, making a great show of gestures and sign talk full of ridiculous errors, until a man became ashamed of both himself and the white man.

But this Powell had his own casual way. When he had seen that each of the four of them had a pair of posthole diggers out of the wagon, he did not wait to check their work, but took a pocket compass out of a leather case and began sighting along the line ahead. Then he took an armload of stakes and an ax and started out walking. Later they could see him out there a mile away, chopping down a bush or driving in one of the long stakes.

The soil was not hard to dig. Shortly the four of them were producing holes, each with its small mound of earth beside it, proceeding in ten-step intervals along the line where the fence would be. Each time the rear man finished a hole he would step off another ahead of the head man, so that each dug an equal number. The Chickasaw boys were chattering and sometimes giggling.

Joe became aware that a kind of challenge was being offered. When one of the Chickasaws was next to last, with a Comanche behind him, he would hurry to finish his hole, then stand yawning, staring insolently at the one behind him. They thought it was funny.

Slow Tom said, "These jackasses are having a lot of fun."

"I noticed that," Joe said.

"Do you think they could outdig us if we tried to keep them from it?"

"No, I don't hardly think they could."

Slow Tom was chunky of build, slow and stolid, but surprisingly strong and even agile if he had a reason to exert himself. He attacked a hole, his heavy diggers tossing up and down, causing the dirt to fly out onto the mound. Soon it was his turn to wait with exaggerated disgust for the slow Chickasaw behind him to finish and move up so that he could move up. At this, the race was on. Even the lead man had to dig fast lest he be caught too far behind at the rear.

The hot sun had come halfway up the sky. They soon dripped perspiration. It was a ridiculous competition, but none of them wanted to be the first to surrender.

Mr. Powell had come back to the wagon. He watched them awhile, grinning. Then he came over to Joe and said, "You fellows are going to be sore as a boil in the morning if you don't slow down."

"All right," he said, relieved.

Mr. Powell got another ax out of the wagon and motioned to one of the Chickasaw boys. "Come on and help me chop brush awhile."

The basis for any racing had been removed. Joe

thought that Mr. Powell must either favor new workers over old or Comanches over Chickasaws, or perhaps it was that he had been able to understand exactly how the foolish competition started.

He had not been around cattle workers before enough to study them. He had gone sometimes in past years to watch them drive their great, strung-out herds across the western edge of the reservation and to stand behind the chiefs while they demanded beef. The cattle drivers had seemed grim and distant, hardly human.

The men of this cow camp wore pistols at their sides, but they seemed friendly with one another. The cook and a redheaded boy stayed at the camp all the time. The riders came in at midday to eat a hurried meal and to change horses. In the evening they came in tired and sweaty, but some of them would be laughing about something. While they were eating they made jokes on each other, and afterward, lounging around the cook's fire, one of them might tell a bragging story about something he had done. In some ways they seemed like Comanches.

Mr. Powell was older than most of them. He fitted into their easy going ways, as if he belonged among them, but while they called each other Slim and Ace and Shorty and Buck and Baldy, they called him Mr. Powell.

The number of the cattle workers varied from day to day. Sometimes only three or four spent the night at the camp; another time it might be as many as ten. Joe gathered from their talk that they had another camp farther down toward Red River where they sometimes stayed.

The fencing work was not disagreeable. It made their muscles sore, but the soreness melted away in the heat and labor of the following day. Mr. Powell kept them working steadily but with no mood of urgency. Sometimes, when Joe had worked in silence awhile, aware only of his own movements and of the smell of the clods of virgin earth, he sensed that certain questions and worries flitted like moths about the outer borders of his mind. They sought his attention. He would not examine them, for they concerned Lottie and his mother. One advantage of the fencing work was that it took him away from them. Sometimes, to avoid the pestering thoughts, he would begin talking to Slow Tom.

One evening, sitting on their blankets out of earshot of the others, they talked about the horse band, which always roamed within a half mile of camp. Slow Tom agreed that there were at least fifteen excellent riding horses among them. Joe asked him, "If someone drove the whole bunch off some moonlight night, how long do you think it would take them to find out about it?"

"Next morning, I guess, when they went to catch up the ones they want."

"That redheaded kid that helps the cook—he watches the horses."

"Reckon he checks on them at night?"

"I doubt it," he said. "One of these nights we'll stay awake and see. What do you say?"

"All right with me. You're still real serious, are you?"

"This might be the place, Slow Tom. These people are just begging to have their horses taken."

"Well, there's one staked out right over there in the edge of camp and one with hobbles down on the creek—you can see him down yonder. They've always got two or three that way. What about them?"

"It would be best to take them."

"What about the mules? They're always hobbled or in the pen."

"Take them. Us with four or five hours' head start, and them afoot, what could they do?"

"Which way would we go?"

"North, then go out around the west end of the mountains. Maybe out into Cheyenne-Arapaho country. They'd be nervous following away out of white man's country, especially afoot."

"I don't mean to object all the time, Joe, but—"

"That's all right. Like I say, I'm serious, but we've got to think about objections; you can't do a thing like this without a good plan."

"Well, what I was going to say—what would we do with the horses then?"

"Some things you've got to handle when they come up. We would hide out awhile. What does anybody do with a good bunch of horses?"

They sat there in the twilight with their arms resting on their knees, thinking about it; then Joe asked, "What do you think about Bill Nappy and Spike Chanakut?"

"You mean will they come in on it?"

"Oh, they'll come in on it. I mean what do you think about them."

"They're a couple of coyote pups."

"But seriously."

"Seriously? Hell, I can't even tell how serious you are yourself, Joe."

"Well, I want to tell you," he said. "Before the winter hits—that's not far off—I mean to be rich in horses. All I'm looking for is the way to do it. I was never more determined about anything in my life."

"All right. I wouldn't want to leave out Spike and Bill, would you?"

"No. Spike is a good man, only old-fashioned. Bill is too, only a coyote pup, like you say. Listen, what about your uncle?"

"I don't think it matters much about him. I wouldn't want him to get hurt. The horses don't belong to him."

After a moment's silence Slow Tom asked, "You know who I wish was here to go in on it?"

"Who?"

"George Longwater."

He was surprised that Slow Tom, rarely sentimental, should mention their one-time friend. They never talked about him. At least it meant that Slow Tom was taking the scheme seriously. He said, "Yeah. I do too."

"You ever try to figure out why he did it?"

"Naw," Joe said. "He was friendly. He liked to laugh and joke. Smart as hell too. You can't figure a thing like that out. Sometimes I think maybe it was an accident of some kind."

Slow Tom said, "I can't hardly see how a man could cut his own throat by accident."

"No," he said, "but I can't hardly see George doing it on purpose either."

"I guess you can't figure a thing like that out," Slow Tom agreed.

Like other white men, these had one day in the week when they did not work. They rested, or did any activity other than work, according to the instructions of their god. He and Slow Tom decided to ride back to the Armstedts' for the day. Mr. Powell offered to advance them some money if they had any personal needs. Joe quickly accepted and asked for four dollars, which the man gave him.

The free day was uneventful, except that they went to the Red Store below the fort, and he spent his money on a full box of shells for his rifle. He filled the magazine of the gun and left the remaining supply of shells at the Armstedts' before they rode back toward the cow camp in the evening. It had been a bother to carry the rifle around and take care of it, but now it seemed different, since it was loaded. He might run into some game. But it was more than that; he had taken the first step, beyond speculation and tentative planning, toward the horse raid. He told Slow Tom that all four of them who would be in the scheme must have guns, shells, blankets, water bags, food to carry.

One day the following week they were working on a particular fencing problem to the east along the fence line. To here the posts had been set and the wire strung, but at this point a broad dry wash had to be crossed. Longer posts had to be used, set deeper and closer together, braced. Mr. Powell had all four of his workers engaged on it. In the middle of the afternoon they saw three horsemen dressed in cavalryman garb riding toward them from the north.

The riders entered the wash and rode across the gravel bed to where they worked. It was a young white lieutenant and two black-faced soldiers. Mr. Powell finished twisting the wire he had been working on, then straightened up and said, "Hello."

The lieutenant asked, "Are you Mr. Powell?"

"Yes, I am."

"The colonel would like to talk to you, Mr. Powell, if you can come up to the fort. Right now. Or as early tomorrow as possible."

Mr. Powell was grinning, as was his custom. He asked, "What does he want?"

"I'm not privy to the colonel's thoughts. He wants to see you as soon as possible. Those are my instructions."

"Well, Lieutenant, as you can see, I'm a working man. I can't drop my work just any time anyone wants to see me. I don't even know your colonel."

"I'm pretty sure, Mr. Powell, that he wouldn't have sent for you unless it was necessary."

Joe noticed that Mr. Powell's grin had slowly left his face. The man said, "I'm not a soldier! I don't jump when the colonel yells at me! Who does he think he is?"

The lieutenant was confused for a moment. He dismounted. The two other soldiers dismounted and one of them held his horse.

"I think you have got the wrong impression," he said. "It's not an order. It's just a matter of being cooperative. You might consider it an invitation."

"Well, I'm not taking the colonel up on his invitation. Who runs this reservation anyway? The Bureau and the Indian councils and the agent, or is it the army?"

"Mr. Powell, I'm only bringing a message. I don't know anything about it. I'm just trying to do my duty."

"All right, thanks for the message. Maybe I know more about it than you do. Maybe we are starting in to find out who has the last word on this reservation."

"Then, sir, do you refuse to come?"

"I damned sure do! Tell him he can let me know what he wants to see me about. Or *he* can come to see *me*. I've got a fence to build."

The lieutenant stood there a moment, finally said, "Thank you," then mounted and rode off with his two soldiers.

Mr. Powell was quiet for a while, but before time to go in for supper he had become as good-humored as ever. He said nothing against the soldiers, or in explanation. He seemed to consider it a closed matter.

Later in the week, when they had only one day to work before their day off, the two Chickasaw boys quit their jobs. Joe had gathered that they intended to do so, from bits of talk between them and Mr. Powell. It seemed that they had found work closer to their homes, over east of the Kiowa-Comanche reservation. They got their few belongings at the cow camp and left before supper.

While they were eating Mr. Powell brought his plate over, squatted down and asked Joe, "You haven't got any friends that want a job, have you? We'll be short two hands."

"Yes, sir, I know two men who could do good work building fence."

"Reckon you could get them for me?"

"Yes, sir."

"I'd appreciate it. You can take off in the morning. Me and Slow Tom will haul a load of posts. Then the next day is Sunday. If you could have the new men here Monday morning, we'll be in good shape."

He had entertained various ideas as to what luck is, being willing often to think of it in a cynical way as did others of the young people who were suspicious of the oldsters' superstitions, concluding that it was nothing but an attitude about what had already happened and meant nothing. But again, alone or touched by the influence of one of those oldsters, he would see patterns in events, as if all the spirits, all the invisible duplicates of creatures and things, favored a certain way and contributed to it, or perhaps as if the Earth Mother herself smiled on a man and his project. It did seem more than coincidence that he should desire to bring Spike Chanakut and Bill Nappy down here so that they could learn the lay of the land and help plan his scheme and that Mr. Powell had conveniently asked him to find two men for the fencing work. It could be that, if unseen forces were working, they meant to raise him up only to dash him down; but he did not want to believe it was true, even if it was possible. All of that depended on uncertainties anyway. The thing for him to do was take advantage of whatever offered itself.

6

HIS MOTHER MAKES
BOUGHT MEDICINE

HE RODE north on the Armstedt pony early in the morning, following the course of Pecan Creek. To the west a mile or two ran Blue Beaver Creek, alongside which in the edge of the mountains lay the camp where he would expect to find his two friends. The issue of where he was going and whether he was headed directly there did not arise, for, though he had two free days and nights before him, he had not thought of doing anything except go after Spike Chanakut and Bill Nappy. Yet he did not cross over the slight divide to the other creek. The Mountains of the Wichitas rose higher before him and he rode on, daydreaming and remembering. He came to the headwaters of Pecan Creek where it divided into nothing but small gullies with no trees along them, and he was annoyed to see Bald Mountain due west of him. He had put a mountain between himself and his destination. He came over a divide in the southern mountains where he could have turned back down Blue Beaver, but he did not, and at last, irritated, he admitted to himself that he was headed for the camp of Old Man Iron Lance in the north edge of the mountains.

He did not want to be troubled by the troubles of his

mother. It was not that he did not love her, nor that he was not willing to aid her if he could, but that he wanted to be free of her. She would cast a net over him made of the strings of her affection and her ideas of what he ought to be. What did he care for her White Buffalo? The man had probably been a weakling nobody.

It was to some extent to take his mind from her that he turned back to his memories. Though she was in them, his going to see her today was not in them. He thought that if he knew every fact of his own beginnings he would be better satisfied with himself, but more than knowing facts it was a question of finding a sequence and a meaning.

His memories were of various kinds. Some were sharp and positive images, limited in their extent but certain, known without recourse to any other person, often begging for explanation but not for confirmation. Then there were things known that he must have got from other people, or from solid confirmations themselves forgotten, things beyond doubt that had fixed themselves in his mind. But some memories were less knowledge than impression, perhaps the result of childish ignorance. And he understood that his sorting and seeking was hindered because he had engaged in remembering in years past, sometimes in an atmosphere of mistaken impressions, because now he might not be remembering original things, but only remembering memories.

The image of his father came from one specific time and place, what time and place he did not know. There was no picture, only the feeling of being next to a large man. Belonging and familiarity were a part of it. The certainty that the man was his father was not part of the image, but one of those facts whose proof is lost. It seemed his earliest memory, but he could not be sure, for other memories did not arrange themselves in time.

His childhood was full of war and rumors of it, of havoc, flight, the deprivation and hardship that go with it. The spirits of their camps were attitudes relating to war: The Bluecoats are out of their forts! We shall have victory next time! We must move camp! What will we do for food now? Our allies will save us! A Comanche can whip five white men! Be prepared to save the horses! How can we fight in the winter? All of it urgency amid disruption. Much of it seen from the side of the women and children, fearing, hiding, waiting. His mother's voice often saying, "This is a dangerous time when we must all be brave and follow the orders of the chiefs." Then, occasionally, sudden action, the dashing of men and horses, the whack of guns and the whip of bowstrings, shouts, screams, the blood of men and horses spilling on the ground. The end of that hectic time had come with women putting it thus: We are sick of war, so now we will go live on the reservation where it's safe. The reservation is peaceful and one can draw rations. It had been hard for a boy to recognize that there was more in it than that. Indeed, he had been uncertain for a long time whether they camped on the reservation or whether they only went there to draw food. He remembered seeing the Bluecoats and thinking: Even the white man is tired of war and has come to the reservation where he can get rations and live in peace.

A good amount of that was connected in his memory. One important early battle was not. He and his mother had been in a camp of people by a river—he had come to understand later that it was the upper Washita—and they had not belonged in the camp. He had stayed near his mother, but he was not afraid, for though they were a strange people, she seemed to be familiar with some of them and at ease; he had figured out later that he must have been about five years old. They spoke a garbled and meaningless speech, and his mother spoke a few words of it and made a lot of hand signs with them; he had later learned that they were Cheyennes and that his mother's grandmother had been one of them. The wind blew cold and snow covered the red land around the camp.

The people danced in the snow one night and sang and shouted their peculiar words. But one morning, in the still dawn, havoc burst suddenly all about, as if it had come out of the sky, from whence the snow came. Dogs barked, men shouted, horses ran, women screamed. They were running and he saw all the bright blood on the snow in patches and sprays and drops. His mother was shot in the thigh and he was nicked along the neck, enough to make a small white scar that he would carry forever. Through luck and her strength, they crawled out of it, through the river slushy with ice, and they pushed south on a long, difficult walk to safety.

This battle was important in his memory because he had not only the certain personal images, but also many miscellaneous facts that he had been able to add to it through the years. He knew the names of some of the people who had been there: Two Bows, a distant kinsman, Black Kettle, Old Smallstar. The leader of the white soldiers had been Long Hair, defeated later by the Sioux and Cheyennes up north.

He did not believe that the long walk to safety had been the same as that other long walk. That other one might have been earlier or it might have been later. It was an event, or not so much an event as an awareness of a process, to which he had been unable to add anything during later years. As for the actual memory, it was that of a thought which had persisted in his mind:

My mother and I, we walk across the earth. We walk every day and sometimes during the night. I knew it the day before this and the days before that, I had it in my mind and thought about it, I understand day after day that this is our way of life. In the cool dew we walk away from the sunrise; after the hot sun is on our heads, it comes before our face and we walk toward the sunset. When my legs hurt she carries me.

That was all of it. He had not questioned about their place of departure or their destination. The propriety of it he had somehow absorbed from his mother without question.

There were memories of later times which were clear and connected, but unsatisfactory, part of an unfulfilled promise. Of these, a crucial one had been the great buffalo hunt. He had been thirteen years old. The men still talked war, but did not go. Their hunting party, led by Chief Tabananica, came upon a great herd. He had seen the glorious sight of the herd himself, a wealth of challenge, brown-black shaggy creatures, moving, grazing, bunched, scattered, stretching into the distance to suggest an inexhaustible plenitude. He knew two boys, only a couple of years older than himself, who were to ride with the hunters, one with a bow and one with a gun. The two of them were greatly excited. He had forgotten whether they were successful, but he remembered his own admiration and envy. There was much planning and agreeing and busyness as the men mounted up for the surround and hunt. He got to watch part of it, the wild riding, the stampeding beasts, the rising dust, got to hear the thunder of hoofs and the exultant yells. After that he had to help his mother with the skinning and butchering. The men killed all the meat anyone could use.

Sometime later, it might have been a year, he got to

go on another big hunt, and he had made a strong bow, actually stronger than he could pull, had also two good arrows that he had found and a dozen crooked ones that he had made. He had not yet solved the problem of a trained hunting horse, and therefore knew that he would not get to ride with the hunters. But anyway, the party found only seven buffalo, alive. They found many bare and shriveled carcasses scattered on the land, stinking carrion.

They went again and again. When he was seventeen he went with a party, and he was ready. He had a beautiful new gun—the ten-year-old rifle that he now carried across the withers of the Armstedt pony—and had made arrangements to borrow a first-class buffalo horse from another boy's father. He had ammunition. The hunting party found white bones in the valleys. They went on and found bones on the crests of the gentle hills, they searched on and found bones in the alkali flats, in the gullied wastelands, across the sweeping grassy prairie. When their supplies gave out and they became too hungry to go on, they returned to the reservation. That was the last communal hunt they attempted.

He felt resentful of all he had been thinking as he threaded his way through these mountains of mossy granite. Not the past events; only their hold on him. Had they been inconsequential it would be different. They had their claws in him, like the sharp nails of a hawk fastened into a ground squirrel. It was not their evil, but their persistence. It was that memories are not things of the past, but of the present. It was that they clinch a man's existence and his nature and twist him. He resented his memories the same way that he resented the persistence of his mother and his sweetheart, in a kind of tender and anguished way. Why should a man be a creature of women and a creature of his own childhood, especially when the childhood is a chaos of unexplained or lost or meaningless events?

His mother's lodge was empty and the ashes of the cook fire were cold. He took a string of dried beef to chew on and walked along the path which wound among the oaks into the main part of the Iron Lance camp. The place was quiet, except that down alongside the creek a woman was scraping diligently on an iron pot. He saw Freddy Bull brushing a horse.

Freddy Bull was a Carlisle boy, who could not make up his mind whether to wear his hair short or long. He had once been a friend, but now Joe's friends considered him womanish, and he acted in a peculiar way sometimes or ill at ease. He appreared to concentrate deeply on his work as Joe approached, picking bits of dried mud from the horse's mane and brushing deliberately.

He asked him, "Freddy, do you happen to know where my mother is?"

"No."

"Have you seen her the last couple of days?"

"She was making a lot of medicine with my old man. I don't know anything about it."

"Was that yesterday?"

"I guess it was the day before, or the day before that."

"Did you see which way she went?"

"No."

As he turned away, he changed to English and said, "Well, thank you very much, Freddy." It was a mild reproof, as if to say, Don't think you're better than the rest of us just because you've been away to school.

Actually, the reference to making medicine with old Duncan Bull—buying medicine was more the truth—had been a help, a confirmation of what he had begun to surmise. He went back to the canvas tipi he shared with his mother and saw that the grass-stuffed pad, which she used when she rode the mule, was gone. He remounted the brown pony and started east along Medicine Bluff Creek, the same route he and his mother had followed on the fine paint horses and with great expectations several days before.

He pushed the tired pony down the winding trail to where the creek turns south and out across the bare rolling plains toward where the new trader's store had been built. It was late afternoon and the pony nearly worn out when he topped the last small rise, from which he could see East Cache Creek and sketchily the road to the north agency and dimly, up to his left, the new building.

Dismounting to rest his legs, he stood awhile to consider the lay of the land. Down to his left ran a small stream bed with scattered trees and brush; beyond that, on the next rise, grew a clump of shinnery, somewhat nearer the trading store than he now stood. He walked in that direction, leading the Armstedt pony, and before he had gone a hundred steps he saw his mother's mule staked in the low ground.

As he climbed up the rise toward the green clump, he heard a sound so faint that it did not demand identification; it might be the wind, though the air was still, or a cow lowing, or a distant coyote baying. But it grew louder, more intrusive. It was too varied for any of those things. It was a crooning, broken by interruptions, now high pitched, now hoarse, with an inhuman note in it, but so varied and so full of passion and despair that it could come from nothing but a human throat and mouth. Even as it became a mystery he realized that he was hearing his mother singing a prayer.

He paused, feeling like an intruder. He moved forward quietly, paused again. It went on and on, plaintive and persistent. He did not want to interrupt. Finally he became annoyed at his own timidity. He jerked at the brown pony and shouted, "Come on, you jackass!" Then he strode ahead, cursing the horse and kicking the rocks in his path.

She sat quietly on the ground, waiting, when he came up. The scrub oak and shinnery formed a kind of nest from which a person could look out upon the new trader's store a half mile away. She said calmly, but hoarsely, "Son, I've been hoping to see you. Where have you been so long?"

"What did you want me for?"

"What does any mother want? I wish you wouldn't go off and stay weeks and weeks."

He thought she was trying to make an issue of it because she was embarrassed. He told her, "I got a job."

"That's good. That's a good thing. What do you do in the job?"

"Build fences. Away down south where the cattlemen are."

"Do they give you plenty of food?"

"Yeah."

He could guess by the worn grass and crunched limbs that she had been here two or three days. Things lay around: a can of water, a burlap sack, the saddle pad, and on a clean white cloth two little dusty piles, one of which looked like bone scrapings, one of which looked like crumpled dry leaves with the dust of puff balls upon them. He looked straight at the white cloth and knew that she saw him.

Bluntly he plunged into the barrier of privacy that existed between them. He asked, "What is that?"

She resisted during a moment of silence, then responded, "*Puha.* For love. And for hate."

"Do you believe in it?"

"Of course I do. Why would you ask that? When you know I do."

"I don't know what you believe," he said. "I've heard you talk seriously about it, and I've heard you make fun of it."

"I believe in it," she said, then a little later, "I have to do whatever I can."

"Is she still down there?"

"No, I haven't seen her at all."

"Has he come to his store?"

"No. I haven't seen him at all. Something's wrong."

"What did you pay Duncan Bull for all that stuff?"

"For the words and everything, I paid our issue for four ration times."

"What in the world are you going to eat?"

"Well, that's all right. If nothing else, the acorns are ripe."

"That bitter stuff?"

She stared out through the leaves toward the new store, clearly visible, and the new house, which could partly be seen toward the rear. She said, "Maybe the medicine went wrong some way. Maybe I hurt him by mistake instead of her. Something's wrong."

"I think you ought to go back to camp," he said.

"I don't hate her," she said. "I thought about it all last night. I don't really hate her if she treats him like she ought to." She glanced up briefly at him, then back down. "Some men have two wives. I should be the *paraibvo* because I was really first. It would be only right. But if it had to be that way, I would be willing to take the place of second wife. I'm not too proud; I just want to be around close to him."

He wanted to slash through her sincerity and humility.

"Be close to him! What was he anyway? Wasn't he what they called a squaw man?"

"Joe, you don't understand."

"I wish you wouldn't keep on telling me that! Why don't I understand? Was he a squaw man or wasn't he?"

"What is this squaw man? I don't know anything about that. You don't understand." Suddenly she thought of a thing to tell him, and rushed to relate it. "Once there was trouble over an antelope that was killed. A man started shoving and arguing, and White Buffalo knocked him down, and then gave the meat away. They said there would be trouble over it. They said it would come to a bad fight in our camp. They came to our lodge and talked about it, and your father told them he didn't want a bad fight, but he was in the right, and if trouble was to come, let it come. But the trouble didn't come. You know why? That other man took his family and left and went to join another band. So you see? He was very respected, Joe. I've always taught you that, and it's true."

"I don't say it isn't true. But those whites, they don't do like you say, Mother. They don't have two or three wives. Don't you see what it means?"

"What?"

"He doesn't want you."

She looked out at the lonely trading store for a minute, then said, "I keep asking myself questions like that, but I don't believe it's true. He knows the Comanche ways. He chose them, Joe. He could have lived among the whites. Why did he choose to be a Comanche in the first place? Just because the whites don't have two wives doesn't mean he wouldn't."

"He chose? That was a long time ago."

"What difference does it make? He chose."

"It makes all the difference! You know it's not the

same now as in the old times. Now he has chosen white ways." He thought of telling her more about it that he thought he could understand: that white men can control their lives, that they come and go as they please, that when life is good they enjoy it and when it is bad they change it or leave it behind, that they do not permit loyalty and memory to cause them pain. But even as he was thinking these things he knew that he could not support them with examples or proof.

"Then why has he come back?" She asked this question so that it was not an argument, but a plea. She repeated in her hoarse voice, "Why has he come back?"

"He wants to make money selling things."

"He could make money selling things lots of places. Why has he come here? Maybe he has chosen again."

He felt it a necessary cruelty as he said, "He came here because it doesn't make any difference to him. It shows how little he thinks of us."

"No. You don't know how it was between us."

"Maybe it's you who doesn't know."

"Maybe so. And maybe it's you. Do you know everything? Could you be mistaken about it? Sometimes a person can be sure about a thing and still be wrong. I know how it was with White Buffalo and me. I think you ought to trust me about that and believe me."

"Why should I believe you?"

He felt certain she was going to say, Because I'm your mother.

But she said, "Because I love you."

He was taken aback for a moment, then slung his arm toward the small piles of powder and burst out at her, "Then what's all this? Why doesn't it work? If he was so pleased with you, where has he been? If you're willing to crawl to him and be his second wife, why are you using hate powder against that woman? You're going around in circles. If you think he wants you, why don't you hunt him up instead of sitting out here in the bushes?"

"I don't know," she said. "I'm afraid."

"You're ashamed of being an Indian."

"No, I'm not."

"I'm going to kill him as soon as I get the chance."

"No, you're not, Joe."

"You'll see. As soon as you find out what he thinks of you, then you'll change your mind, and you'll tell me to go ahead."

"No, I won't. You shouldn't talk this way about your father, Joe."

"He's no father of mine."

"He is too."

"If you believe in these things you bought from Duncan Bull, why are you willing to be a second wife?"

The shadow of the rise on which they sat had lengthened so that it reached the new store beside the creek. All of the rolling land was a patchwork of shadows and high spots lighted by the failing sunlight.

"I don't know what's the matter," she said. "Maybe the medicine is no good. Maybe I did something wrong. I'm afraid maybe I caused him to be hurt some way. I just don't know."

"Hasn't anyone been down there since you've been waiting here spying?"

"No. Two men came along the road and they nailed a white thing on the door of the store. Then they went back. It wasn't him. That's all."

He didn't feel as if he had accomplished a thing with his day of hard travel to see her. He said, "I have to go, Mother. I wish you would go back home. You can't live out here in the open. I have a job, like you're always telling me. Now why can't you do something I want you to do?"

"I've been thinking about going home," she said. "I don't seem to do any good."

"Then go on home."

"Will you come home, Joe, whenever you can?"

"Yeah."

"And don't do anything foolish?"

"I'll promise you one thing," he said. "What you do is your business. That man wouldn't take you for a second wife and that woman wouldn't allow it either. But if they are willing and you do it, that's the last time you'll see me. I'm not a mat for a white man to step on."

He started to mount the Armstedt pony and she said, "Wait, Joe."

He turned back to her.

"I want to tell you something."

"Tell me. I've got to go."

"I guess you'll hate me. But I can't help it. You think he left me. I left him. I took you and ran away."

He thought that she must certainly believe that he was stupid.

"Why did you run away from him?"

"I was scared of Saint Louis."

"Where is Saint Louis?"

"It's away out east."

"What were we doing there?"

"The whites had a big war when you were born and we also had a lot of fighting. We had so many strange allies coming into our camp. . . . They didn't know your father, so he finally had to leave, and he took us to white country."

"So then you ran away."

"Yes. He had to go somewhere three days, and I

couldn't stand it. There were too many new things and white people."

Though he did not believe any of it, the story seemed elaborate to have been made up suddenly. He asked, "When we ran away, did we go on horseback or in a wagon?"

"We walked," she said.

"Was it a long walk?"

"Yes. We walked to the mountains. Then I wanted to go back to Saint Louis, but I couldn't find the way. I couldn't find out how to go. And I thought you would die from too much walking. I thought he would come and find us."

He did not want to believe it. She might be lying for her own reasons. If it were true it would make a difference, but not any difference that would do either of them any good now.

He mounted and rode toward the new store in the dusk. He crossed the road and paused immediately in front of the building. A white piece of paper with white man's writing on it was tacked to the door. He stared at it desperately. Here was some meaning, some intention to give a message. He felt as if someone were speaking to him a thing he had a right to know, but he could not hear them.

Suddenly he felt unreasoning anger at the frustration. It was unfair. Like dangling meat before a starving man. Why should they have a thing called writing when Indians couldn't read? He ought to rip it down and tear it up. But, of course, Freddy Bull could read. It was a chastening thought, to which he had no answer.

Except for the paper the place looked the same as it had. He could tell, even in the fading light, that little or no tracks had been made in the dusty soil around the building for several days.

He tried to imagine the looks of White Buffalo, starting with a man like Iron Lance, only bigger and stronger and younger. But white. He envisioned an Indian with white skin. His vision had no face. The trouble with it was that it was a boy's dream instead of any kind of possible reality, and he felt sure that no man's face could ever really belong on it. If a man appeared now and said, "I'm White Buffalo," it would seem like a lie, no matter who it was.

He turned the reluctant pony and urged him along a half mile downstream, where he crossed East Cache Creek. He dismounted in a secluded spot where the grass would provide forage. The pony he hobbled with the rope which had served for bridle reins. Then he went out on an open gravel bar beside the water to lie down to rest and pass the night.

Out of the long-ago time of Comanche magnificence and dominance, one thing which stood out to him as a tantalizing mystery more than any other was the nature of medicine. It was an example and a symbol to him of how one can know all the answers and find them not sufficient, knowing that vague and unasked questions hide in the shadows; of how one can see the facts in all their surface detail and find them pitiful, knowing that somehow at the heart of it all had been certain essential matters of the spirit that transcended the details. He was skeptical with that healthy doubt which was typical of his people, but he knew that his forefathers, powerful and effective men, had possessed a pure faith in one medicine and another, and he believed that such medicines, then at least, had possessed potency, though not of a kind easily explained. Were they magic? He didn't know what he believed, and when he followed the question he came not to an answer, but to another question as to what magic is.

He had seen them act in contradictory ways. He had once seen an old, honored man die, and that man's wife and aged brother take the dead man's medicine bundle and place it in the rushing deep water as tenderly as if they were putting a baby in a mother's arms and as sadly as if the baby were dead, not dead in the sense of worthless, but precious and holy and belonging to another world. The brother's shaking hands held the bundle until it filled with water and would barely float, then thrust it out into the grip of the current. They watched it move away, nearly hidden in the water, and wept with the sorrowful and solemn faces of old age. Seeing it, he understood their faith and the propriety of what they did. Under the water was mystery and the destination of a thing in the water was a vast uncertainty. Somewhere in the midst of the uncertainty the spirits who had given the medicine would receive it back unto themselves again. A life was gone and the power which had assisted that life was returned to its proper place. The transitory and the wholesome everlasting were come together.

He knew that many medicine bundles had floated during his lifetime down the streams north toward the Washita River and south toward the Red. Some the property of men who had passed away. Some the property of hopelessly frustrated and surrendering men who followed a form which could mean nothing to them, only nonsense, for gods who can die were never gods.

He had heard men scoff and joke and talk sarcastically about each other's medicine, as they sometimes did about the ceremonies of the Kiowas. One time when he was half grown, when he was asking himself the meaning of the reservation and medicine and such, he had

seen a man named Smoky dispose of his bundle. Of the
man's reasons he had no idea. He saw Smoky walking
away from camp among the trees, a small bundle in
his hand, and he followed to spy on him. He expected
to see a religious act or rite. Smoky sat down on a log,
held the bundle in his two hands and stared at it. Peering through the leaves from forty steps away, he could
not see that Smoky did anything except sit calmly and
stare. Then the man untied the thong, unrolled the strip
of dark blanket, and at last took out small objects one
by one and dropped them on the ground between his
feet. All of it he did slowly and thoughtfully, until he
stood up; then he looked down, obviously at the objects
he had dropped, and suddenly swung his foot to scatter
them. The man immediately turned away and walked
back toward camp, trailing the strip of blanket in his
hand. He went forward to the log and searched the
ground in front of it. He found three of the objects:
the shell of half the cloven hoof of an antelope, the
dried leg and foot of a hawk or owl, a small bone from
a rabbit or prairie dog, shiny from handling. The bird's
foot, dried with its claws spread, he kept several days,
contemplating it in secret, but he could not forget the
previous owner's contempt for it, so was not able to
imagine any value in it. He threw it away.

Then, more recently—it had been two years now—
the suicide of George Longwater had come about because of, at least as a part of, a medicine search. The
young man had been good-natured, thoughtful, hand-
some, with deep-set black eyes and an easy grin. He
liked to joke and never showed himself to be worried.
Joe had not thought him serious about religious ideas.
Yet one morning he had burst out in anger at his father and mother and sisters for no reason, they said,
and when one sister ran after him to ask where he was

going, he said he intended to pray four days on the top of Hawkhead Mountain. He had no food and no clothes except moccasins and breechclout, a knife stuck in the rope belt around his naked waist. It was the last time they saw him alive. On the fifth day, believing he would be weak from hunger, the sisters prevailed upon a neighbor man to carry food to him. The man found George Longwater dead. He had been dead about a day. He had killed himself with his knife.

Now, only in the past few months, rumors of new religious ideas were in the air. They were based on an understanding that a Messiah had once come to the white people long ago, but the whites had not given him a place to be born, so his mother bore him in a trough where cattle are fed; the whites had not believed him when he taught, and finally they had tortured him to death. Now an exact time of years had passed, and the Messiah had come back, this time to the Indians. He was waiting somewhere west of the mountains, so the Arapaho and Cheyenne said, and the scars could still be seen in his hands and feet where the whites drove nails in him. If the Indians would believe in him and dance *Apa Nekara*, the Ghost Dance, the new earth would come and on it all the Indian forefathers and wild horses and elk and buffalo. It was difficult for most Comanches to believe. They had come to have a kind of nervous appreciation that the world is full of monstrous jokes.

7

FENCING TROUBLES

HE FOUND little difficulty at the Blue Beaver camp in persuading Spike Chanakut and Bill Nappy to go south with him and join the fencing crew. All it took was a hint of the horse-raiding scheme. Spike, the more eager of the two, even went so far as to put on a pair of trousers over his usual breechclout. They walked into the cow camp late Sunday afternoon, Joe leading the exhausted Armstedt pony. He himself was as tired as if he had worked. During the past two days he had traveled some sixty miles horseback and afoot.

Mr. Powell grinned and shook hands with the new workers, saying, "Howdy," and seeming to pay no attention that they did not answer him in English. Later, while they were eating, he came and squatted down to talk. Joe thought it was for the purpose of making friends with the new men, even though they could not understand his words.

The man asked, "Have you fellows been in any good arguments about the land allotments lately?"

Joe said, "No, sir."

"Did you say you were against it or for it?"

He didn't remember saying and, though he was against it, saw no reason to commit himself. "We haven't given it much thought, I guess."

"Well, here's what I think," Mr. Powell said. "They're going to try to buy the land too cheap. Then the white farmers will swarm in. The money will soon be gone, and by the time the Comanches find out what a dirty deal it is, it will all be settled. This is too dry for farm land. And Comanches can do better ranching anyway. Don't you think so?"

"Most of them don't like farming," he said.

"Who is this Quanah fellow?" Mr. Powell asked.

"A big chief."

"The army made him a chief, didn't they?"

"No, sir, I don't think so."

"I wonder what he thinks about dividing the land?"

"I don't know," Joe said.

As Mr. Powell rose to go, he said, "Well, I hope they give it plenty of thought. They can hold every acre of it if they all stick together." He had spoken in a casual and friendly manner, but left no doubt about his opinion.

After supper as they lounged by themselves, Joe reported the English conversation to his three friends. He and Spike and Slow Tom agreed with what the white man had said. But Bill Nappy said, "Maybe if they paid for the land everybody would have plenty of money, and we could buy all the horses we want."

They looked at him in great disgust.

Spike asked him, "Who have you been talking to?"

"Well, plenty of people agree to it. What's the matter with money?"

"Sounds like he's been talking to Great Eagle, that soldier-lover," Slow Tom said.

"I'm not trying to say they should do it," Bill Nappy said. "I just say that plenty of people agree to it and they say we ought to grab the money while we can." Obviously he had not thought about it much and now was uncomfortable in the position he had taken.

Joe said, "If they paid for the land, it would be years before we saw any of the money."

They sat and lay on their blankets in silence for a minute, then Bill Nappy burst out, "You know something we ought to do sometime? I've got a buffalo gun. A Big Fifty. It'll shoot a mile. Well, we load her up good and go up to the fort. See? We get all ready. Then we blast away and shoot a hole in the water tower. We hide the old Big Fifty. Then we go running up to the soldiers and say, 'What happened? We heard a loud sound! What happened?' "

They could not keep from laughing.

"What do you think about it?" he asked.

"It would be all right," Spike said, "if we didn't have anything else to do."

"Well, something else I thought of. Over east, these Chickasaws have got these fields full of pumpkins and stuff. No guards. We could slip over there and fill up a wagon and be gone before they ever knew what happened."

"Oh, boy," Slow Tom said. "A wagonload of pumpkins."

Joe sat up and asked Bill Nappy, "Do you know what we're doing down here?"

"Where?"

"Right here, dammit! What are we doing? Are we here because we like to build fences, or what?"

"To steal horses, I thought."

"That's right. We're here to look things over and plan. Now, do you want to be in it or not?"

"Sure I do."

"I thought we ought to give you a chance to get out. Then you could go and steal pumpkins or something by yourself."

"No, I'm serious. I just didn't know it was all worked out."

"We're going to get some first-class horses," Joe told him. "If you know where the Chickasaws have a big bunch of horses, we'll go over there and look at them. We're going to take a good look at the cavalry horses at the fort and study how they guard them. But this looks real good to us right here, so far."

"It looks good to me," Bill said. "You're the boss."

Spike asked, "Who is the boss of this raid?"

"Joe is," Slow Tom said. "I've got all I can do just to boss myself."

Bill asked, "How much experience has Joe had leading horse raids?"

He seemed to have a gift for saying the wrong thing without thinking. They all looked at him in disgust.

But the question of experience set Joe's mind to work on an idea, which he developed as he proposed it to them. "What if I talked to some of the old men? There are tricks to horse raiding. Old Iron Lance, for instance. I'd put up a good front and get him to talking and act like he was a big hero. I might learn plenty."

"It might work," Slow Tom said. "You'd have to do it right. We don't want our scheme spread all over."

"Talk to some medicine man," Spike said.

"I know some old men that like to brag," Bill said.

Slow Tom said, "You better leave it to Joe. This is delicate business, touchy. I think we ought to agree to let Joe handle it and we won't have so much danger of spreading the word all over the country."

Joe told them, "I figure old men are funny; suspicious and hardheaded, but gullible, you know. It'll take shrewd questioning, but not too much. They're long-winded and like to give advice. I won't even mention horse stealing. I'll hear about a hundred big lies, and out of that maybe I can sort out some stuff we can use."

"Iron Lance would be good," Slow Tom said. "Only you don't have time to get back up there if we only get off one day a week."

"I'll have to think about it," he said. "Any time I get ready I'll take off two or three days if I need it."

"Talk to some medicine man," Spike said.

Mr. Powell evidently did not think it necessary to go through his teaching routine with the two new workers. He left the four of them digging postholes alone all morning. But in the afternoon he stayed with them, taking the diggers of first one then another, while they took a short rest.

Joe was thinking, Why doesn't he just tell us what to do and then go sit in the shade of the wagon and let us do it? He actually liked the man, had found him the most friendly white man, the easiest to be around, that he had ever known. But the very liking was for some reason a source of irritation, as much toward himself as Mr. Powell.

They were working no more than a mile and a half above the cow camp. In the middle of the afternoon, the horse band strayed out toward them to graze, strung out in clear view. Joe finished a hole, walked past Mr. Powell with a grin, and said to the others in Comanche as casually as if he were commenting on the weather, "I get the big bay with the white nose."

Slow Tom paused to wipe his forehead, gazed out across the land in the opposite direction from the horses, and said, "I'll take that long-legged dun on the other side."

"I haven't had a chance to study them," Spike said. "Is that dark paint any good?"

"He's big," Joe told him. "I haven't seen him ridden. That paint away back in the rear is a good one."

"I'll take him," Bill Nappy said.

They took delight in this game of mild revenge against the white man who worked beside them. Joe thought that the others probably found it sweeter than he did. How many times they had faced the language barrier when they were around whites and felt their own shortcomings! They discussed the merits of the horses—which ones might be best for a fast getaway, which ones appeared to have stamina, which ones were most beautiful. Sometimes they looked at the horse band, in order not to appear to avoid them. They enjoyed the sense of their own cleverness, the audacity, the hint of danger in it.

The next morning they worked in the same place, extending the line of postholes across the nearly level prairie. Mr. Powell briefly checked his stakes ahead against his compass, then began to take a hand with the digging. High gray clouds covered the sky and made the day dim and cool.

Joe caught movement in the distance to the north and paused to look. Three horesemen were coming at a trot. They sat like soldiers. He said to Mr. Powell, "It looks like some soldiers are coming again."

The man looked, frowning, then laughed. "I reckon so." He went ahead working until the riders had come up between them and the wagon and were dismounting. It was a white officer with a black moustache and two black-faced soldiers.

The officer stepped forward to shake hands with Mr. Powell. "Hello, Mr. Powell."

"Hello, Major."

They both grinned in a friendly manner. The officer's

moustache seemed to have tallow on it to make the black hairs stick together and form stiff points at each side of his face. He said, "You have a nice cool day for this kind of work."

"Pretty nice," Mr. Powell said.

"What I wanted to see you about . . . What was the trouble with the lieutenant the other day? Maybe he wasn't very diplomatic."

"No, he seemed like a nice fellow."

"Well, what was the trouble?"

"I don't guess there was any trouble, Major. He was sure polite. A clean-cut young fellow."

"Maybe he didn't make himself clear."

"No, I thought he spoke real well. A credit to the army."

It seemed as if they were trying to outdo one another grinning.

Mr. Powell asked, "What did you do? Bring me another message from the colonel?"

"Not exactly in the same way the lieutenant did. I have the authority to discuss the matter with you. Explain the official position."

"What is the official position?"

"That you are meddling in Indian politics. That you comment on the land-division question frequently. That this is undesirable and even dangerous."

They had stopped the posthole digging and stood watching. All three of the strangers wore revolvers at their belts. They wore blue clothes with yellow stripes up the trousers, large gray hats and high boots with dust dulling their shine. Unlike the major, the two black-faced soldiers did not smile. They had a way of standing reared back without being stiff and they tilted their heads back and moved their cool gaze over everything. Their manner seemed to state: We've got you outnumbered; there's three of us and only five of you.

Mr. Powell said, "My official position is that it would be a crime to divide this reservation. That these people ought to have all the facts. That they ought to have every chance to know what's happening before it's too late."

"Isn't your word 'crime' a little harsh? Maybe it's only a matter of opinion as to whether it's best to divide the reservation. I don't know anyone who's trying to suppress the facts. I want to discuss this in a reasonable manner if we can."

Mr. Powell was still grinning. "All right, I can be as reasonable as you can. This is not farm land. Plow it up and you'll have a grand dust storm from one end to the other. It's too dry. Even a white man couldn't make a crop every year. It's good grazing land. Why not leave it more like these people are used to? They're damned good horse breeders. They can be good stockmen. It's their nature. What right does a bunch of land-greedy white farmers have to this land?"

"Do you figure I'm greedy for a homestead here?"

"I don't suppose you are."

"Not at all, Mr. Powell. You might be right in your opinion. You could be. Of course, the experts don't agree with you. But here's the point: you're more or less a visitor here. This is a reservation. All you are being asked to do is this: stay out of politics. If you don't, I must tell you in all good humor, I think your permit will be denied."

"Do you *think* or do you *know?* What's the army got to do with my permit?"

"Oh, come on, Mr. Powell," he said, flashing his teeth beneath the stiff moustache. "We were going to be reasonable. I don't think I have to explain the army's presence here. The question is your presence here. The colonel has his responsibility. You know as well as I do that he is consulted on all these decisions. But we're not a bunch of devils. Look at the other side of it. I know you don't want to be known as a troublemaker. Do you?"

Mr. Powell had finally stopped smiling and he reddened at this question and said, "I damned well may turn out to be a troublemaker."

The smart black-faced soldiers seemed not to be listening to the conversation, but they moved their eyes over everything in a cool manner.

The major chuckled. "Well, if you make us trouble, that will be one more. We have one commission after another and the Bureau and the War Department and the Indians."

"Anybody that would try to hook a spirited race horse to a plow ought to have trouble."

"Hell, don't you see we're just trying to do a job? Mr. Powell, it may be dangerous for you to go around talking like you do. Did you ever think of that?"

"Is that a threat?"

"Not at all. I got orders to put a man off the reservation once and I put him off as gently as I could and wished him luck. But some of these damned Indians are liable to kill you. You know the Indians are stirred up all over? Something's eating on them. They've got these native superstitions all mixed up with this wild Messiah idea and this Ghost Dance religion. They're trying to twist Christianity to their own use, and they get all excited."

"That's strange. I thought that official policy says everything is fine and peaceful on this reservation."

"Well, we want to keep it that way."

"I don't think the Comanches are going to join any Ghost Dance religion. And I know I've got a right to talk about the facts as I see it on this land division."

"Well, that may be your trouble, Mr. Powell. You're on a reservation. Why don't you go to Washington and talk? You're not arguing with me. Not at all. I'm just talking sense. Your permit is held up. And you're standing on this land at the pleasure of the agent. Right?"

"And the colonel has a veto whether it's legal or not," Mr. Powell said.

The major chuckled. "Well, at least I don't. I'm not any inspector or judge. Listen, you know what I think? I think the colonel is closer to your point of view than he is to some of these damned Quakers on this latest commission. But he's got to keep order around here. That's about the size of it. Try to look at the other side of it, Mr. Powell."

"You try to look at the other side of it."

"I have, but what does that matter? You're not arguing with me. Not at all."

"In other words you're just like that lieutenant. You're just a messenger."

"It could be, Mr. Powell. At least I think I've pretty fairly explained the official position. Please give it some thought."

Mr. Powell's talk had become shorter, less cooperative, as the interview proceeded, and now he did not answer at all.

The major stood a moment smiling, then turned and said gruffly, "Mount up."

In a moment the three of them had departed toward the north on their trotting horses, the two black-faced soldiers flanking the officer as precisely as if they had been all harnessed together. The dust from the iron shoes of their horses hung low in the humid air.

They went back to work. Joe was aware that there had been a sense of two opposing sides, the five of them against the soldiers. He supposed that the permit had to do with the fence or with bringing cattle onto the reservation. Two or three times his mother had received small sums from Iron Lance called "grass money." He actually knew as little about it as he did about the proposed land allotments. Probably the sense of being on Mr. Powell's side had come from the fact that the soldiers were armed and the rest of them were not. He thought, everything considered, that it would be well to guard against building up any loyalty toward their fencing boss.

The man was quiet and moody, completely unlike himself, until an incident that evening in the cow camp restored his good spirits.

Everyone was watching one cowhand's troubles with a half-broken horse, a black, raunchy-looking beast with a nervous eye. Evidently, two of the men intended to ride down to the camp farther south after chow, and they had caught fresh horses. The one with the black spent several minutes putting a bridle on his mount, with all the men laughing and shouting advice, then found it necessary to take off his shirt and tie it over the horse's face before he could put on the saddle. He left the horse, cinched up and ready to go, tied to a tree some thirty steps from the chuck wagon.

The cook dropped an iron pan full of bread onto the table at the end of the wagon and bawled out, "Come get it!"

The black horse jerked his head, broke the rein by which he was tied, and bolted, bucking across the prairie. The cowhand thoughtlessly ran after him on foot, crying out, "Help me catch my saddle!"

A rangy bay mare, unsaddled, was tied to a wagon wheel around on the other side. Joe moved toward her, uncertain whether to intrude into the white people's business, but as he came around the front of the wagon,

Mr. Powell came around the rear, ahead of him. The man deftly slipped loose the knotted rope, cast a half hitch about the mare's nose and was already urging her forward while he was clambering onto her bare back. The mare lined out into a hard run, and Mr. Powell hunkered low over her neck, guiding her after the runaway horse.

One cowhand said, "Would you look at that old man ride!"

Another said, "Anybody can ride old Queenie."

The first one said, "Can't just anybody get her to run like that."

Someone else said, "I got a dollar says he catches him," but no one took the bet.

They saw him come up to the black horse a half mile away and, after several passes, catch him to lead him back. They returned trotting, the half-broken black subdued. The second rein had been broken in the running, and Mr. Powell had a grip on the bridle itself.

It was the kind of incident that the cowhands enjoyed. During supper they teased the man who had lost his horse and one of them said to Mr. Powell, "You ought to help us on the roundup and leave that fencing to fellers that can't ride."

Mr. Powell grinned and said little about it. To Joe, the man was a puzzle, a better rider than he would have thought. He found nothing in him to dislike but was suspicious of him, or was suspicious of his own opinion of him. Already, there was Slow Tom's uncle, not now at this camp but farther south working for the same people, who must not be harmed. He and his three friends did not need another man around for whom they must feel loyalty or concern. He said to himself, Let this white man look out for himself; I didn't ask to be his friend.

It had been cloudy for several days, with now and then a flurry of rain. One morning they had been digging postholes an hour or two when a buggy came from the east along the fence line carrying two white men. Mr. Powell seemed to know them. He went to them and reached up into the buggy and shook hands. Joe could hear only a little of their talk. He heard Mr. Powell ask in a loud voice, "What?" After they had talked a minute Mr. Powell came back and said to his workers, "You may as well hold up, I guess. I ought to be back before chow time." Then he got into the buggy with the men and went east with them.

They sat around on the damp ground and waited. Their talk turned to horses, how the cavalry horses at the fort were guarded day and night, whether the cattlemen might have another good remuda farther south. It was a dim day with little wind. The sky was low and gray, seeming to accent the broadness and flatness of the prairie land. To the north the Wichita Mountains rose faintly, hardly visible through the misty air.

The buggy came back at midday. Mr. Powell got down laughing. The other two followed. One was a young man with a cap on his head and pencil behind his ear, like a store clerk. The other was an old man with white moustache and white pointed beard, with watery pale-blue eyes. He stood straight and stiff. He wore a large clean gray hat, a white coat with fine black stripes, and cowman's boots, highly polished. Mr. Powell seemed ill at ease, though he laughed.

Joe and his friends had risen and they drew back a few steps as the others approached.

Mr. Powell asked, "How far off would we be here?"

The younger man took a small book from his pocket and wrote in it a minute, then said, "Nine hundred feet. Maybe more."

Mr. Powell kept shaking his head as if he couldn't believe it. "Damn! You see, after I got to where I couldn't see your flags, I thought I could go on the compass. How much difference would it make in acres?"

"Maybe sixty acres. At this point."

Mr. Powell did not think it was funny, though he was laughing.

The older man had been kicking some loose dirt into one of the postholes with his polished boot. He said quietly, "We can't accept it, Powell. You contracted to build a straight fence. I'm afraid it's your error and your expense."

"It's my fault, all right," Mr. Powell said. He went to the wagon and got his compass from its leather case and said to the younger man, "Go over that once more."

"It's about ten degrees here," the man in the cap said. "Like this. Let her point about ten degrees east of north."

"I'll be damned," Mr. Powell said.

The old man said quietly, "Go back to the wash about a mile back, Powell. Start from there. He'll put you in some flags on the line."

Mr. Powell asked, "You want us to fill in these holes?"

"I think so."

Mr. Powell was still laughing in a peculiar way and shaking his head as the two strangers got back in the buggy and drove east. He stared down the line of empty holes and said, "Seems like I have the sorriest luck, everything I try to do here lately." He stared at the compass in his hand and said, "Damn a contraption like that anyway!" He threw it hard against a wagon wheel and smashed its glass.

For a minute he stood with his hands on his hips, then finally he grinned at Joe and the others and said,

"Let's go to dinner. Looks like we've got to fill in some holes this evening."

The morning's developments did not alter his feeling of puzzled suspicion about Mr. Powell. He had assumed the man was a cattle owner, but evidently the other old man was. He had assumed for no reason he could name, that Mr. Powell knew exactly what he was doing in the mysterious matter of which way a fence should run. In a way it was a relief to see a white man make a bad mistake. And for a white man to curse one of his own "contraptions" and smash it! It was a pretty good joke.

They brought shovels that afternoon and worked in a drizzling rain filling postholes. The mud stuck to their shovels, making them blunt and heavy to work with, and to their moccasins and shoes, making walking clumsy. The rain had a chill in it. They worked hard in order to keep warm, but Spike's bare skinny chest turned purple from the cold. They hurriedly worked back along the line, came to the place where they had stopped setting cedar posts, and began to push these back and forth and wrest them from the ground. Finally Mr. Powell decided that they must quit for the day; it was too wet.

Back at the cow camp the cook and his helper had stretched up a tarpaulin between some trees, and this, along with the big tent and the covered wagon, provided shelter from the rain. Late in the afternoon the rain fell steadily and showed no sign of slackening. Mr. Powell came to where his fencing workers sat under the tarp; he gave a yellow slicker to Spike and told them that they would not work for a few days. They could stay around the cow camp or leave. He would not start back on the fencing until the rain had stopped and the ground had dried a couple of days.

When he had gone, Joe told them that they should

take this opportunity to gather their equipment for the raid. He wanted each of them to have ready a gun and ammunition and food and a water bag—either bring them when they came back or have them ready to pick up at a minute's notice. And coats. And each should have a rope. He would try to talk to some old men and pick up any horse-stealing tricks he could.

They left early the next morning, Slow Tom northeast toward the Armstedt place below the south agency, the other three toward the camp on Blue Beaver Creek. Joe parted from Bill and Spike there and rode north in the drizzle and mud toward the Iron Lance camp deep in the mountains.

8

SHREWD QUESTIONS ABOUT
HORSE STEALING

HE HAD SUSPECTED himself of wanting to see his mother,
though he had assured himself that it was not the reason
for his going back to his home camp. She fixed him a
big meal and seemed to be trying to enjoy his presence,
but one of her moods was on her, evidently interrupted
by his arrival, and she soon retreated into a stolid shell,
as melancholy as the gray weather. He wondered whether she felt as unhappy as she looked or whether she
had developed a way to close off her feelings. He was
inclined to say, Maybe your medicine against the woman
did work. Or, He will surely turn up one of these days.
But he had determined to abandon her problems.

He insisted to himself that his reason for coming was
the brazen plan to extract information about horse stealing from Iron Lance, perhaps Duncan Bull. That, and
to put together his raid gear.

In the morning of the day after he arrived in camp,
he moved among the scattered canvas tipis, watching
the lodge of Old Man Iron Lance. The paths were muddy and thin sheets of water seeped along them. Where
he could, he walked on the grass. The leaves of the oaks
dripped water. The smoke of the camp hung like a fog

around the tops of the tipis and among the upper branches of the trees. The camp smelled soggy.

The two wives of Iron Lance were putting rocks and mud around the base of their big tipi, weighting down the canvas, shutting out the air in preparation for the coming winter. The old man was inside and could be heard shouting gruff instructions to them. Joe watched, standing under a tree thirty steps away. Evidently a stream of water started seeping under the edge of the canvas, for Iron Lance bustled out through the flap and, staying under the shelter of a broad awning in front of his lodge, shouted more urgent instructions to the women. He sent one of them to the model house for a shovel. Then, as things were going in a manner to satisfy him, he folded his arms and stood surveying the area around his domicile. He had a craggy face and little black eyes. When he stood straight, he seemed to have a powerful figure for his age.

A new flurry of rain began, and Joe took it as an excuse to walk over and take refuge under Iron Lance's awning. He asked, "Is it all right for me to stand here a minute, Mr. Iron Lance?"

The man grunted.

"I've been thinking I'd like to talk to you sometime, sir. When you have time."

"I don't have any horses to lend you."

"No, sir, I didn't want to borrow any horses."

"You came in on a little brown gelding yesterday. Is that your horse?"

"No, sir. It belongs to the Armstedts."

"Who's that?"

"They live on East Cache Creek down below the south agency. They let me use a horse sometimes."

"I know him," Iron Lance said. "Those people down

there, white man says, 'Nice doggy,' and they wag their tails. Bunch of damned farmers."

A small fire pit was dug in the center of the area covered by the stretched tarpaulin. In it were a few live coals. The butt of a dead limb extended into it to keep it going. Being wet, Joe felt chilly. He held his hands outstretched over the faint warmth.

"What did you want to talk about?"

He felt clever, also bold. He thought he could read the mood of the old man and anticipate what he might be almost ready to say. He said, "Nothing especially, sir. I just think young people don't listen to their elders enough these days. If young people would listen to those with more experience, they could learn a great deal."

Old Man Iron Lance stared at him with black suspicious eyes. He unfolded his arms and seemed hesitant a moment, then he thrust aside the flap and went into the tipi. He came out shortly with a mat woven from cattails, which he placed on the ground and sat upon, crosslegged. He began to whet a hunting knife on a gray whetstone with deliberate strokes. "I'll tell you the worst things these days," he said. "School."

Joe could see that the old man was willing to talk. He asked, "How's that?"

"You know how the Penatuhkas are? When those white people came to kidnap the children for Carlisle, the Penatuhka mothers and fathers cried and closed their eyes; their kids whined. But the Nawkoni and all the others, those parents cursed and clawed like wildcats; their kids screamed and ran. It took two grown men from the Bureau to carry off each Nawkoni child. They say it took three and a rope to carry off each Kwahadi child, but that's exaggeration. Kwahadis like to exaggerate. All right. Finally they got out of Carlisle and came back. You know what? They were all Penatuhkas when they came back. Every last one. School does this. Stay away from schools. Look at Duncan Bull's boy. Just look at Freddy Bull! School does that."

Joe sat down on the limb which extended into the fire.

Iron Lance slipped off his moccasins and said, "The time to cut your toenails is during wet weather. A day like today." He began working on his toenails with the hunting knife. "Never let a woman cut your toenails. They ruin you. Let them comb your hair. Pick off ticks and lice. Maybe pull hairs out of your face. But never let them cut your toenails."

Joe waited a minute, listening to the old man grunt at his task, then said, "Sir, I guess some of the older men could tell a man my age a lot about Comanche history, the way they used to do things. . . ."

Iron Lance looked up. "You ever hear of Mad Wolf?"

"No, sir."

"You talk about history of the old times! Old as the hills! A grand old man. He never surrendered. Anything you wanted to know about the past, old Mad Wolf could tell you."

"I guess there's plenty of knowledge a man like you would know that men my age don't know. About raiding. Getting horses."

Iron Lance alternately whetted the point of the knife and dug at his toenails. "The biggest thing to remember," he said, "is to take care of your arms and your warhorse. Take care of them and they'll take care of you. Don't get your bowstrings wet. I could tell you plenty of advice along that line, and I learned it all the hard way."

He picked up a small stick of wood and threw it at a yellow dog that was raising its leg to a post of the awning, then went back to whetting the knife. "Always pick up your arrows if you can. An arrow shot at a mark is the owner's. An arrow shot in the hunt is the owner's. But an arrow shot in war belongs to the man who picks it up."

He was thinking that he was not getting much useful advice. He said, "I guess there are quite a few tricks to know when a party is out raiding or getting horses."

"If you cook on the warpath," Iron Lance said, "move in the dark before you sleep. And here's a thing you should always remember: strike your moving enemy on his right flank. Always on his right flank."

"Why is that, sir?"

"Because it's best. And when it's turned around backward, watch out. If you're moving and he hits your right flank, stop. Right then. Or turn into him." The old man had been cutting off his fingernails; now he was paring off the horny skin from around an old wound on the edge of his hand. "Another good rule is this: always carry extra moccasins on a raid."

"Sir, suppose you have taken some horses from the enemy. What's the best thing to do then?"

"Head for home country," Iron Lance said. "Head for home country." The old man sat there, alternately whetting the blade and whittling on his toes and hands.

"Mr. Iron Lance," he said, knowing that he was only casting about at random, "do you think the Ghost Dance is any good?"

The old man snorted. "We danced the Sun Dance with the Kiowas one time and followed a prophet named Isatai, and got nothing but dishonor out of it. Why should we take a Ghost Dance figured up by some fish-eating Paiute? And what would a live man want to mess with ghosts for?"

Suddenly it occurred to Joe that he would not get any useful information here. He wanted to ask a hypo-

thetical question how Iron Lance would go about stealing the cavalry horses from the fort, but it did not seem
worth the risk to ask it. He needed to consider it more.
The old man still had a trace of suspicion in his glance.
Also, it was difficult to tell to what extent the old man
was slow-witted, and to what extent he might be purposely making his advice inconclusive.

He rose from the limb and said, "I enjoyed talking,
Mr. Iron Lance. I have to go now."

"You ever get hard up for a horse to borrow, I got a
little black mare I might let you use a short time. If
you take care of her."

He said, "Thank you," and walked out into the rain.
He did not think he had learned anything of value, but
he had demonstrated to himself that he could question
an old man deliberately. He would try Duncan Bull,
who, as a practicing medicine man, might have some
more thoughtful advice.

The next day was a ration day, and he refused to go
with his mother on the trip to the south agency. The
beef issue had once been a wild sport which all the
young men loved, with the excitement of killing the cattle in the open; but now the white preachers and the
Quakers had changed all that, and the animals had to
be shot in the head while they were penned up and
dragged out of the chute by a team. Where once it had
been an exhibition of riding skill and shooting skill, now
it was just a man from the agency and a few soldiers or
Indian police and women butchers swarming over the
meat. Some of the men went after rations and beef in
order to assert that they were the head of their families
and entitled to them by treaty, but he had gone during
the past year or so only to help his mother; now that he

had determined to stand aloof from her, unaffected, he thought that he should not go at all.

Some of them went by wagon, over a rough round-about route. They would stay the night. His mother left early with the mule. On the beast was an empty pack saddle and tie ropes and her butcher knives rolled up in a piece of burlap and some empty cloth bags. She mounted and whipped the animal into a trot along the muddy path. It was no longer raining, but the sky was low and gray.

The camp was still. He sat outside the lodge awhile, musing on his mother, wondering what was in her thoughts, whether she had any intention of asking about her precious White Buffalo at the fort or the store or anywhere. He wished that she would keep up enough pride to let the matter drop. In her things in the tipi she still had magic items and medicine, and he had no doubt that she had continued her prayers for spiritual help. It was hopeless. He had mastered his own troubled feeling about the mysterious man by turning his back on all thoughts of it. Why couldn't she do the same? Maybe he would go away. Maybe he had already gone. Why pick at it and pick at it? He deliberately forced these ideas from his mind.

He brought two blankets outside and spread them on the platform rack woven of small limbs at the side of the tipi. He lay down on his back, stared at the sodden sky, and thought about horse stealing.

A certain quality of the plan was peculiar, if the tentative possibilities and cautions could be called a plan at all. It was that the plan, the intentions, did not seem to match future events in the way that one looks forward to expected events, intending to enjoy them or suffer them. When one of his companions had asked, or even intimated the question in a roundabout way—Are we

really going to do it?—then his best, most sincere answer had been, Yes, we certainly are! The implication
was that though the plan might be subject to adjust-
ment, they were certainly going to carry out a desperate
project, and any details that seemed to present dif-
ficulties would simply be taken care of in some way,
rather than reducing the certainty. Yet in the face of his
determination, the strange quality pervaded it all: it
seemed like a dream which has already been dreamed.
Not like a thing to come. It seemed inevitable, as if he
vaguely knew the whole, but only could not call it to
mind.

Because of the peculiar quality of unreality, he was
anxious that they plan carefully, discarding ideas that
were bad, considering every eventuality, yet at the same
time anxious that they fix upon the plan and go ahead
and settle exactly what they would do. At times he felt
a flush of desperation, because of his leadership in it.
They must have confidence in him. It wouldn't work
any other way. He could not attempt to explain his exact
attitude or impression to them, and thus he knew he was
in some sense disloyal to them. They must see the whole
thing as a certainty in the near future and take it seriously. He himself willed that it should be so in spite of the
dreamlike quality, and if he had to, to justify his assumption of leadership he would give his life to force
it all to come to pass.

He vacillated in the matter of the completeness of
the plan. At one time he was ready to hurry back to his
friends and say, Let's do it! Let's just go! Forget this
quibbling! They could do what needed doing when the
occasion arose. Just head straight for the nearest horses.
Take them! It would be risky, but that was certainly
supposed to be part of it. If they didn't intend to act in
a daring manner, better to forget the whole thing. His

friends ought to know that he meant to lead them boldly and make quick decisions; that was inherent in being
a good leader. They should not think that he worried
over trifles. And if they would do that, just get up and
go, it would be a crushing defeat of the dreamlike
quality. What is being done is no dream. And yet there
was the question as to whether it was necessary to be so
rash. A leader ought to be shrewd as well as bold. With
another flush of desperation, he would realize that he
must not allow himself to be forced into any precipi-
tous foolishness by his own uncertainty. He detested the
example, but it came to him: how, according to his story,
that fool Great Eagle had seen the danger of the cess-
pool and, acting careless on purpose to keep from seeming too careful, straightway fell in.

What kind of valuable knowledge about taking horses
could he possibly get from Duncan Bull? One thing: if
a man knows what it is he wants to learn, he probably
already knows it. What he needed to do was to get the
old man's confidence first, smooth away every bit of suspicion. Whether the medicine man had ever done any
successful horse stealing he did not know—he could have
—but he must have been involved in making medicine
for many a raid. It wouldn't hurt to get more evidence
about the value of medicine; he could always discount
what Duncan Bull might have to say about it.

What if he just pretended that he was completely lost
mentally and spiritually? Didn't know what to think.
Didn't know what to believe in. No way to turn. Didn't
know what to do. Didn't know what is good. What is
bad. What is worth living for. A medicine man is supposed to know about final things, large things beyond
the sky, why people are here. He had never spoken in
any careful way to Duncan Bull, but believed that
with such pretense he could engage him. For some

vague reason it seemed that among all the things the man might say must be those that had a connection with horse stealing.

He dug out a chunk of the pemmican his mother had lately made and ate it. About sundown she came back leading the loaded mule, tired, her moccasins hardly distinguishable because of the mud on them and on her legs. He began to untie the ropes, and she said, "I have to take it to Duncan Bull. It's his."

"All of it?"

"Yes."

"I'll do it. I'll turn the mule loose and carry it over there."

She started into the tipi, obviously tired, but turned to ask, "Did you have anything to eat?"

"Yes."

"I'll cook something."

"I tell you I don't want anything!" He felt angry at her because he had lain on his back while she slaved all day for nothing. She went inside.

The pack held a front quarter of beef, a tin of lard, a heavy sack of meal, and smaller sacks of salt, sugar and coffee beans. He took the meat, which was wrapped in burlap, under one arm and the sack of meal under the other and went down across the steppingstones in the stream and toward the lodge of Duncan Bull.

He had seen the man's younger wife and Freddy Bull and Freddy's older sister go south that morning in their covered wagon. They wouldn't be back tonight. If the old man was home, only his older wife would be with him, a tough old *puhawe*, a woman who had reached the age when it is all right for her to go into the medicine tipi and handle sacred things. She was the medicine man's helper sometimes, but a woman with a mind of her own.

Duncan Bull was feeding his two dogs, throwing scraps of bread and meat to one then the other for them to catch in their mouths. He was an overweight man, sloppy of build, loose-jointed, and his hair was notable, a grizzled loose mass, long and bushy, like bunches of thin dry grass growing out of his head. He was clumsy of movement, but an impressive man who spoke loudly and with assurance. He was known to be partially deaf.

The woman came out to look at the food. She quickly asked, "Where's the sugar? Where's the coffee?"

Joe laid his burden down and said, "I'll bring them. There's lard and salt too."

She unwrapped the burlap a little and said, "If your mother will strip out this meat and dry it for us, she can keep the lard and meal."

He carried his burden back across the creek to his mother's lodge and brought the salt, sugar and coffee.

Darkness was coming quickly because of the cloudy sky. Duncan Bull stood in front of his lodge with his arms folded, looking like some strange animal with a hairy head. Joe said, "It sure is damp weather, sir."

"We will have an early winter," Duncan Bull said.

"Can you tell how long before it dries up?"

"It will rain three more days and three more nights. Then it will dry up."

"How can you tell, sir?"

The old man made a grand motion toward the sky with his fingers spread, as if it all belonged to him. He chuckled. "There are many ways to tell, if you know the secrets."

The old woman, squatting in the doorway, mumbled, "It will rain three days and nights if it doesn't clear up sooner." She seemed to be speaking to herself and Duncan Bull did not hear her.

The old man said, "The whole world speaks to those

who listen. But you have to know how to listen. You have to ask. You have to know how to ask. Have you got any personal medicine, Joe Cowbone?"

"No, sir."

Duncan Bull shook his head slowly and the brush of hair swayed. He laughed and said, "Oh, these young men! That's like walking along the edge of a cliff with your eyes closed."

"How would it help me," he asked, "if I had personal medicine?"

"You can get medicine two ways, Joe Cowbone. One way, you can buy it or trade for it from someone who has it and knows all the answers about it. Or, the other way, you can go to all the trouble to get it by yourself. But even if you try to get it for yourself, you might want to buy some advice about the method and save yourself a lot of wasted time. Of course, people don't give away valuable secrets for nothing."

"Sir, my trouble is that it seems like I have a lot of questions about medicine and such. And I don't know where to start."

"Always start at the beginning," Duncan Bull said. He turned to the woman. "Light the candle in the medicine house. I go over there often at night, young man, to meditate and pray. You can go with me if you want to. I'm not giving away any valuable magic for nothing, but as for questions, I don't mind that. I think it's my duty to answer all questions. You don't have any grease about you, do you?"

"No, sir."

"Good. Always keep grease away from sacred things. Grease will drive away good spirits."

The old woman had gone inside, evidently after matches, and now she went along the path ahead of them. She mumbled. It sounded as if she said, "Candles are grease."

Duncan Bull's medicine tipi was back in the trees by itself, in a place which was now so dark that Joe could see nothing and knew how to go only by the rustle of footsteps ahead of him. He heard a fumbling with canvas and the heavy breathing of the old man, then he saw the flickering of faint light and he found himself in the doorway.

"Pass to the right," Duncan Bull said. "Pass to the right. Sit down."

In the center was a small ceremonial fireplace made of stones. He stepped around it to the right and sat down on some kind of skin. The floor seemed dry. Two tallow candles standing on a box at the rear lighted the room, and it was a weird shambles. Bags and bundles and dried gourds hung from the lodgepoles. All around the edges sat boxes of leather and wood, of all sizes, most of them painted with spots and lines of white and yellow and red and blue. He could hardly identify anything in the room because of the dimness and movement of the candle flames.

Duncan Bull grunted several times as he lowered his bulk to sit nearby. He said to the woman, "Bring a few coals for the fire."

Joe was asking himself what good could possibly come out of this ridiculous scene. He had wanted to find a way to talk to the man and now found himself almost pulled into an interview. He could not but halfway consider the old man a faker, yet could not be sure but that underneath it all might lie some bit of valuable information. He resolved to get anything from it he could.

"Ask me whatever you please," Duncan Bull said. "I think if anyone can tell you the right answer, I can."

"It's hard to express my questions," he said. "It's not

so much medicine for one certain thing that I need as
. . . I would like to understand the past and what they
did and how they knew what to do."

"If you find it hard to speak," the old man said, "that's
all right. I've seen many slow-witted men back through
the years, and that doesn't mean you're stupid. Don't
let anyone tell you it does. Just take your time and speak
as well as you can. I'll find out what you mean and give
you the answer."

The man was surely talkative but not very responsive. Joe said, "Away back in the old days . . . you know,
they say all that's gone now, all that's passed away. I'm
trying to discover how it was before it was gone, or
what it is that's gone. The main thing. But, well, I don't
know what to do. Something may have been lost and I
don't see what it is." As he said these words, something
in him stronger than his mind seemed to take over. He
had meant to say some such words, but had not intended quite that. It was too serious and he did not
respect Duncan Bull that much. Yet some part of him
seemed to trust Duncan Bull, or want to.

"Nothing is lost, young man. Some people are mixed
up, that's all. It's true that you express yourself poorly,
but don't be insulted. I think I'll be able to help you.
Actually it's your problem of speaking that bothers you
more than anything else. Just ask your questions as well
as you can." In contrast to the confidence shown in his
words, Duncan Bull seemed ill at ease.

The woman brought in an iron pan of red coals and
dumped them in the fire hole. "A little sage," the old
man said. To Joe he said, "My wife doesn't hear too
well." Then, "A little sage, woman!"

She mumbled something unintelligible as she rummaged in a box at the rear. She brought a fistful of
something and brushed it out of her hand into the old

man's open hands, ceremoniously thrust out. Joe could smell it, faintly spicy; it reminded him of the country out west of the Wichita Mountains. The old man passed his hands several times over the coals, sprinkling the crumbled plant, and smoke wafted up, strong, penetrating. He moved his hands as if sending bits of the sweet smoke to the sky and the earth and the four winds.

He wore a fringed shirt of the old style, not of leather but a dull blanket material. His chest was covered by a breastplate made of four slanting rows of white quill beads. These and his hair stood out in the candlelight, and the rest of him, even his face, could hardly be seen, but his bearing was uncomfortable, like that of a sick man who cannot find an easy way to hold his body.

"Now," he said, "what were you asking?"

"I believe you were saying nothing is lost, sir."

"That's true. What could be lost? Is the earth lost? The mountains? The people? I have magic ways of finding property that's lost, but I have to know what it is first."

He felt foolish in continuing to ask questions, but pressed on. "Forty years ago, sir. Do you think life was good then?"

"Very good. Very good. We had medicine to get the buffalo. Medicine to get the antelope. We trusted in our beliefs and didn't doubt. Didn't listen to the superstitions of foreigners. We had medicine for war and for everything we needed. Those were the good old days, young man."

The woman, squatting back near the candles, mumbled, "Pack, unpack. Move, move, move. Pack, unpack."

"But isn't that all lost now, sir?" he asked.

"I think your problem of understanding flows from your problem of expressing yourself," the old man said. "And that flows from speaking too much English. Now you take me; you can count all my English words on the fingers of your hand. I know some of their names they call each other, like 'ass,' 'son of a bitch,' 'goat.' The *mejicanos* have words for those animals too and they call each other those things. But that's about all the foreign words I know. It's well known that if a *mejicano* tries to become a Comanche he has trouble speaking. Why? Too much foreign language. I knew your mother made a mistake teaching you so much English. She hid you back from school, then taught you English anyway." Again he moved his hand as if sending bits of the sweet smell to the sky and the earth and the four winds: his hand did not move grandly, but jerked awkwardly. When the movement was done, his hand thrust tentatively as if some direction had been forgotten, then started over from the first. His movements seemed as much out of tune with his talk as his answers were out of tune with the questions. He said abruptly, "Aren't you working at a job?"

"Yes, sir." He was thinking he must have been crazy to have expected anything of value out of this ridiculous old man.

"How much do you make?"

"A dollar a day." He realized that he hadn't thought about getting paid since the time he got four dollars in advance.

"For fifty dollars I can teach you and give you instructions so that you can get the power to do nearly anything you want to do. I'll send you up on Medicine Bluff or up to the top of Mount Scott or any mountain you wish." He began to shake his hands and paw at them over the coals as if bits of the stubborn sage would not turn loose. "I'll tell you how long to fast. Exact directions for your sweat lodge, how many poles, everything. Words for prayers. This would include aid from my own personal medicine, and all instructions.

Such as what to answer when voices speak to you. Everything."

Joe became angry. This old man thought he was stupid. That he was so impressed with the bushy hair and the weird tipi that he would swallow anything. His anger contained stubbornness. He would push his questions for spite if for nothing else. He said, "Yes, sir. My trouble is, I'm so mixed up about things, I don't guess I would benefit from fasting. For instance, with all the medicine power they had, why did the Comanches surrender?"

"You're too young to remember Mad Wolf, I guess," the old man said. "He's dead now. There's a man who never surrendered. A great man. Very old." He said this as if it were the answer to the question.

Joe definitely heard in the old woman's monotonous mumble: "Mad Wolf's not dead. He lives at Saddle Mountain." She was whittling on a short piece of tree limb, as large as a person's finger, removing the bark, smoothing it off, sharpening the ends.

"In the good old days, sir, how did they know what to do? I mean a man by himself." When he had asked this, he felt again that he had asked something deeper than he meant to, but no matter; Duncan Bull would never know it. His angry stubbornness remained.

"More sage, woman," the old man said. The nervousness of his body was invading his voice. "Now you take your mother, young man, and her love problems. There's a smart woman. It's a private matter. All medicine is a private matter. That's the beauty of it, to know that you have something working for you, unseen, looking out for you." The old man clumsily shook more crumbled sage on the dying coals, and the woman went back to her purposeful whittling.

"In the old days, sir, do you think a man wanted something different?"

"A man wanted what he wanted. You see, that's why a wise man protects himself by having powerful medicine and observing all the taboos about it. That way he's sure. Say you wanted to stay warm and not freeze, you wouldn't go out naked into the wind. That only makes sense." He tried awkwardly to make certain that he had wafted small portions of the smoke in each of the proper directions, but seemed always hesitantly to remember some power to which he should show deference in some direction of which he was uncertain. He grabbed at the essence of the sage as if it were specks in the dim air and thrust it about as if he fought a swarm of gnats. His breathing was heavy, irregular, as if he had trouble getting air.

"But, sir, does medicine always work?"

"Yes, it does! Certainly! It does! Always. It never fails." He seemed strangely aware of his own nervous activity and determined that he would ignore it or overwhelm it with his words. It had become a battle. "It's trying, you see. It works and other powers work too. That's natural, you see. It works and other powers work too. That's natural, you see. It's all very simple."

"I think my main question, sir, is about the old days: How did a man know what to do?"

Duncan Bull gasped for air as he spoke. "It's your trouble. . . . Trying to express . . . You see? . . . You take that Ghost Dance. . . . See? What is that Jesus thing? . . . He's a white man. . . . He'll kill the buffalo!"

"But, sir, how does a man know what to do?"

"I tell you . . . you are confused. . . . What are . . . you trying to do? They surrendered because they didn't . . . get true medicine! That's all! . . . That's all it is! . . . It

146

was too much power! . . . Against them . . . Evil magic . . . Not me that's mixed up . . . It's you!"

"I'm sorry, sir. It just seems like something may be lost."

"How does anyone . . . know what to do?" Duncan Bull said. His hands had balled into fists, his body shook, his breath seemed to be failing. "How did they . . . ever know! . . . What can I do? . . . You're confused. . . . You're impudent. . . . Disrespectful . . . I know the answers. . . . Sage! . . . More sage!" The old man reached out as if he were falling or as if the earth were in upheaval, then settled back on the floor, his hair spread out as big as a tumbleweed. He lay still. The woman rose nimbly and came to him.

"Are you sick, sir? What is it?" His anger and stubbornness were forgotten. "What happened? What's the matter with him?"

"He's having a fit. Can't you see he's having a fit."

"What are you doing to him?" In the half-light it appeared that she was attacking him with the smooth peeled stick.

"I'm putting it in his teeth to bite on, so he doesn't bite his tongue."

She didn't seem much worried, but in a moment she said, "You're worse than Freddy. Why don't you go away?"

"I didn't intend to upset him that way."

"No, you young men are so smart. What do you know about Duncan Bull? He was an important man in his day."

She was squatting beside the hairy head and holding one of the hands. He moved toward her and knelt. "But, Mother! Please! I didn't do it on purpose. I really need to know the answers to those questions. I really do."

She didn't answer.

He asked, "Will he be all right?"

"What you think he is? A baby? He has lots of fits, living here."

He went out into the blackness and walked with his hands outstretched to guard against running into anything, feeling the path through his moccasins. At the stream crossing he wet his feet feeling for the stepping-stones, then gave up and splashed across. As he walked on, his soft, soaked moccasins made small squashy sounds. He laughed at himself at realizing that he had completely forgotten the purpose of talking to that man —to find out about horse stealing. Where had he ever got the idea that you could find out things talking to old men? He wouldn't make that mistake again. They were all *pawsa*. Great Eagle certainly. Iron Lance was stupid. This one, Duncan Bull, was raving crazy. Both of the latter had mentioned some old man named Mad Wolf, who was dead, except that the woman had asserted he was alive. How could a person know what to believe? This Mad Wolf, if he lived, if he had ever lived, was probably the biggest idiot of them all.

The following morning his mother cut into strips the quarter of beef. The weather was too damp to keep the meat without smoking. She hung it on thongs crisscrossing between the poles inside the tipi, and he brought a supply of green oak limbs to burn for the smoke. That afternoon the clouds broke and began to disappear. The wind blew. He judged that in one more day it would be dry enough to work fencing.

Early the next morning he gathered what he needed: a piece of his mother's pemmican as large as a man's head, a square of clean cloth, a long water bag made of the skin of a horse's leg, his blue denim jacket and a good rawhide rope. He kneaded the pemmican into a long shape, wrapped it in the clean cloth, rolled it and the empty water bag into his jacket, and tied the whole solidly with the rope. He would leave the bundle at the Armstedts' with his extra ammunition. He mounted the little brown pony, carrying his rifle and the bundle, and headed east.

When he came after several hours in sight of the fort, he left the trail and passed south of the fort, near enough to study the fenced pasture and stone corral, where the cavalry horses were penned at night under guard. They had high-quality horses, no scrubs, but the solid appearance of the corral made him realize that any speculation about taking horses here was unreasonable as long as the cattlemen's horses roamed around free down south.

As he came into the valley of East Cache Creek he was aware, with an uncertain thrill, that ahead of him lay, among other things, the Manybirds lodge and Lottie. It would be simple to stop by and see her. Then he caught himself and drew back from the idea. Had he thought that the relationship between them was such that if he wanted something from her, she would say, All right; she would say she disagreed, but if he thought it was best, All right—then he would have been willing to listen to her and even agree. But she didn't have that willingness and it made a barrier, or he was determined that it would make a barrier. He imagined meeting her by accident at the store or somewhere, and when she asked him to come visit he would say, I don't have any turkeys to bring and no time to get turkeys. He would say, And I don't have time to listen to your long-winded father; I've been listening to too many old men lately, and I've decided to start listening to myself. If she asked what he had in the bundle wrapped around by the rope, he would say, You might find out one of these days.

Sitting Bear Creek was off to his right, and as he followed down it toward the Armstedts' the idea occurred to him, from nowhere, that he had passed this way many times before, that for years he had been going around in circles: from the Iron Lance camp in the mountains, down to the fort area, down through the settled area along East Cache, west to the Blue Beaver camp, then north into the mountains again. Only now it was southwest to the cow camp, then north into the mountains again. Around and around in a circle. Getting nowhere. It was not only true that he was going to stop listening to old men; also he was going to stop going up into the mountains to the Iron Lance camp. He might not go back there for a long, long time. Around that place, wherever his mother was, hung a sorrowing, a pitiful waiting, a longing for a man who used to be. That mysterious man who might be. Someday. He wouldn't have it. It was her problem. His bundle wrapped with the rope and his loaded Winchester and the three friends he would soon see were the only things that counted.

Slow Tom was not at home. Mrs. Armstedt thought he had gone to the Red Store. He left his bundle and rifle with some of Slow Tom's things, remounted the brown pony and rode toward the store.

The road which ran from the fort south toward Texas lay about a mile west of the main course of East Cache Creek. In this mile-wide strip of land were scattered the Red Store, over by the big road, another trader's store back near the creek, the agency buildings, the blacksmith shop, the doctor's house, the school, the Reverend Fairchild's church, the farming teacher's house, the carpenter teacher's house, now vacant, and other houses and barns and lodges of whites and Indians. They were not crowded, but interspersed with fields and sandy flats and patches of trees. Roads, consisting of two worn wheel tracks, ran from the big road toward the creek.

Along one of the small roads he saw a horseman, a quarter of a mile ahead of him, riding east. He would have given it no thought, except that it looked like Mr. Powell. The hat, the set of the shoulders. It could be no one but Mr. Powell. He could almost hear the man's voice and see the man's grin just by looking at his figure on the horse from this distance. He thought that whatever the argument had been between the man and the army, Mr. Powell must have given in and come to see the colonel. But what was he doing here? He was two miles south of the post, going east. If he was trying to go around and talk to Indians about his ideas on the land allotments, he would find he couldn't get far without an interpreter. He considered briefly how it would be to act as Mr. Powell's interpreter, then forgot it. He had more important business in the offing.

As he approached the Red Store he heard loud voices and curses. One wagon and team was tied in front of it; another horse with travois poles and two saddle horses were tied to the hitching rails. Some kind of argument seemed to be going on inside. When he was still two hundred steps from the building, a disheveled man burst through the door running and stumbling as if he had been shoved from behind, then sprawled into the dust. It was Great Eagle. He half rose, looking dirtier and shaggier than usual, and began to cast about on the ground for rocks, which he began to throw at a front window of the Red Store. Two Indian women in colored cotton dresses, Kiowas, came running out of the door and toward the parked wagon.

Thinking of Slow Tom, he hurriedly tied the pony

and strode to the door, but he looked in cautiously. A dozen men, mostly Comanches, faced each other, muttering threats. Some had blood on their arms and faces. They held knives in their hands and some brandished the store's supply of new shovels and axes and grubbing hoes.

But above the other noise rose the shrill voice of the trader in English. "Get out! Get out, I say!" He was standing on his counter, towering over the others, with a shotgun in his hands.

"Get out!" he screamed. "I'll get the soldiers! Put my tools down and get out!"

It had been hard for Joe to see in the dim interior at first, but after a moment he saw Slow Tom straight in front of him, sitting on the floor, leaning against the counter. His rounded black hat was crushed in and a trickle of blood ran down the side of his head. Joe ran to him and lifted the hat.

Slow Tom said, "Some crazy bastard—"

"Hey, man, are you all right?"

"Yeah, I'm all right. Some crazy bastard . . . I wasn't even arguing." He lifted one hand to feel the knot on his head.

The shrill-voiced trader had convinced the men. They straggled out the door, each asserting himself with mumbled threats and curses.

"What happened?" Joe asked. "How do you feel?"

"Somebody hit me up side the head with a brand-new singletree."

"How do you feel?"

"I feel like somebody hit me up side the head." But he was grinning and sitting up.

"What's it all about?"

"I wasn't even in it. Great Eagle wanted credit and they wouldn't give it to him and he tried to get everybody to say he'd have plenty of money someday when the government buys the land. Then everybody started shoving. Damn!"

"So it was the allotment business."

"Man, be careful how you say that word around here," Slow Tom said, trying to get the crown of his hat rounded out.

Slow Tom had come to the store afoot. They mounted double on the pony and started back to the Armstedt place.

"You're not going to be in much shape to dig postholes tomorrow," Joe said.

"I could dig two to your one right now," Slow Tom said, "if I wanted to exert myself. I'm ready for anything. Except if you mention allotments I don't want anybody behind me with a singletree."

9

WHITE BUFFALO APPEARS

MR. POWELL paid them each ten dollars, though Spike and Bill had not yet worked that many days. Joe felt strange about the money. He had not thought as he worked that he was doing it for money, though he understood that he would, of course, be paid. It seemed almost like a bribe, to make them forget the horses. He considered giving back the money, then tucked it in his trousers pocket and forgot it.

They worked two days pulling out cedar posts which were on the wrong line. The earth was moist enough to make the work easy. Then they began digging holes west along the new line.

One afternoon after they had eaten and thrown their tin plates into the cook's tub of soapy water, Joe and the three other Comanches walked out near the makeshift mule pen to squat down and talk. Shortly afterward Mr. Powell came out to throw some hay to the mules from a loose stack in a small adjoining pen.

Joe saw, as he had seen twice before, three men on cavalry horses coming down across the prairie from the north. Undoubtedly they wanted to see Mr. Powell again, and he started to call the man's attention to it; then he sensed that Mr. Powell knew it and was pretending to ignore it. He thought suddenly that the man had been watching to the north a great deal in the past few days.

The horsemen came in an easy lope. It was the same major and trailing him this time two Indian policemen, Comanches, dressed in cavalry garb. They slowed to a trot as they came near the camp, and the major stood up in his stirrups, looking it over. Then they came straight to the mule pen. The major dismounted.

Mr. Powell did not show any surprise and he did not smile. He jabbed the pitchfork into the ground and stood with one hand on it as he faced the officer across the flimsy fence. He said, "Major, you're wasting your time."

"I didn't come to argue, Powell. The head agent will be down tomorrow. If you ever expect any action on your request of the U.S. government, you'll have to meet with him in the colonel's office tomorrow."

"You're wasting your time."

"Powell, I don't understand you. When you came in, the army welcomed you. We gave you every consideration. Now, in all candor, what's the matter? What is this army-hating attitude?"

"You're holding up my permit."

"For the love of God, man! Do you think the government is going to put you in a position where you can talk your subversive talk all day, every day, to these Indians?"

"You're wasting your time, Major."

"And you're headed straight for trouble," the major said. The two Indian policemen had not dismounted to hold the officer's horse as the black-faced soldiers had done, but they seemed to Joe to have the same attitude. Their faces reflected the seriousness of the talk, but they looked around with cool impersonal gazes. Each of them wore a revolver, as did the officer, and each of them carried a carbine in a leather boot alongside his saddle.

"You're just not reasonable," the major said. "You're just not at all reasonable. Isn't your wife still living up there somewhere on the East Cache near the agency?"

"What's that got to do with it?"

"Well, it makes it pretty clear to the colonel, if you want to know the truth, that it's not a matter of convenience for you. It's a matter of stubbornness. You've been near the fort a dozen times since this question came up. You just don't mean to cooperate."

"By God! You finally got it through your head."

"But why, Powell? I don't understand you. You've got this cattleman point of view in your head—"

"I'm not a cattleman!"

"You've taken this job down here with the cattlemen."

"Hell, I can't wait forever on government red tape!"

"All right. All right. You better think about what I told you before. Some of these Indians have these wild native superstitions all mixed up with these Christian ideas. Nobody knows what this Ghost Dance means. There was a brawl in a store up close to the agency last week. You're playing with trouble, Powell."

"The Comanches won't accept the Ghost Dance religion."

"I guess you know more than the army does about that."

"I just might."

"You know what I think? I think you'll get yourself killed before we get around to kicking you off the reservation."

They seemed to have come to an impasse. Joe was thinking that each of them wanted to say something else, to say some final strong words, but then he saw that Mr. Powell was not looking at the major, but at the two Indian police, and he was frowning. His voice up to now had been completely unfriendly, but calm. Now his gaze was so intense as to make it seem that he had forgotten everything but the two mounted Indians, and it drew their quizzical gaze to him. Then, with great passion, Mr. Powell burst out at them as if the words were tearing at his throat.

"Why do you wear their soldier clothes?"

He was not speaking English. Not even the polyglot of the reservation. But old-time Comanche.

"Don't you know they are going to take away every good thing you have? You are the kind of fools who are giving away the land! Are you Comanches or a bunch of stinking Tonkawa women?"

It was amazing to hear the language come out of the white man's mouth. A terrible intensity rode in the voice. He became silent. Then, as if he had been caught crying or acting shamefully, he turned his eyes to the ground at his feet.

The major and the two policemen stared in disbelief. The major backed up beside his horse's head and said gruffly, "The head agent . . . well . . . I hope you will see the colonel." He gave up, mounted and swung the horse around. The three of them kicked their horses into a lope going away.

Mr. Powell had come over to the corner of the pen near where they sat. He said, "I want to apologize to you fellows about the English." He was speaking Comanche. He had a wry smile on his face.

"I thought . . ." he said. "I wanted to hear what the People are saying about the land. I'm sorry."

In a moment he said, "That day you were talking about stealing the horses . . . Don't do it. Don't pull any pranks like that. It's not worth it. There are more important things to do."

He stood with one foot on a fence rail, and they were

all silent for a while. Joe rose, acting as casually as he could, and walked to the big wagon to get his blankets, then out toward the area where they slept. Bill Nappy followed him. It was almost dark.

Joe's mind was a turmoil. He felt wordless dread. A scattering of clues in the air with no meaning seemed to be gathering toward him. Those Comanche shouts from the throat of a white man—they sounded like something Iron Lance might have yelled forty years ago. The accent! It sounded like Kwahadi or Kotsotuhka from an old one who lives in a secluded camp and never goes around the agency.

Why did the vision of Powell swinging on the unsaddled horse come back to him? The man was a good rider, as a cattleman was supposed to be. Wasn't a Texas cowboy supposed to be a good rider? It was the riding of a man who, though old, is almost kin to a horse. Who rides without thinking about it. The horse had been a part of him, a thing he used like his own legs. A man who had sported and played on a horse. He pictured Powell at other times, walking in his flat-heeled boots. Why had this one man troubled him? How had he been so sure who it was when he saw him several days before at a distance? But what was missing when he swung on the horse? What was out of place? The hat? Why shouldn't he wear a hat? It wasn't the hat. *No braids of hair were flying.* Why in the name of God should a white man have braids of hair? The movements would fit, without the hat, with braided hair and nakedness. Yes. He was a better rider than a Texas cowboy.

He pictured Powell swinging on the running horse again and he saw a fact of which he had not been conscious before.

Mr. Powell had mounted the horse from the right side. He had run from the front and in that hurried, unthinking using of the horse he had mounted from the Indian side. *I'm not a cattleman!* he had said. And the permit. A permit for what?

The facts all matched in his mind, but not in his heart. It seemed impossible. It outraged his sense of truth and propriety. How could it be?

Bill Nappy was saying something. "What's the matter with you, Joe?"

"Me? Nothing's the matter. What did you say?"

"Hell, I asked you three times."

"I was thinking. What did you want?"

"I just asked you what did we say that day. I was wondering just how much Powell knows."

"I guess he knows too much."

"Yeah. Well, at least he's good-natured about it."

This chatting about it was unbearable to him in this moment and he said, "Good-natured? Bullshit! He says it's a prank. It's no damned prank. If he knew how serious it is he wouldn't be so good-natured. You think it's a joke too about half the time. You're going to wake up one of these days and find yourself right in the middle of a raid you think is a joke, and sure enough it's dead serious to everybody else. Where in the hell's your gun?" He had brought his Winchester .44 and Slow Tom had brought his .22 rifle, but neither Bill nor Spike had brought any weapon.

"My gun? I haven't got a gun. Why are you jumping on me, Joe?"

"That's what I mean. You haven't got a gun. When are you going to get one?"

"I'll get one. I told you I'll get a big buffalo gun. What's the matter with you all of a sudden?"

Slow Tom and Spike came toward them with their blankets under their arms, chattering and chuckling. Slow

Tom said, laughing as he spoke, "Well, Joe, it looks like that's that. What's your next plan?"

"Back to the war council," Spike said.

"You two better not get funny with Joe," Bill Nappy said. "He's sore about something."

"I don't blame him." Slow Tom said. "Our plan is shot. Blown. Gone down the river. Isn't that about the size of it?"

"The raid is still on," he told them. "There are plenty of horses in the world."

"But it's definitely off here. Right?"

"We've got to think about it," he said.

Spike kicked his blankets into a mound and perched on them, his bony legs cocked up so that he looked like a skinny frog. He put in, "I'd say kill Powell or take him prisoner, but I'm beginning to like the old white-eyed bastard. You fellows left too soon. You didn't hear the whole story. That man used to live with the People back in the old days. He says he did and I believe him. He says he *was* a Comanche."

Slow Tom added, "That's not all. He said he had a Comanche wife and baby boy, and they were killed in the big Custer raid on the Cheyennes out on the Washita. I'm about like Spike; he sounded to me like he was telling the truth."

There was a silence for a minute and it was hard to realize that they were at ease, casual, just talking. For him the four of them seemed to sit at the center of the dusty swirl of a whirlwind. He forced his voice to be natural and made himself speak slowly. "If he lived with the Comanches, what were his wife and boy doing at the Cheyenne camp? Where was he?"

"I don't know. I believe they were kin to the Cheyennes a little bit. He didn't say where he was. But I thought he was telling the truth."

He sat there in the darkness with them, after they had made themselves comfortable for a night's sleep, and a couple of times one of them asked, "What's the matter, Joe?" and he said, "Nothing." Then finally Slow Tom said, "How you expect us to go to sleep with you sitting there like you're going to do something? Did you give up sleeping? If you've got something on your mind, what is it?"

He had not thought anything through nor figured out what to do, but Slow Tom's insistence brought on a decision of a kind. He said, "I have to go back up in the mountains and take care of some important business. I'll see you fellows in a few days."

"What you got to do?"

"Never mind."

"Is the raid still on?"

"It certainly is."

"But not here."

"I don't know. We've got to think about it."

"Think about it!" Slow Tom said, sitting up. "How come all this mystery? What kind of business have you got up north? Are you going to see your mother or what?"

Spike said, "I know what the mystery is, and Joe's right."

"Well, let us in on it."

"He's got to go check his medicine some more."

They were silent after that statement and he let it stand. He halfway expected some cynical remark about medicine from Slow Tom or some joking remark from Bill Nappy, but none was forthcoming. He got his rifle and said, "I'll see you fellows in a few days."

He walked north into the darkness. The night seemed immense and the earth black and hidden, with many unknowable gullies and ridges and thickets of brush and unnamed plants. The sky was alive with stars of every variety of color and every degree of brightness; their differences made their numbers seem even more hopelessly beyond counting. The sky and the earth made one great unknown in which he moved.

When he had walked a few minutes he stopped and turned around toward those he had left. The land behind him had already become a part of the unfamiliar vastness, but somewhere in it Mr. Powell sat or lay, awake or sleeping. The Winchester '73 hung heavy in his hand, a cold, balanced, deadly weapon. He tested his desires. He could go back and find them, approach each dark figure on the ground, with his rifle cocked, and ask, "Mr. Powell?" "Are you Mr. Powell?" "Mr. Powell?" "Where's Mr. Powell?" But he had an equally strong impulse to throw down the rifle and go back. And evidently he had a feeling stronger still that he should walk up into the mountains toward home, or toward such home as he had.

He turned and walked on north, scarcely able to see his own footing on the dark earth. He could feel the brushing tug of grass and weeds against his feet. Once he walked into a patch of prickly pears and was not aware of it until he smelled the crushed leaves and broken thorns under his moccasins. He backed out, ignoring the stickers that stung in his feet, and walked on. The mountains ahead, and finally to each side, fitted into the black sky, outlined by the absence of stars in them.

Then he forgot the night and moved into another black and vast and unknown world, *toka*, the dark place of his soul. He was two creatures, one a savage Comanche man, no less dangerous because he did not know the source of his anger or where it was directed—furious, uncaring, hungry for violence, like a beast of prey stalking. The other creature, not one to move forcefully or violently, but rather to wander, lost, like a five-year-old boy, was jerked along by the first on a journey under a black *herkeead*. Neither part knew a sensible purpose or direction.

Some force guided him twenty miles that night, mostly uphill. The labor of it wore him out and saved his life, for when he found himself approaching his mother's lodge it occurred to him that George Longwater's act had been right and good, but he felt completely tired, incapable of anything other than sleep.

10

THE BOOK

IT WAS ODD how the question of White Buffalo had come
toward him and away, toward him and away, since his
mother first announced the news that day. He had first
been impressed by the idea of a father; then as his
mother had dressed up and worried about meeting the
man, he had thought it was a much greater question
for her than for himself. After the ridiculous confrontation with the skinny white woman in the house that day
he had been determined that it was all her problem
and that he should not feel involved at all if he could
help it. Now, upon his realization of the identity of Mr.
Powell, it had become entirely his own problem again,
his question, his perplexity; and it was only when his
mother woke him after his fitful sleep that he saw that
all of it belonged to both of them.

She seemed to have changed her mood and was now
friendly, solicitous, motherly. He was not going to tell
her what he had discovered, not until he had himself
decided what it meant and what he should do. The
time for doing just what other people wanted was over.
He felt the poignancy of the meaning of the secret for
her—in that the man thought they were dead. Only one
string of causes could have brought such a result. His
mother must have run away from Saint Louis as she had

said. And the man must have followed and searched for them. How else could he have known that they were in the Cheyenne camp? It was cruel to keep it from her, but he was determined to be as cruel as necessary until he could understand what to do.

The horse-stealing raid seemed no less desirable than it had seemed before. The fact that Powell knew—he could not immediately see what difference that would make. What he needed to do was have a few days to think in a quiet place, not going around in circles and not in a strain. He did not admit that it might be because of the presence of his mother, but something about the Iron Lance camp appealed as being less tense, more peaceful than any other place.

She had not awakened him until well after the middle of the day, and she had cooked for him a good meal of thin bread cakes out of flour. She bustled about in the dimly lighted tipi chattering at him while he ate, then she became quiet a moment. She finally said softly, "Joe, can I ask your advice?"

"About what?"

"Do you think Duncan Bull's medicine is worth it?"

"You know what I think. Why do you ask me?"

"Sometimes I forget how old you are, Joe. I just thought I would ask you. Maybe if I paid him more he would give better medicine. We'll have some grass money coming again someday."

He knew that she had not yet come to the point. He said, "Anything you pay Duncan Bull is wasted."

"Well, I have to do something. So what can I do?"

He didn't answer.

"Joe, I've told myself a hundred times through the years: This is all right. I can stand it. Because someday White Buffalo will come back. And I've almost waited too long. If he doesn't come, I guess I'll give up."

Even though he thought she was being devious, he felt her simplicity and directness.

She asked, "Will you do something hard and important for me?"

Part of him wanted to give her an agreeable answer but another part was saying silently: No, I won't do anything that somebody else has figured out for me; I'll do what I figure out by myself.

"You're big and strong, Joe, and you know how to go places and talk to people. You could find him. You could ask the army people and all the agency people, the freighters, the stagecoach people, the people who sell hay. You could go up to the north agency. Somebody knows. You could find him or find out what happened to him. You could even go out into the white man's world."

He thought that he could not listen to her forever without speaking, but he had to be careful not to reveal what he knew. "What about the white woman?" he asked. "Have you figured out what to do about her? I know that white men don't have two wives."

"All I say is what I said before, but I remembered something else, Joe. The white preacher in Saint Louis said we would have each other till death. And we both agreed to it."

"Who said it?"

"The white preacher."

"What white preacher?"

"In Saint Louis. When you were little."

"Did you get married in Saint Louis?"

"Yes. We got married first in Palo Duro Canyon. Then we got married again in Saint Louis."

He asked, "When people get married by the white man's way, are the army people there?"

"No. It was just us. I held your hand on one side and

your father's hand on the other side. The preacher said White Buffalo and I would have each other till death, and we both said 'yes.' "

They had digressed from her question: Will you do something for me? He thought it just as well. The less he had to say, the better. If she pressed him, he would tell her that he would do what he thought was right whenever he got ready. She didn't ask him again. The question hung in the air, as if she was willing to have him think it over; and he wondered whether, since he had been resisting her lately, she was beginning to see him as a different person. The point of the meaning for her of his secret seemed to stab deep into him. He was relieved a little upon thinking of the ten dollar bills in his pocket. He took them out and gave them to her.

"What's it for?"

"It's my pay. You can have it."

"I'll keep it for you."

"No, buy a dress or some beads."

"I'll put it up for you," she said.

He wandered in the vicinity of the Iron Lance camp, thinking, allowing attitudes and moods to sway him. Only one thought which seemed to have depth and pertinence crossed his mind: I ought to think less and act more. I ought to do things. He was purposely avoiding other people, even the children who played along Medicine Bluff Creek. He walked up the rough rise south of camp. Here oaks grew thickly. The ground was littered with broken granite. A small dry stream bed ran a jagged course down the slope, almost hidden by trees, its bottom filled with boulders. This place was no good for grazing and rarely visited by anyone, though in yelling distance of the camp.

He was surprised to see through the trees a man sitting cross-legged on a large chunk of rock. Freddy Bull. The young man was reading a book. He was aware, because he had been deliberately avoiding other people, that Freddy was doing the same.

He had a peculiar awakening at the sight. A man thinks. He searches in his mind to try to capture dim things. Memories crowd in, interrupting one another. He talks to himself. The sky and the earth talk silently to him. Moods come through him like pieces of wind. Sometimes he sorely needs peace and privacy to try to resolve whatever is stirring him up inside. But here Freddy had sought out this place and was devouring a book with his eyes, taking in other people's ideas from the book.

He walked backward as silently as he could. A feeling surged in him, envy. He could imagine possibilities as large as another world. As he wandered in another direction, he could not escape the overwhelming idea of the advantage of reading. Who could tell what might be in it?

The piece of paper on the door of the new trading store, for instance. Maybe it said nothing of importance; maybe it said everything. If it said nothing and a person could read it, at least he could put it out of his mind.

But there were other ideas, more subtle, less immediately useful, which might be explained by reading. Some of his people had always tried to talk to the whites. *Puha*, they had said. A way to walk. A way to live. A guide. A marked-out trail. They had made the sign for "walk" and pointed at the ground. Then, in deference to the whites, they made a sign for "wheel" and pointed at the ground. In answer to all this, the whites gave them the sound "road." The missionaries had strongly identified it with their religious faith and practices, so that those of the Indians who were trying to understand called the preacher *Puha-rivo*, or when they tried to say it in English, "road teller." What he said in church was "road talk" and every seventh day was "road day." The whites seemed to understand these sounds, and it was all right. But when the Reverend Fairchild's church was built and they called it by the English words "road house" white men thought it was hilarious. It was so funny, they couldn't explain it for laughing, or wouldn't. There was an error somewhere, and it was assumed to be an Indian error. So the people drew back from the word and wondered how large their mistake was and where else in their thinking mistakes might lurk.

Then for many years there had been the matter of the written recommendations. Perhaps they had begun as a good thing, a piece of paper written upon by a white man, which an Indian could show when he wanted a job or when he traveled off the reservation. But they became something else, a joke, and the owner of one would quickly know. When he showed it to strange white men they would laugh and slap their hips and show it to each other, then carefully refold it and solemnly hand it back to him. A Comanche could speak to a dozen foreign people without uttering a sound, yet they would suppose that he did not understand. Exactly what it said he would never know, whether "This man is a scoundrel" or "This Indian is a liar"; but what it meant was always quickly clear: "This man cannot read." Some of them carried the papers, knowing what they were. When the laughter came, they would laugh too; and for their assumption of simplicity, their willingness to be the butt of a joke, they might be aided or given directions or allowed to pass among white people in peace. Some Indians didn't mind, for they knew the value of laughter, and they saw two sides of the joke, where the whites saw one. But for others, the price seemed too high and laughter about this kind of thing made them sick.

Joe had walked a half mile away from the solitary reader before he stopped and deliberately started back. Why should Freddy Bull know how to read and not himself? The thought came that he had been vaguely wanting to read for years and had never realized it.

He had difficulty finding the place, for no paths led to it. Then he found the small crooked stream bed full of boulders and was able to retrace his steps. Freddy Bull sat motionless. He moved forward boldly.

Freddy straightened suddenly and whipped the book behind him as he stared.

"Hi, Freddy."

"Hi." He stood up and his eyes flicked about as if to see how many intruders were coming or to find a route for escape. The book was gone. He had dropped it behind the rock.

"Your book fell off the rock," he said.

"I've got to go," Freddy said. He hesitated, then awkwardly leaned over the large flat rock and retrieved the book. He started off in the opposite direction from the camp, saying, "Well, I guess I'll go on."

"Wait a minute." He went forward. "I'll go away if you want me to. You were here first. I just saw you reading and I thought I'd speak to you."

"No, I wasn't reading."

"What does that book have in it?"

"I don't know. I found it."

"Whereabouts?"

"At the fort. I mean the agency. I found it by a road. I guess some white man dropped it, or something."

"What's in it?"

"I don't know." Freddy edged to his left toward a dead limb which lay on the ground. It was crooked, as thick as a man's wrist.

"You got it at Carlisle."

"No, I didn't."

"You've been sitting right here reading the book for hours."

"No, I haven't, Joe. Sure enough."

"I don't know why you say that. They taught you to read books at Carlisle."

"No, they didn't. I never did go there." He stooped over without looking at the limb and picked it up with his left hand. Looking straight ahead, he fumbled with it, trying to move it to his right hand while he moved the book to his left.

Joe was thinking, What in the hell is he doing? The piece of limb was so rotten that it had fallen from the tree of its own weight. It was worthless as a weapon, which was obviously its purpose. And that was senseless. He was embarrassed for Freddy and for himself. It seemed best to ignore it. He said, "Where did you go for years and years? I've been knowing you since you were ten years old."

"I went to visit some relatives."

"Do you speak English?"

"No."

"Freddy! for the love of God! You have spoken English to me. Everybody knows you went to Carlisle. What's the matter with you?"

"I don't want any trouble. Why don't you leave me alone? I never did anything to you."

"All I'm trying to do is ask you a few questions."

"What's so funny about reading? What's wrong with it?"

"Nothing. I didn't say anything is wrong with it."

"Then why are you making fun of me?"

"I'm not. I only wanted to ask you a few questions. Do you think you could teach me to read?"

"I've got to be going."

"No, wait, Freddy. I'll go away if you want me to. Just tell me, what would you take to teach me to read?"

"I can't read."

"I don't understand why you keep saying that."

"I don't want any trouble."

"Am I giving you trouble?"

"You're making fun of me." Freddy seemed to be himself trying to ignore the limb in his hands, to pretend that it meant nothing, that it was just something which he happened to be holding.

"But why do you think I'm making fun of you?"

"What did I ever do to you?"

"Well, wait a minute, Freddy. Listen a minute. You've got me wrong. Think about the other side of it. Did I ever do anything to you?"

"I don't know. You're trying to make fun of me right now."

"How do you know?"

"I just know."

"If I never did anything to you, what makes you think I'm against you? I'd like to know. What am I doing to make you think it?"

"You act like you're so smart and tough. You have a lot of friends. You go around everywhere. You have all the friends you want. And they act like they're so smart."

"Freddy, I swear you have me all wrong. You really do. I thought you always acted big-headed. I'm serious."

He realized that he had not looked at Freddy closely in years. The young man was dressed in white man's clothes and his hair was now barely long enough to plait at his shoulders. How many times had he cut it, then let it grow out, then cut it? He had fine features for a Comanche, and the permanent wrinkles of a frown between his eyes. His stance now indicated uncertainty, as he held the book and the limb with both hands in front of him. The book had dark-blue covers, somewhat faded. Finally he said, "Well, I'd better go. I don't know whether you're making fun of me or not. I suppose you are."

"Wait. What did they teach you at Carlisle? Don't you see? I don't know anything about those things. What did they teach you there?"

"They taught me that my father is a big fool. And he is. He knows it too. Nobody comes to him for help any more except old women. He hates me because I know it. And I don't care, because I hate him worse than he hates me."

"But at least they taught you to read."

"Yeah. And now I don't belong anywhere." He dropped the limb to the ground, still pretending that he was not aware of its existence.

"But it's better to read than not read, Freddy. How would you like it if you didn't even know what it was about? If you just wondered and wondered what writing says? Listen. You know the new trading store on the north agency road? It has a piece of paper on the door with writing on it."

"I know it. I saw it."

"Well, I wanted to know what it said. I thought it might be important. But what could I do?"

"It said: Closed. No buying, selling or trading permitted here. By order of the colonel. That's all it said."

"At least you knew what it said. Listen. Did they have the army at Carlisle?"

"What do you mean?"

"Did they have cavalry and a colonel there? Do white people have an army to watch them everywhere?"

"No."

"Do you think you could teach me to read?"

"No."

"I could probably learn by myself if I had a book. What will you take for that book?"

"I couldn't sell it."

"I'll give you ten dollars."

"No, I better not sell it."

"Listen. I'll give you ten dollars now and twenty dollars later. If I don't give you twenty dollars in the next year, I'll give you the book back."

"It's not worth that."

"That's all right. I'll give you ten dollars just to let me use it for a year."

"It's harder to learn to read than you think, Joe. It takes a long time."

"How long?"

"You start with easy things. It takes several years."

He couldn't tell whether Freddy was being truthful. "Maybe you could help me a little, then I could study several years by myself."

Freddy stood in uncertainty a minute, though he seemed less distrustful. He said, "If you'll keep it a secret, I'll bring an easier book up here in the morning and show you a few things in it."

They agreed upon it. It was nearly dark. He understood that Freddy did not want to walk with him back into camp, so he turned and made his way back alone. The reading, for him, if he ever mastered it, would not need to be so much a secret. Though he could understand Freddy in a degree. He himself certainly would not want Slow Tom and Spike and Bill to know about it.

He anticipated it greedily. At least he was taking action, doing something more than just worry. This thing he was going to try out was large enough and also the right kind of thing so that he was justified in putting aside other problems.

The next morning as soon as it was convenient he went up the rough rise to the same spot. The sun was hardly high enough to have taken the chill from the shady spaces. Freddy was there before him, standing by the granite slab, his hands behind his back. "Joe, maybe this is all a mistake," he said. "Maybe we should just forget it. I don't think it's a good idea."

"Sure it is. It's not a mistake."

"I think you're going to be sore at me."

"Why?"

"Because it's harder than you think."

"That's not your fault." He laughed. "Maybe you'll get sore at me because I learn too slow."

Freddy brought from behind his back another book, with a worn gray-back, laid it on the rock and opened it. It was a book of stories about people and animals made by a man named Aesop. Freddy read: "Once upon a time a man and his son were driving their donkey along a country road to sell him at the fair." He read it three times, pointing at each word. Then Joe tried it and was elated that he could do it.

They proceeded with three more statements in the same way. Then Joe tried to read it beginning at the first, but found that he could not. He had forgotten some of the words. The two of them took more comfortable positions, sitting side by side on the rock, each holding half of the book, and Freddy prompted him until he could read through the first four statements without an error. It would be harder than he thought.

They went ahead further. The more words they passed the harder it became to remember them all. He was staggered by the thought of how many words existed, written down, in this book. Freddy was patient. He would sometimes say, "Look at it hard. Read it. What does it say? Try to guess what it says." Sometimes he did guess right. And he saw another aid; sometimes the words repeated. When it was the same word, it looked the same on the page. He began to peer at each separate word intensely. But the overwhelming impression that built higher and higher in him was that reading was an enormous undertaking.

They finished the story. It turned out that the men tried to carry the donkey and they dropped him in a river. They went over the whole again and again, but Joe always found it necessary to guess or be prompted several times.

Freddy remained eager but concerned. He seemed to have a pathetic desire to make the work a success in the face of the near impossibility. It was past midday when he said, "Well, you see it will take a long time."

"What will you take for this book?" he said.

"Oh . . . I thought maybe you could see what a big job it is. Then after this book, there are harder things to read. Joe, it may be impossible for a grown person to learn to read."

He thought that his new friend might be right, but he said, "If I had this book I could study some by myself. I've learned a lot already."

Freddy said, "You can have it."

"I'll give you ten dollars."

"No, you can have it. If you give up, I'd like to have it back."

176

"I believe you're right about it taking years," he said, "but I don't think I'll give up."

They came back later that afternoon and studied more. They went over a short story about two goats that met on a narrow bridge. They went over the donkey story again and again. Freddy had brought a pencil and he wrote the ABCs, large and small, in the back of the book. Joe learned the names of the first half of them.

He believed that it might require the remainder of his life to learn to read. That seemed more clear the further he went. At the same time, it was a consolation to know that he had the rest of his life. He meant to pursue reading. The good in it would wait for him until he came to it. Yet this resolution of his attitude toward reading left him in sore need of some action that might produce earlier results.

The book of stories by a man named Aesop fitted tightly into the back pocket of his trousers.

He awoke that night and lay staring at the night sky. A mood was over him, under which his mind seemed as clear as the spaces between him and the stars. He was making things more complicated than they needed to be. He thought, Why not just go down and tell him? I'll just tell the man the truth. I have a surprising thing to tell you, Mr. Powell. Wasn't that man friendly and thoughtful and considerate, as good a white man as he had ever known? The man might say, Can it really be true? Yes, sir, it's true.

Why had he ever thought that it was his problem or that there was any reason for shame or anger on his part? He had not done anything to cause it. But could it be that this was one of those ideas which look different at night from how they look in the day?

He would do it, but he should not allow it to seem urgent. He had rushed up here. He should not rush back, certainly not as if he had a desperate duty. He needed to relax and think over things more calmly. Let his buddies believe that he was engaged in a long consultation with his medicine.

Somewhere out through the trees toward the other edge of camp a baby cried, a sad, small, lonely sound. Then a woman sang a lullaby, so patient and low that he would hardly have been able to hear the words if he had not already known them.

> *Ya-hi-yu niva-hu*
> *Hi-yu niva*
> *Hi-yu niva-hu . . .*

It seemed simple and peaceful. But as his mind became hazy, unfocused, drifting toward sleep, one incongruous thought crossed it: of a man called Mad Wolf, part rumor, part legend, who might or might not be alive.

11

OLD MAD WOLF

EARLY in the morning he stalked along the paths of the camp, keeping his eyes open, watching, until he saw Duncan Bull's older wife walk toward the creek with a water bag. He quickly followed her and intercepted her as she came up the rocky path with wet legs and wet moccasins and a full, dripping bag.

"Mother, can I give you a hand?" he asked.

She grunted something like "No."

"I wonder if you have time to answer a question or two?"

She stopped and her manner indicated that she might have time.

"Is it true that an old man named Mad Wolf is still alive?"

"Of course it's true. If he hasn't died in the last week or so."

"Is he a very old man? How old is he?"

"I guess he's the oldest man that ever lived."

"I wonder how I could find him. Do you know where he lives?"

"It's no secret, young Cowbone. Just because some people go through life half asleep doesn't mean that everyone does. I know his granddaughter well. Saw her at the last ration day."

"Where does he live?"

"Up yonder a ways." She nodded her head up toward the headwaters of Medicine Bluff Creek. "You know where Saddle Mountain is? Just south of there, where a spring runs out of a hill. A young couple and his granddaughter live there with him."

"Is it only a short walk from Saddle Mountain?"

"The first hill this side."

"Thank you, Mother," he said.

It was still early. He set off afoot, not entirely convinced, and yet with more conviction than doubt. The woman's words "If he hasn't died in the last week or so" had struck him as important. If such a man existed, what a shame it would be to miss seeing him. He would certainly know plenty about techniques of horse stealing.

As he walked along, he found in himself contradictory ideas about what his attitude should be. One moment he thought he would pretend to have enormous respect for the old man; the next, he thought that he did indeed have respect and would, until he was proved wrong. One moment he thought he should use trickery to gain the useful information he desired; the next, he wondered whether he might get sincerity and honesty in return for these in himself. One trouble was that he couldn't specify even to himself what useful information he desired. While he was thinking in this vein, an unreasonable thrill grew in him. The oldest man that ever lived!

As the woman had said, the location was no secret though it was remote. Before the middle of the morning he found it, a large tipi and three makeshift brush shelters backed up against a lone elm tree. As he approached he noticed a strangeness in the texture of the tipi covering and he realized that it was buffalo hide, the only one had had seen for several years. It was spliced and patched with newer skin, probably horse-hide. A young man, a few years younger than himself, emerged from one of the shelters and came out to meet him a hundred steps from camp. Following him came a young woman, bending over holding to the collar of a gray dog that looked like a wolf, lightly scolding the dog when it tried to bark. The young man spoke pleasant greetings, but the way they came out was almost as if they were protecting the camp.

He felt foolish as he asked, "Does Mad Wolf live here?"

The young man asked, "What did you want with him?"

"Well, I just wanted to talk to him, if he has time. You see, some men mentioned him and about his knowing so much out of the past. I would like to ask him some questions, just general things. I don't want to be any trouble. Maybe if I could just find out when he would have time to see me."

"He likes to talk," the young woman said, smiling, "when he gets going." She turned the dog loose. The animal came and sniffed of his feet, then turned away, satisfied.

"You wouldn't argue, would you?" the young man asked, as if to show that he had the power to say yes or no.

"Oh, no. I have a lot of respect for an old man that way."

"I think he would enjoy it," she said.

"You can't argue. And if he says Go, you must go right away."

"That's fine with me. I sure don't mean to trouble him."

"All right," the young man said. "You wait here. It's

too early now. We'll bring him outside when the sun is higher. He needs the sun on him."

He saw an old woman, stooped and gray-haired, puttering among the shelters. He asked, "Is that his wife?"

"That's his granddaughter," the young man said. "Will you wait here?"

"Yes."

"What's your name?"

"Joe Cowbone."

He waited in suspense while the laggard sun made his slow way toward the center of the heavens. The man for whom he waited took on more stature with every passing moment. Finally he became aware that something was happening. The stooped, aged granddaughter swept the ground in front of the tipi with a bundle of dry grass on a stick, then spread a robe, hair side up, and smoothed it carefully. The young man and woman, one on either side, brought out a hulk wrapped in a Navajo blanket. With much arranging, they sat it down on the robe, and it began to appear more like a man.

The young man came out to him and said, "He'll talk to you, but you must be patient. You can ask any question, but don't argue. Don't shout at him or make any sudden moves. He can hear all right, and if he doesn't answer, you must wait for him. Walk up where he can see you and smile and stop and speak to him, just about three or four steps away from him. He'll talk plenty when he gets started. Don't speak any modern slang if you can help it; you know what I mean. And, please, if he says he's tired, you must leave at once."

He went forward with all these instructions in his mind, aware of the incongruity of his situation. He was strongly impressed and at the same time, observing himself, amused. Here sat a quite ordinary, poor camp, no apparent wealth, no beautiful setting. Brown soil, scattered pebbles, areas of loose dust trod up by moving feet, scant grass, one lone tree, all plain and common under a moderate autumn sun. And yet he went forward feeling nervous, wondering, thirstily eager. He smiled and said cautiously, distinctly, "Hello, sir. I'm very glad to see you."

Mad Wolf's hair was white with a tinge of listless yellow, broken and straggly at his neck, not long enough to braid. Across the smooth washed-brown skin of his upper forehead some tufts of grizzled white stuck up untamed. The skin fitted tightly on his forehead, on his hooked nose, across the expanse of his broad cheekbones. On his cheeks it made a delicate pattern of wrinkles. At his lower jaw and throat it loosened to folds and pouches, fine brown, translucent. His mouth was sunken. His eyes were dark caverns, with a point of light in each. He seemed infinitely old, not senile so much as worn and molded. His body gave no shape to the carefully arranged blanket which covered it.

"I'm pleased to have a chance to talk to you, sir. You have lived so long and know so much about the past."

"Yes," Mad Wolf said. "Yes. I'm very old." His voice was toneless, curiously casual, but not facile.

The others seemed to have gone about their business. He slowly sank down to squat directly in front of the old man. "Do you know how old you are, sir?"

"No. I might be a hundred winters. I don't know. I was already a warrior when the white men from the east first came in wagons to go to Santa Fe."

"Someone told me that you remember almost everything that has happened to the Comanche people for a long, long time."

He seemed to be nodding faintly, but he said, "No

one could know what all the people did. The *Nuh-muh-na* was always split into bands and sometimes the bands split. We were scattered from the timber country to the big mountains, from the Arrowpoint River to Horsehead Crossing. I've seen plenty. Some I recall, some I don't.

"But I've had time to look at my memory. My mind is like a field of flowers. You know how a flower bud looks? I have spots like that in my memory. You take your thumbnail and dig into a bud, and you can't get a flower out of it. You can't smash it or scold it and get it out. But the bud knows when. And the sun knows. The green spreads and just a crack of color shows. When it gets ready it unfolds. And there it is. Often these days that happens in my mind. A closed place opens and spreads out and I see it all as if it were yesterday. I remember a battle, or the lay of a winter camp, or a certain horse, or a love affair, or a feeling I had. These memories are as numerous as flowers across the prairie."

He seemed, as he spoke, so insubstantial that he might knock himself over if he shouted or if he let himself become too deeply involved. And so the dry, superficial nature of his voice doubtlessly came from the precarious condition of his chest and throat and tongue. But his speech was deliberate also, lending an ironic note to all he said. It was as if he spoke timeless, unhurried truths, as if the words themselves carried such meaning that no strength of expression was needed.

"Sir, someone told me that you have never surrendered. Is that true? To the whites, I mean?"

He laughed silently, a small shaking of the blanket and jerking of his head. "That's true. Some of them kept on surrendering, but I never did, and I was with two or three different bands when they did it. We were on Otter Creek one time where the old white soldier camp

184

was and we had a council and they said, 'Well, we'll go on in and surrender,' but I said, 'Not me.' They said, 'But you must; it's all over.' 'Not me.' 'We're all doing it, Mad Wolf.' 'I'm not.'

"Then one time a white colonel got all worked up and he was fussing at some young men and asking them whether they wanted peace or war, and someone told him that I had never surrendered. He kept saying to me that I must, and I kept telling him that I wouldn't. The people laughed, and he got angry and cursed the interpreter. He couldn't imagine that I would keep on saying 'No.'

"I was camped away down there by *Pu-hi-ti-pinab* one time and they came and told me that I must go and give up to the soldiers. They had a bunch of Comanches and Kiowas in a stone pen there. They said I was on the list too, and I must go to a prison in Florida. 'But I don't surrender,' I said. They kept hounding me so much I had to pull stakes and move out here this side of the mountains."

When he laughed the only sound was that of broken blows of air from between his sunken lips. He was not carried away by any humor, rather it was as if he recognized it with his mind and not with his heart, or perhaps it was that his body was too much worn out to respond deeply. The laughter was an interruption, not because it expressed dominant and overriding emotion, but because he was not careful of time, and it would not have been surprising to hear him say, We'll rest awhile and think awhile and talk about it some more later on.

"Sir, I have a question. . . . Maybe it would sound funny. But could you tell me what it was like to be a Comanche man a long time ago. I know some of it. . . ."

The black eyes with the points of light were focused on him. "You're a strange young fellow. People don't

185

ask me questions like that. I talk to myself about it, but not much to others."

"I know it sounds foolish, but I just thought . . ."

Mad Wolf was not listening. He had closed his eyes and it seemed for a minute that he had shut out the world. Then he opened them slightly and began talking, at first slowly, then at a normal rate.

"Five times made up the life of a Comanche man. First he was a baby. What can you say about a baby? They clean them and feed them and carry them and hug them. And the difference between a boy baby and a girl baby was this: 'Give him a little more meat; remember he will grow up to be a warrior someday.' The woman would sometimes try to hold him back, keep him a baby, but one could not hold him back. He would fret to be out of his cradle board and would toddle about, poking into grass and leaves, looking around, always touching and looking. And when he had less than four winters his father would put him on a horse and he would cling there, looking at the horse, then looking at the world, understanding in his little mind that the world looks different from horseback. And on that day when he did not want his mother to take him down, perhaps he kicked his tiny heels against the horse's shoulders and cried out; then he was a baby no longer.

"The second period was boyhood, a long and good time of life. The camp and the country around it became his range. He played shinny and ball and the games that would make him a warrior. He learned to shoot the arrow at a mark and throw a throwing arrow at a mark. He learned to know the bones of a horse and these moving so that they seemed like his own. For a time he was a wild and free boy, exulting, with no worry.

"Then he came to a difficult time, a hard change, for

he had to learn from his father, yet he wanted to be a man of his own. Of course, when I say 'father,' I mean all his fathers and his grandfathers. It is impossible for a boy to invent manhood. He saw his father as his beloved teacher and also his enemy. So he came to pull pranks, stealing out at night with the big boys to ride their fathers' horses, race them, disobeying the rules of the older men and the council. How he loved and hated them! They were his gods and for him it had come to be thus: to live is to be one of them, a warrior. You see, he thought he saw himself in the future as a powerful man, but can you imagine a thing that has never been at all? What he saw was a thousand examples of his father's glory, and all these attached to himself. He was a scoundrel. But he was still like moist clay which can be molded. Then on a certain day that he would always remember, when it seemed his breast would burst from waiting, his father would look over his untried weapons and say, 'All right. You can go.'

"Or it might be, if his father waited too long, he would go without permission. Sneak after them, you know. Follow behind. Stay hidden and then show himself when it was too late to be sent back. They would let him continue and give him the task of gathering firewood and maybe holding horses.

"When he broke through this difficult period, then he would come to like his father and become his comrade."

Though Mad Wolf did not speak violently, he would become out of breath and would pause as if he had been running. He would make faint, airy whistlings with his hooked nose as he exhaled. This calmly, with no apology, hardly noticing what he did. Then he would proceed as if he had never stopped talking.

"In the third period, he became what he had waited for; he was a man on the hunting path and the warpath.

He went into danger with the others. He did not know the arts of war, the raiding tricks, the landmarks, the nature of a dozen enemy peoples, but he had a high place before the women and children and the friendship of the greatest Comanches alive. Wisdom and the ability to lead warriors could only come with the passing of many events through the years. It might be that he became impatient of his slow reputation in war. The older warriors would caution him, 'Watch out. You're going to get hurt.' But he would break away and dash like the *pukutsi* into the very face of the enemy, flaunting his contempt for their power to hurt him. Then the older warriors would laugh and shake their heads and whack him on the shoulder and pull the eagle feathers out of their hair and offer them to him. I remember when young Darting Hawk—but that wasn't his name then—I remember when he counted two coups against the Mescaleros. We were scattered all over that battlefield and had trapped eight of them; they were crowded into a buffalo wallow, with only that shallow hole and a little sagebrush to hide behind. They had two guns besides their bows. Darting Hawk came up late, having wasted time painting himself, and he was afraid he had missed too much. 'I'll give them something to think about,' he said. We tried to stop him, but he broke loose. He swerved in a circle, then came straight into them. They raised up to receive his charge, but he came on so fast that they had to fall on their faces to keep from being hit by his horse's hoofs. He struck downward with his lance, flailing like a woman beating a dog, and glided over them and on to safety. He brought back a bullet burn across the back of his hand, a hole in his breechclout and one arrow in his horse's hip. I remember we asked him, 'How many did you hit?' and he replied, 'I hit two and my horse hit one.'

How he must have felt at that time! That was the day he got his name. He'd been known as something or other, but that night, standing by the fire, he told us he wanted to be known as Darting Hawk. Not many men can name themselves, but on a day of victory a man who has done a thing like that can give himself a name that will stick with him forever. I have a picture in my mind of that event with the motion stopped. The enemies have fallen to their faces and his horse is over them in the air; his slender bronze arm is descending as he strikes with the lance. I kept the picture because of the thought I had in that moment: that the Comanche people will surely live forever.

"In the fourth period of his life, a man became an older warrior. I don't know that it was the best period, but it was the time he had worked toward. He no longer had to prove himself. He might be a war chief or he might not, but he was consulted in matters of war. He knew a thousand trails and water holes over our vast country and deep into enemy country all around. He knew decoy and ambush, their planning and counteraction. He knew the holding of fire and the drawing of fire, flanking, orderly retreat, surprise and guarding against surprise. Off the warpath, he might boast or he might not, letting his silence speak for him. I remember such a time for me. When a certain Cheyenne party came south, they had an important chief who spoke a little poor Comanche with a lot of hand talk, and he was planning war along with us. I spoke up about something. The Cheyenne chief said, 'Who are you?' I said nothing. Then some of them told him, 'That's Mad Wolf.' He looked back at me fast and said, 'Oh! Mad Wolf.' It was a proud moment for me. Here was a strange chief from hundreds of miles north, but when he heard who I was, he jerked his eyes back to me and said, 'Oh! Mad Wolf,' then he asked my thoughts on this and that in our plan.

"No one knew exactly when he had come to the fifth period of life. He tried to keep it secret and succeeded for a time. No one knew how his body felt except himself. He would choose a traveling horse, not for its speed or stamina, but for its easy gait. Then the pipe for war would come to him again and again and he would pass it, offering some excuse. No one would blame him. We *Nuh-muh-na* were never sheep. Who could object if an honored warrior wanted to choose his own time for the warpath? But after several refusals, they would cease to bring the pipe for war to him. Even then no one knew for sure. The active war chiefs might be killed. This one might possibly take up his weapons again and with his long-gained knowledge lead us gloriously against our enemies. But he could not keep up the pretense forever. He would begin to keep company with the old men and would pass his time stringing beads or perhaps making arrows for others. Finally the day would come when it was time to move camp and the long horseback ride would be too much work for him and he would hunker down in a travois basket behind a gentle horse, to travel like an old grandmother. Then everyone knew that he was a warrior no more.

"They've taken it all away from us, all that lies between the baby who wants to stay on the horse and the old man who can no longer keep up the pretense. I don't think the white man understands. Must we pass straight from babies to old men?

"They've cut away so much of our lives that we are like bees when the honey tree is cut down. What will draw the bright eyes of a girl to a man and make her admire him? There is no hunting nor war nor victory. For what reason shall we dance?"

Mad Wolf's hand had been sticking from the recesses of his blanket and grasping a fold, clawlike. His arm was bone and tendon and vein, with no more muscle than is seen in the lower leg of a bird. It had not been conspicuous until, as he paused a minute to breathe, his hand slipped from the fold it was gripping and dropped down. When he raised it, the member shook uncontrollably. He pulled it against himself to steady the trembling, then edged it back to hold the blanket again, all without seeming to give it any thought, as if such action was a long habit.

"They told us the answer is the Jesus road and the corn road. The first I cannot understand and the second I cannot like.

"They take a straight stick and put a lance point crossways on the end of it and call it a hoe. Then they tell a man like me to take this hoe and go around the corn with it, chop weeds, stir up the dirt. Pet the corn. Say to it, 'Please make food.'

"Why should I pet corn? Let the corn pet me. I'm more than corn is. They don't know me. It has been my way and the way of my fathers to ride like a thunderbolt against the buffalo, a great beast with horns, and demand of him, 'Give me your blood and flesh!'"

The old man stopped talking and remained silent so long that he ventured a question. "Sir, do you believe there is any advantage at all in living on the reservation?"

"I don't accept the reservation, young man. I don't even know where it is. When they try to tell me its borders, I close my ears.

"But I did think for a while that the reservation might be an advantage to an old man. In past times an old man might become bitter when he knew his strength was gone and others in the band discovered it. Some of them found relief in patient work. It's good to carefully make a strong, useful thing, and if it takes long hours, what better does an old one have to do? I've made many bows since I've been old, but I had a problem in them that no one understood. I would cut and patiently scrape and wonder, for I could not test the bow. The *bois d'arc* wood lay silent in my hands; its taper slid through my fingers as I tried to gauge it and remember its strength. I would try to remember how my arms and shoulders had felt thirty winters before and the secret they knew of bending hardwood. The danger was this: that I would try to trade it and the warrior would test it and say, 'What's this, old man? This is a bow for a child.' So I learned to leave it heavy, and if the warrior said, 'It's a little stiff,' I would say, 'Yes, I have a little more scraping to do.'

"But some old men could find no relief in making things. They would gather to smoke and talk. They might sit all day, part of the time silent. I know such talk. They come to say the same things over and over. They have experience but it lacks life because it's all over. To have a loud voice one must have experience and still be able to act. So they would talk slowly and sadly and repeat themselves. It was hard that they did not get the respect they deserved.

"Some of them would become bitter, always ready to argue and cast blame or complain about their treatment in the band. One of them would spit on the ground around where he sat as if he made himself unlovely because he wanted it that way; if they would not come near him, he would make it even harder for them to come near him. Also, they would make evil medicine against one another. They dishonored their own great names by becoming bitter and caused life to pass them by even more.

"So I thought for a time that the reservation might make it easier for the old men. If no more war honors could be gained, they would become more precious. That they could not go hunting or warring would not be so much trouble; no one else could go either. But it didn't turn out that way. I believe war honors decreased in value. How could a man of warrior age revere a thing that he could never attain? War honors became unreal. A great gap came into our lives, and it is filled with nothing but confusion.

"I foresee a time when there will be only a few ancient Comanches who have ever counted coup on an enemy. They will lie down one by one, like old feeble bulls that are deserted by the herd. Then I don't see what can happen after that."

The old granddaughter came and stood nearby for a minute, examining Mad Wolf, then, satisfied, went on about her business.

Joe asked, "Sir, what do you think was the most important thing in the mind of a man back in the old days?"

"Bravery," he said. "And pride in himself. In his family. In his band. In the Comanche people.

"Let me tell you something about bravery. It always has to do with other people. And not just an enemy. And not just the friends who might praise you. Other people must be in the deed itself. Most coups are not acts of bravery; they only show that you might have it in you to be brave.

"I'll tell you the bravest thing I ever did. You know Tabananica? A kind of a chief now, I think. He was much younger than I. We were in this war party and got ambushed. We got one man killed and Tabananica clubbed in the head. We spread out and began to surround them. There was Tabananica, stunned, right among them, walking around on his hands and knees, on all fours like a sick dog, and blood running out of his head. They were too busy to knife him and take his hair. I was riding a strong horse, a big *awdutsunaro*, and I had practiced hundreds of times picking a man up. My comrades knew that. They feinted from the other side, and I rode in and got him. Didn't even slow down. Got an around around his shoulder and neck and brought him out of there. I broke his shoulder, but a moon later he was as good as ever. That's a hard trick for one man to do, but that's not the point; the point is that it is true bravery. Such an act strengthens the entire Comanche people.

"Forty winters ago it would not have been necessary for me to relate that story. People knew it. I specialized in being modest in those days."

He began his silent laughter, the barely perceptible shaking of his blanket and head, this interspersed with his words. "Here I sit . . . bragging about my bravery . . . and my modesty . . . but that's all right . . . I am very old."

Then he went on. "Let me tell you a good story about that. It's true. We went on a long raid out into Jicarilla country. About two moons. In the summertime. You have to stay out of that country in the winter. There were only eight of us, so we had to keep moving and stay on our toes. We fought a dozen skirmishes. When we got home, they had a big celebration for us. The second day at home they were getting ready for a scalp dance that night under two scalps we had brought, and that morning they had a ceremony where each man tells what he did on the raid. This was Yamparika Comanche custom at that time: each man laid down his marked arrow in a row, and in this way he knew his turn to brag. When I brought my arrow, the other seven were ahead of me. I told my wife to take it back to the lodge. She said, 'No! You must tell it. You did as much as anyone.' I told her I wouldn't talk. 'Take my arrow back to the lodge.' 'No! No!' I had to threaten to hit her before she would obey me. She did it and came back and stood behind me, looking spitefully at the others.

"The seven stepped up one by one and talked. But every one of them had a certain thing in his speech. One said, 'Then I sprang out of hiding along with Mad Wolf and . . .' Another one said, 'There I was out in front of the others with Mad Wolf . . .' Still another said, 'Only two counted coup that day, I and Mad Wolf.' One said, 'Two of us took the risky job of fighting a rear-guard action, I and Mad Wolf.' Another said, 'I was in the front of the battle; only one man was ahead of me . . .' About that time someone out in the crowd shouted out, 'Mad Wolf!' And they all laughed. The seventh man ended up his speech like this: 'Of course, I also took one of the scalps we brought home.' Some voice out there yelled, 'Who took the other one?' And the whole crowd thundered, 'Mad Wolf!'

"They came and got me and pushed me up into the air with their hands. Everybody. Pushing me up, all around the camp, shouting and singing my name. Around and around. I got black-and-blue spots on every place on my body. My wife stripped me off in the tipi and rubbed my body with salve. It was like a herd of baby buffalo had run over me. She said, 'I'm pretty dumb. If you had spoken like the others, I guess they would have killed you.' I said, 'I may go back to Jicarilla country where it's safer.' I was so sore I couldn't dance that night. But I was an important war chief from that day on.

"And you see, that wasn't all of it. It sounds like all

of it, but you don't know old-time Comanches unless you know the rest. I was not the raid leader, but I actually had fought eagerly and gone into danger and been lucky; so the seven others had judged me in secret and made it all up. I found out about it a year later. We were in a raid camp and horsing around, and they started shouting my name and trying to push me up in the air. Then they said, 'Should we tell him?' 'Might as well.' 'Mad Wolf, you modest bastard, you never guessed.' They had stayed near the truth in their bragging tales, but they had planned exactly what to say. They had fooled my wife, me, the whole camp. It was a joke, but it was dead serious too. How they laughed! How it pleased them! What fellowship! What magnanimity! They were human gods, young man. They were gods of the earth. And someday soon I am going to see them again."

He paused, and though no particular sign showed in his aged face, it was clear that he was lost in reverie.

He said softly, "Sir, did you ever know a man named White Buffalo? He was a white man who came among the Comanches."

Mad Wolf's sunken mouth formed the name silently and slowly two or three times, then he said, "Yes. Yes, he got that name. He was one of the Bent's peacemakers. You know they had two or three log houses on the Colored River, and one time they brought a wagon train and a gang of *mejicano* workers down there to build a big mud trading house. The *mejicanos* tromp up mud and grass and dry it to make soft rocks and build houses. *Adobe.* A white youngster came with them. Not grown. Fifteen or sixteen winters. We used to come around to watch and joke them and get coffee with sugar in it. The Comanches liked that boy.

"During the years after that he used to travel around

with a wagon or a string of pack horses to trade with the different camps. He would dance and enter into sports. I remember he won a horse race one time down on Trading River. They gave him the name of White Buffalo.

"We always had trouble off and on with the Bents. It was all peace and trade with them, you know. At this new mud store, some men thought the trader cheated them, so they killed him and the others there. We had peace meetings and treaties and councils, and finally the Bents got mad and went down there and blew up that mud house. We had a lot of skirmishes those days with white soldiers and wagon trains making a road along that river. Plague too. It got many of us. All of Bent's men went away or holed up in the north mud fort. All except White Buffalo. He turned his back on the whites. I think he lived with a Kotsotuhka band and maybe the Kwahadis too. I don't know what ever happened to him."

As the old man stopped talking, the skin about his eyes seemed to wrinkle slightly, as if he were about to frown. "Did they say your name is Cowbone?"

"Yes, sir. Joe Cowbone."

"Speaking about the Bents reminds me. I knew a man named Cowbone. Knew him slightly. His mother had been a slave taken from the Cheyennes. We had this big peace, Comanche, Kiowa, Cheyenne, Arapaho. It's the same peace we still have. We met just below the north mud fort—that other one wasn't built yet. Big feasts. Big councils. Cowbone's mother decided to go back with the Cheyennes, because he was grown and her man was dead. So she went back to her people. Cowbone had a baby girl, just off the board, toddling around. Prettiest little thing. She cried. Didn't want the old woman to go with those babbling strangers." Mad Wolf paused to laugh silently.

Joe realized with a thrill that the old man was probably remembering his mother. He asked, "What did the little girl say?"

"I don't know. I just remember she was cute. Pretty as a little doll. Beads on her dress. And she cried."

Without any great change, the old man's face took on a stern aspect. "Young man, you shouldn't have taken a dead man's name."

He said, "They do that these days, sir."

"I know. You do it at your own risk. If anyone takes my name after I'm gone, I'll come back and scare the wits out of him."

It didn't seem to require an answer.

The old man said, "The big peace. That reminds me. Call one of the youngsters."

"What's that, sir?"

"Call one of the youngsters over here."

Joe stood up, looked around, and called to the young woman, who was grinding some grain or other food on a stone ledge a hundred steps away. "Will you come here, please?"

Mad Wolf said to her, "Bring out my old *natsakuhna*."

She brought from the tipi a worn rawhide case, placed it on the ground in front of him, then went back to her work.

Mad Wolf did not point, nor lean over, but sat straight, as if he were carefully balanced. "See the lacing all around?"

"Yes, sir."

"What do you think of it?"

"It looks like good work. It's old."

"What is the lacing made of?"

"Horse hair. Black tail hair."

"Look again."

"What is it, sir?"

"Cheyenne hair." He went into his mirthless laugh for a minute. "After the big peace we were supposed to respect our allies. You understand. Throw old scalps away. But I thought, Why throw away a good case? It's nice work. I didn't keep it for spite, but only to be a little devilish.

"Ah, the Cheyennes! How I hated them! What a dangerous and wonderful people! I never cared much for some of their northern friends. The best allies, of course, were the Kiowas. But even they are peculiar. Superstitious. Strange customs."

Remembering the warning that the old man might become tired and the talk might be cut off, he felt impelled, with no good reason, to ask probing questions. He asked, "Mad Wolf, what would you do if you were my age?" It seemed abrupt and he expected either a rebuff or a long pause.

Mad Wolf said immediately, "Of course, I'm not your age."

"But if you were?"

"But I'm not. That's really the answer. Maybe I would do just what you will do."

"No, sir, I mean if you were my age and know all that you know from your long life."

He said slowly, "Young Joe, how should my soul speak for yours?"

It seemed necessary to find some way to probe the question, and, thinking of the old man's fancy allusions and his pride in his deeds, he said, "I think I'm like Tabananica was, sir. I feel stunned, as if I'm walking around among my enemies on all fours like a sick dog. Is there no way that you could ride in and pick me up."

After some silence he said, "I can answer, but the

words are not worth the breath it takes to say them." The cavities of his eyes seemed to darken and the light in them to become more a contrast. His body straightened slightly. It was as if he were preparing for the answer that would come in the worthless words. Then he said, "I would go back on the warpath."

"Against the whites?"

"Yes. And the others. The Sauk and Fox. The Utes. The Apaches. The *mejicanos*. The Osage. The Pawnees."

"If I go against them, do you think I will be beaten?"

"We are not speaking of you, but of me."

"I don't understand, sir."

"I like you, young Joe. I like your questions. You're more thoughtful than most men. I pity you too. I cannot be your age. Do you know the fact that stands in my mind greater than anything else?"

"No, sir."

"Soon I go to the Other Side. I must and I shall and I want to. As for you . . ." His words became even more deliberate. "You must go on alone."

These words were like an announcement of doom.

After a while the old man said, "Do you know who took the horses from the gods?"

"Yes, sir. They say the Comanches did."

"You ought to say, 'We did,' young man. Our fore-fathers did it. Before that the women and dogs had to carry our things. We had no one to carry us. We had to walk. Maybe we will have to walk again. Who knows? Maybe we will have to stagger around on all fours with blood running out of our heads. Or maybe we will learn to ride the clouds. Who knows?

"But when I say 'we,' I don't mean Mad Wolf. I go on a long journey soon, and I own a good traveling horse and a war-horse, which I shall take along to ride in that place where I go."

The pause after that was long, and he began to try to think of another question, a difficult thing after the sense of finality in Mad Wolf's words. Then he studied the old man carefully and realized that he had gone to sleep. He stood up and started to call to the other inhabitants of the small camp, but saw that they were already approaching. They raised the old man up delicately, and he could see the old brown bare feet were not flat on the earth, but dangling, trailing, as the young man and young woman supported him. The movement woke him and he said, "Young man, you are invited to come back to see me again. You are an interesting talker."

He thanked him and said good-bye.

He walked home more slowly than he had come, and had forgotten whatever uncertain practical benefit he had told himself he might gain from the visit. All ideas of utility were engulfed, drowned by a strong impression of the past. What all that man had known! Those very eyes that he had looked into, they had seen it all!

His words about going on a long journey and owning a good traveling horse and war-horse which he would ride in that place—had he spoken symbolically or literally? Or did the old man recognize any difference in the two ways of speaking? What did it matter? From some depth in him a voice was crying, "Let me go with you, Mad Wolf!"

Certain thoughts—about never surrendering, not accepting the reservation—pecked at his involvement. The old man did not know the borders of the reservation, yet he was well inside them. He had never surrendered, and yet Duncan Bull's wife had seen his old granddaughter at the last ration issue.

But he pushed back these nagging objections. They

seemed disloyal. He submitted himself to the luxury of sadness and awe and wonder toward the grandeur of the past, while the sense of it was still fresh, allowed it to surround him and dominate him and cleanse him like thick sage smoke. For an hour as he walked, the Mountains of the Wichitas seemed to be the topmost point of the world and they seemed to bless him. There would be plenty of time for petty, unavoidable objections another day, when Mad Wolf's words stopped ringing in his ears.

12

THE TRUTH

HE WALKED down the winding wagon road beside Medicine Bluff Creek in the direction of the fort, carrying his rifle in one hand and his book in his back pocket. He had decided to settle something. It seemed that many things in his life he had not understood. That this is a trouble and a fault in all people. They don't get together and explain and pass on facts that others should know and have a right to know. He would settle something for the sake of his mother, for the sake of Mr. Powell, and perhaps even in some vague way for his own sake. He was going to tell Mr. Powell the truth. Other problems and possibilities would face him later, but this was a clear and certain thing that could be done, and he did not know but that it might have some effect on the others.

He passed across the sandy flats, over the ridges, through the groves of elms and pecans and cottonwoods and through the scrubbier patches of oaks. Where the pack trail left the wagon road to cut off some of the windings, he followed it. When he was an hour above the fort, he asked himself, Why am I going this way? His destination was the cow camp, and he was making the distance twice as long.

It was the circles again. Without planning his route

he was finding that he must pass by the fort and the agency, the area where Lottie lived, then turn back out southwest on the prairie. He wondered whether it was a force inside himself or outside himself that led him. It seemed the story of his life. Why should a man go along so many windings and circles? Why couldn't he have a straight trail, his own, which he understood and agreed to? He did not know whether to be angry at himself. But at least now he was taking action. After he had settled the truth with Mr. Powell, then he would face whatever truth lay in his response to the words of Mad Wolf.

He removed his moccasins to ford the creek, then walked up the rise south of Medicine Bluffs. The squat stone buildings of the fort lay below them. A trail of dust pointed from the fort out along the north road. There, clear in his view, rode a column of cavalrymen followed by three wagons and six pack mules. Here and there a small sparkle of light came from a brass button or other polished bit of metal. He counted. There were fifty-two riders. And fifty-two beautifully matched bay horses.

He walked on past the fort and was strongly conscious of the stone corral and the stables, of how they guarded their stock, of how they would not even turn the horses out to pasture and had to buy hay for them. But fifty-two of their horses were cantering up the north road, away from the protection of the fort.

It was late afternoon when he came to the Red Store. To conceal his purpose, he asked the storekeeper whether he had seen Slow Tom Armstedt lately.

The man said that he had not.

"I wonder," Joe said, "why some of the soldiers are riding toward the north agency."

"Fussing and fighting all over about the land," the

storekeeper said. "Say, ain't you the one that come in after that Armstedt boy when he got hit on the head? I thought you was. Top of that, them Kiowas and Pena-tuhkas up north is taking up the Ghost Dance. Hell, it don't mean nothing, but the soldiers is scared of it."

He shook his head soberly and went on: "All them soldiers running around with guns, I don't like it. It's one thing to play war inside a fort. Something else to go riding out half scared and trigger happy that way. I don't like it."

He was hungry, but had no money to buy anything to eat and did not want to ask the storekeeper for anything. He walked on down East Cache Creek and slept that night beside it on a gravel bar.

When he had decided to confront Mr. Powell with the truth, he thought that his main problem was to get the man alone so that the talk could be private. But it turned out to be no problem at all, as if circumstances conspired in his favor, while another obstacle, unex-pected, reared its strange head and almost prevented his speaking.

He had wasted time trying to find a rabbit for break-fast, and he walked down across the flat autumn prairie toward the cow camp just at midday. No sooner had he come in sight of the fence line and the place where Spike and Bill and Slow Tom were digging postholes, than the three of them stopped work and headed for the camp on Pecan Creek, no doubt to eat their noon meal. And when he had come to where they had been working, he saw his good luck: Mr. Powell was coming toward him in the wagon, driving along throwing off the last of a load of cedar posts beside the line of fresh postholes.

He picked up a pair of the diggers, stepped off ten

steps on the line and started digging a hole as if he had never quit the job. Mr. Powell could not possibly fail to stop and speak to him. Then, with the confrontation definitely before him, with nothing between him and the man except a minute of time, the new problem thrust up, so sudden as to be frightening. What would he say? I'm the boy, Mr. Powell. I'm not dead. My mother isn't dead either. We've been alive all these many years. How improper it seemed to say such things!

His nature as a Comanche had never seemed so important as it seemed now. It was not that his nature was identified or defined, but that it was subject to that. He was a particular kind of human being.

And his clothes. He had on white man's trousers, a vest but no shirt. He had passed a comb through his hair the morning before and replaited his braids. He resented his own concern about his appearance, but he could not suppress his gladness that his hair was combed, nor his sadness that he wore no shirt.

Mr. Powell threw off the last of the posts and drove the team straight toward him, waving one arm in a rough greeting. He yelled, "Whoa!" at the mules, deftly tied the lines to the stake in the corner of the wagon box and clambered down, using the doubletree as a step. He grinned broadly and pushed his big hat toward the back of his head.

"Hi there, Joe."

"Hi, Mr. Powell."

"How's everything going?"

"Fine."

"I'm sure glad to see you come back to work."

He was determined to speak about the matter in English. He could speak it as well as any white man and would be careful to make no error. He would not use any expressions which some white men use in speaking to Indians, such as "heap big." He would speak naturally. He could do it.

He must have certain words with which to begin. It was not like talking about something else, where any words that come out will do. He must not say anything foolish. And yet he must begin. The words would not reveal themselves. Could it be that there was no way he could find a beginning? He must do it by blurting out something. Words were in his throat, stuck, and he did not even know what they were so that he could judge them. He took a deep breath and found himself wondering, arguing, whether it would be better to wait, to think all his speech out alone beforehand, at least a beginning. But what was this man here? Only another human creature. Why should he be afraid? He was not afraid. He would not be afraid to strike the man square in the nose if there seemed a good reason. Why, then, did he hesitate to speak? What did he expect? Would Mr. Powell be angry? Walk away? Fight? What did he expect, to make him afraid? What did it matter? He must keep it before him that it really didn't matter and keep the urgency out of his voice and out of his mind. It would get worse if he didn't go ahead, and so he resolved to say anything he could.

He said, "Can I talk to you about something, Mr. Powell?" His voice sounded queer; he was trying too hard to make it natural. But the words were all right.

"You can talk to me about anything, Joe."

"At Black Kettle's camp out on the Washita, Mr. Powell, when the Bluecoats came in the snow . . ."

A quietness came over the man like a little wave, and he stood a moment as if he were suddenly alert to danger; then he relaxed and said, "You want to ask me about that? I wasn't there."

"I want to tell you about it, Mr. Powell."

"How old are you, Joe? That was before your time."

"I was five years old."

"No, you must be wrong. You must be thinking about something else."

"A woman was there, Mr. Powell, with a boy. She was not a Cheyenne, but she had a Cheyenne grandmother who was dead at that time. Her man, a white trader, was not with her. She and the boy camped with those below a bank, just beside the flat where they held horse races."

The man was alert again, and uncertain.

"She ran with the others and carried the boy and their two covering robes. It was early in the morning. Many horses were running and the guns were firing. A snow lay on the ground. The earth is red there and it showed through the snow at the bank and where the paths were beaten out. But the redness of earth, it only seems red. The blood that morning—it was very bright on the snow, in patches and sprays and drops, so red that you could see it all your life."

"Why are you talking about this? You know nothing about it, Joe. Why are you saying all this?"

"She was shot in the thigh. She fell down and covered them with the robes. When the horses ran over them, he heard a shot. It made two holes in the robe and also cut his neck. He thought, I have been killed. But—"

"What is this? Who put you up to this, Joe? What's the meaning of it?"

"She crawled, Mr. Powell, through the willows, and the boy with her. The firing and screaming and horses running were behind them and downstream. They came to the river. It was slushy with ice."

"Stop it!" he said. "What do you expect to gain from this?"

"She picked the boy up and carried him through the

water. She groaned because of her leg. Then they walked up to a place where two small red hills stick up. The little hills had snow banked on one side and were bare on the other. Between them, that's where she fell down and passed out. The boy bled on himself from the cut on his neck, but it was not bad. He was cold. He thought awhile that his mother was dead. He was too young to know whether a bullet in the thigh will kill a person."

Mr. Powell put his two hands out in front of himself as if he were pressing down a pile of hay and making it stay down. "Listen, young man! Someone has told you to say this! I know more than you think I do about it. Those camped under the bluff near the racetrack were Two Bows' people. They were all killed or taken prisoner."

It was necessary, in telling it, to go straight ahead as much as possible. "But she woke up, Mr. Powell. She said that they must walk and they would get warm. She kept on saying they must walk. They walked up the long sloping prairies out of the valley. The ground was lumpy white, because the sagebrush had caught the snow and made little mounds. She limped. The boy had put his hand on a dry nettle when he crawled and she laughed at him and kissed his hand. They walked in the daytime and at night; I think it was three days. Then she lay down on some high ground and sent the boy ahead."

"That's enough, I tell you! I don't know who put you up to this! I've got nothing against you, Joe, but I don't like this! I knew every Cheyenne in that camp that day. I had traded with them and hunted with them and gambled with them. I knew them. I know what happened. Those who lived near Two Bows—they were all killed or taken prisoner. Don't you think I talked to the people?"

"She sent the boy ahead, Mr. Powell, to a creek. It was a certain place where, if you didn't have meat in the winter, you could find straggling buffalo or deer. As he walked, he kept his eyes on a tree, as his mother had told him. When he got there, a family of Kotsotuhka people were there."

"Don't you think I know? I tell you I talked to the people! Why do you insist on saying things like this? I talked to a sister of Saying Horse. And to Bullhide, and his brother. And when Old Smallstar was kept prisoner, before he was sent away to Florida. I talked to him. He saw it all with his own eyes."

"And the Kotsotuhka people, Mr. Powell, came back with the boy and found the woman and took care of her."

"Can't you hear me? Why don't you listen? I tell you Old Smallstar saw it all with his own eyes. He was there!"

It seemed impossible to think of the proper thing to say next. He was not making it connected in a good way so that the man could understand. He said, "Old Smallstar was camped a long walk downstream, past the island, Mr. Powell, almost where the river bends north."

"Dammit! I didn't mean he could see it all with his eyes! But he knew what happened! This is nonsense. Three days! How could she walk three days with a bullet in her thigh? I know what I know!"

"Do you know if she was good at walking, Mr. Powell? Could she walk a long distance?"

"Why should I argue with you about this? Dammit! Can't you understand that I know what happened? Why do you ask me questions like that? Didn't I say I knew those Cheyenne people? I knew them like brothers! I asked them and asked them. They told me! I know what I know!"

"Why did you ask the Cheyenne? Do you know what the woman would do when she was hurt, Mr. Powell?"

"You damned right I know! I know what happened!"

"If she was hurt . . . if she thought she might die, where would she take the little boy, Mr. Powell? To the Cheyenne or to the Comanches?"

"Who told you to ask these questions? How do you know to ask these questions? Where do you get them?" The man's face had slowly drained of color so that it was ashen. The man was uncertain, saying, "I know . . ." but wondering whether he knew. His eyes gaped intensely and were filled with wonder and surprise and piercing questioning.

But he turned away and his voice contained assertive doubt as he said, "If she wasn't killed on the Washita, when did she die?"

"Was she older than you, Mr. Powell?"

"No."

"She's younger than you. She is still a very young and beautiful woman. She lives alone out through the mountains, in the camp of Old Man Iron Lance." His eyes were watering and his nose was trying to run, though he had no kind of cold or sickness, and he felt hot blood in his face. He was not ashamed of the lie about his mother's youth and beauty; it was an assertion which had a kind of defiant truth in it. She might look old and fat and ugly, but she was not.

"What was her name?" Mr. Powell asked, mixing the doubt and a serious question.

"Some called her Little Brown Girl, but later she took the name of Mary and her father's name of Cowbone to please the white men who keep records."

After a minute the man said, "I'm sorry about this, Joe, because I thought you were my friend. I don't believe any of it. I know you. You probably have a dozen names, and you use whichever one suits you. You may have a dozen schemes in your head, and you expect to tell a big joke about how you fooled a white man. That's all right. But go fool somebody else. I'll laugh about it too." He stopped talking as if that were the end of it and not another word should be spoken. But in a moment he said, "Now, what is it you want from me?"

"I don't want anything."

"Go ahead. Whatever it is. Whatever you had in mind. What did they tell you to get from me?"

"Nothing."

"Then what in the hell is all this story? What is all this ridiculous story about out on the Washita?"

"You asked and asked twenty years ago, Mr. Powell, and you asked the wrong people."

"All right! God damn you! Say it's true! Now, what do you want?"

"I don't want anything, Mr. Powell. I was there and saw it all with my own eyes. Her man wasn't there. He was safe. And now I have answered the question you were asking and asking long ago. I guess it's polite to answer a question. I don't want anything."

"This is no place for joking and scheming! Can't you understand that?"

"It's a true thing, Mr. Powell."

"No, it's not true! And I won't have it! What do you want?"

"I want to tell you something that's true."

"But I know it isn't true! Can't you see that?"

"Yes, sir. You know it. I see that. But it's true anyway."

"No, it's not true anyway! You say it's true for some damned reason! What do you want?"

"I don't want to be friends with you."

"Well . . . that makes a lot of sense. What kind of sense does that make?"

"I don't know."

"What do you want from me, young man?"

"What do you want from me?"

"I'd like to make a little sense out of it. You come up with this farfetched and outrageous lie, and you don't have any idea what you're meddling in. How could you expect to get away with it? You ought to know this is the kind of nonsense a man wouldn't put up with. There's not a word of truth in it, now is there?"

The uncertainty and unreality of it had reached a peak of tension; he felt as if something released inside his stomach, as if taut stitches gave way and left him defenseless. He said, "No."

"It's all made up, isn't it?"

"Yes."

"Then what's the meaning of it?"

"It's a big joke, Mr. Powell."

At that point, he could not bear it any longer. Pride that tasted like old gall had welled up in his throat. He was angry and strangely weak and afraid his voice would break in a sob if he spoke again. Whatever bright expectations had moved him at first were completely darkened by now. He dropped the posthole diggers and walked abruptly away.

"Wait!" the man said. "I don't aim to hurt your feelings."

He waited.

Mr. Powell waited and then said, "I didn't aim to hurt your feelings."

"Hurt my feelings?" he asked stupidly.

"I think I see it, Joe. Maybe I got the wrong idea. Maybe you don't want anything. You believe what you say is true. A lot of Indians don't know where they belong. They got split up and scattered and lost touch. You heard this and thought too much about it and got it mixed up with things you remember when you were a kid. I don't hold it against you."

He had a series of thoughts then, which went into the depths of the thing further than he had gone before. This man was sincere and would believe what he believed no matter what he told him. This man denied that his wife and son lived, and yet he put himself back here in this part of the world, where, if they lived, they would certainly rise up before him. So this man must believe his denial. He felt like taunting the man, saying, Mr. Powell, White Buffalo, if you are determind to escape your wife and child, you had better get away from this Comanche country and go somewhere else. Talk cannot convince you, but you have been lucky so far; one of these days you will meet your wife face to face on a path. Then your shell of certainty will be broken.

But there was the mystery of what had brought the man back. Out of a wide world of places where he might live with his second wife, he had come back to this one place, as if he were drawn back by something. And he might not even know why himself.

The maddening denial, he had a vague understanding of that too, of why the man could do it and be sincere. He himself undoubtedly looked as strange, as unkin, to this white man as this white man looked to him. That memory of a man on whose knees he sat, a man who was not any kind of appearance at all, but only a large body of warmth and joking—that man, though poorly remembered, had been like a part of himself, a thing with which he belonged without even thinking about it. What had Mr. Powell to do with that? They could not possibly be the same man. It was obvious, right on the face of it, that they could not be. He had an insight then that he had been idiotic, mad, to attempt this telling—that the truth is the gulf, the impossibility, rather than the pitiful fact of connection. How unacceptable it would have been to have the man call him "son." Powell, though hatefully mistaken, was right.

He had no good way to end their confrontation. To lash out at the man, to turn and flee, nothing expressed himself. And so he did what was partly habit, and inconclusive, and at least no more a lie than anything else he might do: he grinned.

"What we need is some chow," Mr. Powell said. "Let's climb on the wagon and see if we can get down there before they eat it all up."

They went to eat. Slow Tom, Spike and Bill were obviously pleased to see him but, being in the presence of a white man who could understand their speech, said little other than to greet him. He felt their questioning gaze, and it was in imagining their potential questions that he realized that he had made up his mind and had answers ready for what they would ask. He felt assurance.

After the noon meal, Mr. Powell let them off at the fence line, then drove east alone to pick up more posts, which were evidently being delivered by the freighters to some point along the Texas road.

As soon as the wagon had rattled off across the bunch grass, they were upon him. Slow Tom demanded, "Where the hell have you been?"

"We were ready to quit and come after you," Bill said.

Spike asked, "Did you get an answer?"

He laughed and said, "Did you ever notice the horses of these cattle outfits? Most of them are scrubs."

"What's that supposed to mean?" Slow Tom asked.

"Wouldn't you rather have big beautiful matched horses, *ohaiekas* and *ehkakomas?* Strong geldings. No scrubs. About fifty of them." He could see them grow excited at his words.

"Who's got any such horses?" Slow Tom asked.

"How about the United States Cavalry?"

"Yeah. We going to take them from behind that thick stone fence or out of those stables where they've got a half dozen guards?"

"Man, fifty-two of those fancy-dressed soldiers rode for the north agency yesterday. Supplies and everything. I wonder if they have a good place to keep their horses up there."

"Not much," Bill Nappy said, grinning.

"Not any at all," Spike said.

"That's right," he told them. "We're leaving here tonight. Tomorrow night those fifty-two horses are going to be ours."

They did not know whether they did any posthole digging that afternoon, because of their talk. Joe felt a welling in his blood. And he could see it in them; they were as eager and confident as he. When they saw Powell coming toward them in a wagon to pick them up in the late afternoon, Slow Tom wondered how they were going to get his two ponies from the remuda without rousing the cattle workers' suspicion.

"I'll take care of it," Joe said. "Settle down; don't act excited."

As they drove into the area of the cow camp, he said to Mr. Powell, "Slow Tom and I are going to catch our ponies. We may sell them to Bill and Spike."

"Watch out for them," Mr. Powell said good-natured-

216

ly. "They look like slick traders." The man seemed casual, but Joe realized that the man was looking at him, studying him. It was that way during the evening meal. Mr. Powell kept looking at him out of the side of his eye.

As he and Slow Tom rode the two Armstedt ponies into camp and toward the place where they usually slept, Mr. Powell called from the mule pen, "Joe!"

He slid off and tossed the rope to Slow Tom, who rode on toward where Spike and Bill waited.

He walked over and asked, "Did you want something, Mr. Powell?"

"I hope you don't mind me asking," he said, "but where do your folks live? Are your parents still alive?"

He did not want to say yes and did not see any reason to say no. There was nothing to say, but the strong sense of self-consciousness did not trouble him as it had.

"The reason I asked, Joe—maybe I used to know them. I used to know a lot of Comanches."

There was nothing he could say and he was defiantly determined that he would not be embarrassed. He grinned.

"Cowbone," the man said. "Cowbone. It sounds familiar, but I can't seem to place where I heard it before." Finally he said, "Well, you go on to your horse swapping. We'll talk about it again someday."

The interruption had seemed as nothing to him because his great plan was under way. The three who were waiting for him were buzzing with questions. He was surprised at how clear his mind seemed and how certain he was about what they should do. "If anybody has anything in the wagon or around this camp, get it now," he said. "We won't be back.

"Now, listen. I'll go with Slow Tom to get my stuff

at his place. We don't want to forget to get some matches. You two fellows go home and get your equipment. Say, can you borrow a couple of horses up on the Blue Beaver? Don't steal them. We don't want any damned Indians down on us now."

"What do we want with them?" Bill Nappy asked.

"What do you think we want with them? We're going clear to the north agency tomorrow. Get two if you can."

It was dark. Over in the center of the cow camp they could see the cook's fire reflecting on the tent and the gray tarp covering the big wagon. No one was moving around much. They could barely hear the hum of talk, broken by laughter.

"All right," he told them. "Does everybody know where Stony Point is, up on the north road? Straight across the road from there is a slough of water, before you get to the creek. We'll meet by that slough. In the morning. As early as you can get there. Before the middle of the morning."

"We're not going to get much sleep tonight," Bill said, grinning.

Spike said, "We can sleep when we get old."

Quietly they gathered their few belongings and led the Armstedt ponies away from the cow camp, then parted and traveled north.

13

THE RAID

HE AND SLOW TOM got to the slough below Stony Point an hour after sunrise. He was satisfied with their progress. Slow Tom's weapon was only a .22 rifle, but at least he had plenty of shells. They picketed the pony and, making sure that they were out of sight of the road, lay down to get as much sleep as possible.

In the middle of the morning they were awakened by Bill and Spike yelling, "Ah . . . h . . . h . . . heh! Let's go get 'em!"

They were riding an old heavy-footed paint horse with split ears and the Armstedt pony. Bill Nappy carried a single-shot buffalo gun called a Big Fifty. Spike had left off the trousers he had been wearing as a fence worker; now he wore only moccasins, a belt, and a piece of soft leather pulled through it for a breechclout. He had a good knife in his belt. Over his shoulder was slung a quiver with a dozen arrows and an unstrung bow protruding from it.

Joe had hoped that they would borrow two horses at least. The two Armstedt ponies were already tired. He certainly had not expected Spike to come attired as he was and with only a bow and arrows for weapons. But Spike had a streak of seriousness unlike the other two, which would not bear much criticism.

Slow Tom said to him, grinning, "You going to sell those Indian trinkets for souvenirs?"

Spike said, not grinning, "Load up your peashooter and I'll string my bow and we'll step off twenty steps and see who stays on his feet the longest."

"Let's get going," he told them. "You and Bill ride double on the paint. We'll take the road and keep a good lookout not to meet anyone." He suspected that the bow was as formidable a weapon as the .22. His Winchester was the best, but the buffalo gun would make a good, loud noise. They were well enough armed.

They proceeded up the road, which followed the general course of East Cache Creek. He was pleased to see that the dusty road appeared considerably cut up with wagon tracks and hoof marks. The cavalry tracks of two days before were there, but blown enough by the wind so that it was hard to tell whether they pointed north or south. If they brought the horses back along this road, any pursuer would need to do a careful tracking jo' to find where they left the road. He told the others, and they looked tentatively at spots for a turnoff, well sodded, where horse tracks would not plainly show.

It was a long ride. They left East Cache and passed over the sweeping plains, which bore a coarse bluish buffalo grass in bunches and had gray rocks here and there breaking the surface of the soil, thence into the drainage of the Washita River. Far out to their right the bare Tonkawa hills stuck up with sketchy streaks, which were patches of dark cedar.

The two Armstedt ponies were exhausted and had to be constantly flogged on the rump to make them drag their feet fast enough to keep up with the big paint, which was carrying double. They were less than an hour's ride from the river, and Joe judged that they should pause to rest the horses. They pulled off the road, down a branch of Tonkawa Creek, and dismounted. The animals, all three of which were too little spirited to run off, they turned loose to graze. They themselves sprawled on the ground. Joe felt tired, as he knew the others did, but their goal was almost within sight and he felt a stirring of excitement in his blood.

They had grown silent, when the paint horse whinnied. They sat up. A light clink of harness came from toward the road, and the clonk of wheels rocking on an axle. Joe realized with disgust that the horses could be seen from the road.

Around the point of trees came a buggy pulled by one hairy gray horse. It was the Reverend Fairchild. He guided the horse toward them, stopped and, feeling carefully for the step with his foot, got down.

The man was tall and spare of form. His most notable feature was a sparse gray beard that hung down his chest, as straggly as if some animal had been chewing at it. His hair was shoulder length and gray, topped by a straw hat with a small brim. His black clothes were dusty. His eyes seemed hidden behind his glasses. On his mouth, the large mouth of a speechmaker, was a pained smile, a permanent expression, so that it was difficult to discern his feelings.

He held up his hand and said, "How!" He pointed at himself and said, *"Puha-rivo,"* then began to make clumsy signs.

The intrusion was so unexpected that Joe had no idea what he should do. He stood up. Impulsively he said in English, "We don't understand anything like that. We're Pawnees."

The Reverend Fairchild was surprised at the good English. He was pleased but looked at each of them as he said to Joe, "I thought I had seen you before. May I ask your name?"

"Lone Wolf," Joe said.

"Do you have a Christian name?"

"I don't guess so," Joe said. He was thinking, This old goat thinks he recognizes me, and probably Slow Tom too.

"May I ask if you have a last name?"

"Johnson," he said.

"Mr. Johnson, I'm the Reverend Fairchild, and I'm a minister of the gospel of Jesus Christ. My church is down south by the agency near Fort Sill. I'd like to invite you to come to the services. Are you boys Christians?"

"We're just passing through," he said. "We're Pawnees. We're going south. Down to Texas. We have relatives down there." It sounded ridiculous to him as he said it, but the more confusing information, the better.

"Mr. Johnson, are you a Christian? Have you heard the wonderful news of Jesus of Nazareth?"

"Yes, sir, we've heard it."

"I hope you'll accept it and keep it in your heart. Now, this is not the Ghost Dance, which is a false use of Jesus, but this is the true Jesus, the son of God, who came down to earth to save us. We are all brothers, and Jesus died to save all of us. I'm now on my way south, going back to my church, and we are fortunate to find each other; we can travel south together."

"No, sir, we can't. We'll rest. We have to hunt first."

"Well, God bless you. Remember that you are invited to my church. Whosoever will may come. We have a good interpreter to put the word of God into your tongue." He carefully mounted the step again and settled himself into the spring seat. "God bless you, boys," he said. "God bless you." He pulled the hairy gray horse around and clucked him toward the road.

It was not lost on Joe that the man had mentioned his interpreter when there was no interpretation except Comanche at his church. Whether it reflected the Reverend's ignorance or forgetfulness or doubt, he could not guess. He asked Slow Tom, "Do you think he recognized you?"

"I don't think so. I always stay away from the old bastard as much as I can."

Joe told them as much of the conversation as they had not gathered. They had a good laugh. But the interruption of the preacher had cast an air of unreality over their project. He was anxious to recapture the feeling of movement and purpose. "Let's go," he told them. "I want to locate the soldiers while we've still got some light."

Where the road forked, with a dim trail leading west toward old Fort Cobb, they left it and followed a ridge of low wooded hills. A half hour before sunset, they came out on the bluff southern edge of the Washita valley. The river course was marked with the yellow leaves of cottonwoods and willows. It meandered through broad flats of pink sand. Above it on either side, as much as a mile from the stream, bluffs stuck out, brilliant red in the late sunlight.

Below them and in clusters downstream were scattered the canvas tipis of Kiowas. Straight across the stream they could see the agency sawmill; farther down on the other side, another bunch of agency buildings. The Indian dwellings across the river were the woven grass houses of the Wichitas, *dokanas*, like haystacks.

He was searching the two-mile-wide vista for signs of cavalry. Sometimes a few soldiers stayed in a building at the agency, but not so many as he had seen. Slow Tom grabbed his arm and pointed back to the left, upstream. There were the army tents, less than a mile away, lined up in perfect rows.

"I think I see some horses behind there in the trees," Spike said. "Back toward the river."

"That's where they would be," he said. "In that deep bend."

A thin moon hung hardly noticeable in the sky. It would light up at dark, and it would go down around midnight. The soldiers would be asleep by then. "I'd like to get them just when the moon goes down," he said.

As he stood there with his three companions, a plan unfolded in his mind as clearly and in as much detail as if he had peered at this scene for a month, and he unfolded it to them. Two men would take their three horses and all their gear and slip into the great pasture in the bend. Just before the moon went down they would catch two cavalry mounts, tie the bundles on them, mount up and wait until they saw fires burning near the tents, then stampede the horse band around the curve of the river and out.

The other two would get as close to the camp as they could, spot the guards and all the tied horses. Watch carefully until the moon hit the horizon, then quietly move through the camp, freeing every tied horse if possible, leading one to ride, then proceed to the line of timber behind the tents and fire the tall grass, upwind of the camp if possible, then mount and come out with the stampede.

They must bring the horse band along near the river, then out through the clearing on the other side of the tents, then straight south up the draw which lay off to their left, to keep from collecting any Indian horses, then cut east to strike the Fort Sill road.

Would it work? They thought it would. Except for

Bill Nappy. His eyes were closed and he was swaying as he stood, hugging the Big Fifty in his arms. Dead asleep.

They woke him and, dribbling water from a water bag, made him wash his face. They went over it all again.

They could see two horses tied, also two cavalrymen coming horseback from toward the agency to the camp. It would be well to get every single mount if they could. No firing of guns. They might hit each other.

He looked at his three friends and selected Spike to go in among the tents with him. Slow Tom, heavy-footed in his white man's shoes, but dependable as the day is long, could take Bill around after the horses.

They split up, the other two taking the horses and everything but his and Spike's knives and some matches. The sun had fallen below the trees upstream in the west. Joe agreed with Spike as to who should take which side, and on the floor of the valley they separated. He moved to the left and forward, using for cover a clump of drying sunflowers, a thicket of plum bushes, the undulations of the ground. Daylight was ebbing as he came up behind the low sandy ridge topped with weeds, and he was near enough to have hit the closest tent with a thrown rock. He lay propped on his elbows and looked.

Two guards walked smartly in front of the encampment. Beside the door of a larger tent in the middle stood another, stiff and straight. At the rear, in the edge of the trees, two others marched, probably for the purpose of guarding the horse band, but not doing it well, for the bend of the river stretched back a half mile and its opening was equally wide. Of tied horses, he saw five: two tied to a tree near the rear guards, one picketed by the big tent in clear sight of the standing guard, and two beside a tent over on Spike's side. He could trust Spike for those two.

As darkness came on the thin moon lit up, also the small pale fires in front of the tents. Now and then a soldier walked from one tent to another. He could hear the hum of their talking, sometimes laughter. The wind, stilled at sunset, was rising slowly from the northwest, which was good; he could see the grass and undergrowth back among the trees; it would do for their fire.

When the last trace of daylight went out of the sky, the moon seemed to brighten. New guards came out and took the places of the five he had located. The two new guards at the rear walked a few minutes, then they came together and began to build a small fire. He could hear the snap of dry limbs as they broke them.

The fires within the camp were nearly gone, sunken under their own ashes. A crack of yellow light showed that a light burned in the big tent. The sentry beside its door was a dark stiff outline, and the horse on the picket line was only ten steps from him, clearly in his vision.

The moon fell fast. He rose and walked to the tent line. Standing beside one, peering at the scene in the last of the moonlight, fixing it in his mind, he suddenly smelled the strong odor of white men. He heard their heavy even breathing behind the canvas near him. His heart pounded. He breathed deeply to calm himself. Without looking behind him he was aware of the moon's touching the trees in the west and slipping down.

He moved deliberately then, along the dusty street laid out in squares, conscious of tent ropes over which he might stumble and of the positions of the guards. He approached the big tent from the rear and came up on the side where the horse was tied. He paused and looked intently. The beast's head was down. Asleep. By patiently staring, he made out the rope, leading toward himself, apparently tied to a stake about even with the front of the tent. From inside the big tent he could hear rustling sounds.

On his hands and knees he moved forward until he could see the dark bulge which was the guard, then he lowered himself to his belly. He eased his hands out. The iron stake was there, the rope knotted in its iron circle. He laid his cheek in the dirt and kept his eyes on the dark form in front of the tent, while his hands slowly pulled at the knot. He was in the edge of the sentry's view, but the sleeping horse was well in it. The horse would not know he was free until the rumpus started. Maybe then would join the others. At least he would be free and hard to catch.

He had slipped the end of the rope through the ring and was slowly withdrawing his hands when a hoarse voice called from inside the tent.

A flare of yellow light flooded the horse for a moment. He thrust his head forward to see. The sentry had gone inside.

He sprang forward and retrieved the rope. He tugged, forcefully, commandingly. The horse came. He coiled the rope and led him back along the dusty street, one hand patting gently on the sturdy neck. Their feet made no sound in the sand.

In front of the rear row of tents he turned out of the camp and began to circle toward the horses tied in the rear. The two guards here would be able to see nothing, for they had their fire in their eyes. He satisfied himself that two forms hunkered over the blaze, then kept his eyes elsewhere.

When he saw the two horses at the tree, he paused a minute, patting the horse he led. When he was sure that the two sensed his presence, he walked straightway to them. Each was tied by a bridle rein to a limb.

He loosed them and led the three away. A rustling of leather and sometimes a clink of metal stirrups came from the horses, but he moved on.

The call of a mourning dove sounded from the trees ahead and to his right. So accurate, so like a bird half asleep, that he nearly thought it the real thing. He answered.

It was dark under the elms and cottonwoods. He pulled the horses into a half trot.

A shout rose in the army camp. "Corporal of the guard!"

He called low, urgently, "Spike?"

"Here."

"Hold these three!"

Spike had two horses. "They're yelling back there."

"I know it. Here. Get that rope off so when we turn him loose he won't step on it."

If only Slow Tom and Bill were ready.

"Corporal of the guard! Corporal of the guard!"

The shout was coming from the middle of the camp. He could not see the area of thick grass, but ran toward where it was in his memory, one hand out to guard against tree limbs, one fumbling in his pocket. He heard the grass and felt it with his legs. No time was left to test the wind again. He swept his hand on the ground to find a thick tuft, struck a match on his clasp knife and thrust it into the grass. The flames licked up. It sounded as if a dozen soldiers were yelling now.

Three places he set, ten quick steps apart. As he groped away from the fire, blinded by the light, he smelled the spicy fumes of burning broomweeds.

"Spike, I can't see you."

"Here."

"Keep talking. I can't see you."

"Here. Here. Here."

He ran through a brushy limb, which was not heavy enough to do much damage. Smoke billowed from the fires and was lighted by the spreading flames.

"Here, Joe. Here."

He felt reins thrust into his hands and had to sort them out to tell that he had two horses. He scrambled onto the cavalry saddle. "Lead us out of here, buddy," he said. "I can't see a damned thing."

He gave his horse the reins and bent low to avoid the limbs. Now the commotion in the soldiers' camp was being matched by another down in the great bend of the river, shrill yipping yells, then the rushing of hoofs on sandy ground.

His eyes were regaining their sight and as he came out of the trees he could see the stars, then out ahead the dim white curve of the river sand. At once the whiteness was interrupted by the charging horse band coming out of their pasture in a dead run. He could feel them as much as see them, feel the soft thunder of their pounding feet, smell their sweat brought alive by their excitement.

He kicked into a run as he came into the rear of the stampede, released the horse he led. He didn't know where Spike was, nor the others, but they were there. Off to his right he heard a repressed yell. "Hey . . . ee . . . yah! Go, you devils!" It sounded like Slow Tom.

Out on their left the camp was marked with many small dim lights, some moving, but he could hear nothing from it over the violent rush of the animals before him. His mount ran eagerly with the band. He veered to the right, then pressed in yelling to make sure they did not try to follow the river.

As they began going up the high ground south, he heard the crackle of rifles back there a mile behind. A laugh burst from his throat and turned into an exultant yell at the horses, at his companions, at the wild, beautiful night. Looking around he could see nothing but dim smoke at that place, lighted faintly by unseen red flames on the ground. He could smell it, whether it clung to him or came on the wind, the subtle scent of dusty grass burning, the resinous odor from broomweeds and tumbleweeds, the acrid fragrance from dry gourd vines and sunflowers. He yelled as loudly as he could, meaningless sounds, and when the others answered him, he thought, We are like a tribe, instead of just four men.

As they pushed them left out of the shallow valley, the horses slowed to a trot of themselves. When they came out on top, the horses, the edge of their energy worn, became easy to drive and guide. They had at least fifty. They headed for the Fort Sill road.

Spike's voice came toward him. "Joe? We got them, boy!"

"You bet we did!"

And minutes later he was aware of a horse and the dim form of a rider and on that rider the tall black hat of Slow Tom. "Hey!" he said. "You horse thief! We did it!"

"Sure we did it! I think we got every damned one! You fellows sure set that place on fire!"

"Where's Bill?"

"He's leading this whole parade."

"Good work, buddy. Great!"

After they turned down the road, the four of them came together at the rear and rode side by side. They chattered in the darkness, then, pushing across the sweeping high prairie, became silent.

The regular movement of his mount and the weariness of his body subdued his spirits for a while. He rode for an indefinite time, hardly thinking at all. Then the sky began to lighten in the east, and he became anxious to see their booty. His friends and the broad sweep of the land began to emerge out of the darkness, also the stream of horses ahead. He began to talk and all of them regained their eagerness.

The horses were all bays, most of them with small white markings, a star in the face, a line down the nose, many of them with one or two stocking feet. Some were fine of form, rangy and clean. All were big and strong.

He rode out to the side and counted—fifty-two horses and nine mules. Plus the three they had ridden north.

Back with the others, he outlined a plan for turning west. He would ride in the lead and select a place. As they turned the horses west they should push them into a run, so that there would be less chance of droppings marking the route.

He rode ahead alone. The sooner they turned off, the better, but he wanted to find a good place. The truth was that there was no fully sodded place. Long grass and short grass, all dry, was mixed together here in the headwaters of East Cache, but all of it tended to be in bunches. It was broad daylight. A bank of clouds moved over the sky from the west, ragged clouds with rumples and curls; they might bring weather before the day was over. What good luck it would be if rain fell hard before the cavalry could find their trail!

He picked a place leading out over a rise and signaled to the others. They whipped up their mounts and turned out beside the stream of horses, yipping and yelling. "Hyah! Hyah!" "Hey . . . ee . . . yah!" The horses broke into a run. He stood his mount in the center of the road to help turn them; then, when they had all left the road, turned in behind to keep them going. They kept them at the gallop for a mile. The grass was darker where the band had passed, but it was only because the dew had been disturbed. The sun would burn the marks away.

As they went over the rise, they took the pressure off and the horses slowed to a walk. They herded them loosely down toward a draw with a fringe of trees, where there might be water holes.

Spike rode up beside him. "Look at Bill."

That young man had dropped his chin on his chest and seemed at any minute ready to fall off his horse. Asleep. They laughed.

Spike said, "I'm just about the same way. We didn't get any sleep for two nights."

Joe looked at the draw ahead. The grazing along it was fair and somewhere down it would lie pockets of water. The horse band could drift untended. "We'll stop for a nap down here," he said.

They tied their horses to some willow sprouts. Bill Nappy did not seem to know what was happening as they took him down and laid him on the ground. Two of them had blankets in their packs, but it did not appear worth the effort to take them out. Joe thought that the others fell asleep immediately. He was aware that the sun was coming up and he laid his head on his arm away from it.

It was crazy, he thought, but he was too sleepy to go to sleep. Too tightened up inside. They would need to work out a guard system. He lay for some time, thinking nothing, aware that he was half asleep and half awake, dully believing that he would get up in a minute. He finally came awake with a start, knowing that he had been dead asleep. The first thing he knew was that the sun was straight overhead. Then he knew what woke him: the chink-chink of harness and the light clonk of wheels rocking on an axle.

He whirled over to look. Coming straight toward

them was a hairy gray horse between two shafts, behind
that the painted black top of a buggy, inside that the
erect figure of the Reverend Fairchild.

He kicked hard against Slow Tom's heavy shoe. "Hey,
buddy! Wake up! We've got trouble!"

14

MISSIONARY TO THE
HEATHEN INDIANS

THE MAN felt carefully for the step with his foot and steadied himself by gripping a front support of the buggy top as he lowered himself to the ground. The pained smile on his large mouth, with its long upper lip and slightly protruding teeth, looked serious. "Mr. Johnson," he said, "my heart aches to see this. You boys are surely following the will of Satan."

A quick glance told Joe that most of the horse band ranged in clear view. "We bought these horses from the Kiowas," he said, "and we're driving them down to my uncle in Texas."

"Mr. Johnson, God hates a falsehood worse than anything."

To Slow Tom he said, "We've got trouble; you better get a gun." Bill and Spike were coming awake, staring. He said in English, "To tell the truth, we found the horses. We think they might belong to the army. We're driving them to the fort." He could tell by the twisted expression on the old man's lips that his ridiculous lies were doing no good.

"Mr. Johnson, please don't compound your sin by telling falsehoods about it. You boys come with me to the authorities, and let us pray that we can make amends for this bad act before it's too late."

Slow Tom had his .22 in his hands. Spike, stringing his bow, said, "We're going to have to kill this son of a bitch."

The Reverend Fairchild said with great sincerity, "You must confess and take your punishment like men, Mr. Johnson. It's best. I know it is. I assure you that it is. If you don't go in voluntarily and admit your guilt, you will have a troubled conscience all your life."

Bill said, "We sure can't let him escape. He'll go straight to the soldiers."

"I say kill him," Spike said.

"Or make him go with us," Slow Tom said.

"Mr. Johnson, I don't know what your friends are saying to you, but I'm speaking to you with love in my heart and telling you that your soul hangs in the balance. You must explain to them. You must come and accept your punishment like men. God will stand by you. Jesus will hold your hand. You can bear anything with Him at your side."

Joe said shortly to the other three, "We'll have to take him." To the peculiar, bearded white man, he said, grinning, "Reverend Fairchild, you have stuck your nose in the wrong thing. We've got to take you with us. If you do what you're told, we won't hurt you."

"Mr. Johnson, don't continue this wicked scheme. God is full of mercy toward an humble and contrite heart—"

Joe told him, "Get in the buggy, you old fool! I tell you that you have stuck your nose in the wrong thing! You are going to get killed in a minute!"

The man turned with some dignity and, without any change in expression, went to his buggy, got in carefully and sat down.

"Just leave the lines alone," Joe said. "If you do what you're told, you won't get hurt."

Bill Nappy had brought for his food supply a package of fried cakes and a battered soldier's canteen full of honey. Fearing that the cakes would spoil, they ate them, dribbling a little honey on them as they held them in their hands It was a hasty but full meal. Watching the old man sitting in the buggy from the corner of his eye, Joe decided that it was of no use to offer him any.

Since sunup the rough clouds had grown until now they almost covered the sky and the wind came in gusts. They rounded up the horse band and caught fresh horses to ride. In all there were five cavalry saddles, four of which they used and one of which they threw away in some bushes. They strung out west with three of them driving. Joe had asked Slow Tom to ride behind the buggy with his .22 at the ready and make the old man keep up.

The sky looked threatening. Joe considered it, hoping for rain. But it didn't look like rain. Nowhere could he see the slate-blue veil hanging from sky to earth that meant falling water. Wind maybe. The sky was white and black and turbulent. Scuddy clouds moved in different directions below the solid clouds, as if the winds could not make up their minds. Farther west the sky looked dirty. Sand was in the air. The horses stretched their necks and pointed their ears tentatively in nervous questioning of the weather.

He looked back at the buggy and saw that it was keeping up well enough, though it bounced and swayed on the roadless prairie, and the top was pressed sideways now and then from the gusty wind. The man's straggly beard flattened against his black coat, then flew out and jerked to the side in the wind as if it were alive. He had no plan for the old man, but was not inclined to follow Spike's advice.

They were headed into the low Ugly Mountains. The horses were harder to drive than they had been in the night, as if they were learning to feel a freedom they had not felt in a long time. They were not accustomed to trotting over new terrain except under the saddle. The cavalry mounts wanted to split up into four or five bands, following different leaders. The paint with split ears and the Armstedt ponies and one mule wanted to go in their own direction. The other mules wanted to stop. It took constant pressure to keep them all together and moving west.

The wind seemed to aid the horses' hoofs in striking dust from the ground. It billowed up at times, almost hiding the horses or the trailing buggy or a rider. Joe found himself spitting it from his mouth, picking it from the corners of his eyes, as he raced back and forth to keep the band together. He thought the dust was in their favor rather than otherwise, to help obscure their trail. It was blowing from the ridges, scurrying along the flats. The sky in the west, where the sun was supposed to be, had turned reddish brown, and this coloring of the clouds and the air seemed to grow in extent each time he looked at it. They were moving into a sandstorm.

It engulfed them all of a sudden. He noticed the darkening, looked straight up, and saw that the sky overhead was brown. In a minute it seemed like late twilight. A short time before from a high point he had been able to see the blue outline of the Wichita Mountains to the south; now he could not see a hill a half mile away. The wind blew with erratic determination, and they rode through a completely brown world.

The horse band sobered at the change in light and became more manageable.

He had hoped to drive through half the night, as long

as the moon stayed up, but the night would be completely black. He searched the terrain for possible places to camp and studied the dim light to try to detect any fading. They skirted the southern edge of a hill which might have been the one called Longhorn Mountain, then began to cross a succession of gullies which he believed were the headwaters of Rainy Mountain Creek. Here the land was sweeping plains interrupted by lone hills. The light was failing.

They veered the band to the north up alongside an eroded wash, pushing them into a gallop. When he came near enough to them, he shouted at Spike, then Bill, "Stop at the first wood!"

He could hardly see Slow Tom and the buggy behind them. The wash led into a dry stream bed, shallow, with gravel bars in it, here and there flanked with cutbanks as high as a man's head. A clump of cottonwoods loomed and he could see a whitened log and pieces of driftwood. He sent Bill to circle the horses and stop them, then leave them in the stream bed. As darkness dropped on them, as solid as a blanket, he and Spike came under the lee of a bank and began to build a fire. Spike, fortunately, had brought along in his pack an old, but sharp, brass tomahawk.

They built it large enough to cast an uncertain light out into the blackness. He saw Bill returning. It seemed useless to shout into the wind and dust; he took his Winchester a few steps away from their tied mounts and fired it. Shortly thereafter Slow Tom came into the light, riding alongside the shaggy gray horse, leading it by the bridle. The buggy bounced on the round stones in the stream bed.

The Reverend Fairchild looked tousled as he got down and came to the fire. He held his straw hat on with one hand and in his other hand carried a black-backed book, undoubtedly his Bible. His eyes were red.

"Mr. Johnson," he said, "I hope I have the opportunity to speak to you tonight."

"You better worry about what's going to happen to you," Joe told him. "If you try to escape, you'll get it."

"Escape? Why should I try to escape? I have a message for you. Of hope and love and infinite mercy."

Joe turned his back on the old man. Seeing the book, he had become conscious of the gray-backed book now fitted tightly into one of his back pockets. They had some vague things in common: the understanding that it is useful and good to be able to read, the experience of the long difficulty of learning. He felt irritated that they had anything in common. He was pricked with a brief sense of disloyalty to his friends, and countered the feeling with a determination to show no mercy to the ridiculous old man.

They hobbled their mounts and the gray buggy horse in places where a few mouthfuls of dusty grass were available. As they began to take food from their packs, dried beef and pemmican, Joe thought of the problem of feeding the preacher. He asked, "Have you got any food in that buggy?"

The Reverend Fairchild said, "Yes," and went eagerly into the wind to the vehicle at the edge of the firelight. He rummaged under the spring seat and brought out two gallon buckets, such as lard or syrup are bought in. "I have plenty of crackers and water for everyone. Here, Mr. Johnson." He set them on the ground, took the lid off one, and began pulling it off the other.

"We don't want your food." Joe told him.

"Please, I have plenty for everyone."

"We don't want it. What's in that water?"

"A pint of wine and the rest is water. Please, I have plenty."

Slow Tom asked, "What the hell's in that bucket? It's red. Let's see that." He lifted the bucket, sniffed, took a taste. "That tastes like *bosa-pah*."

"Have some crackers," the Reverend Fairchild said, but they were ignoring him.

Spike took a deep drink and said, "That is *bosa-pah*, but it's the weakest I ever saw."

The four of them sat down and passed the bucket among them until it was dry. It had only the faintest taste other than water, but it was good after the dusty ride. They began to feel as if the protective bank and their fire made this an acceptable camp. The wind came around at times and whipped the flames, blowing the coals so that they glowed intensely. A giant rushing sound came from the black sky and the unseen land around them, and they were aware of being inside the sandstorm.

The Reverend Fairchild kept presenting the other bucket and saying, "Have some crackers."

"Let's tie that old son of a bitch to the buggy," Spike said.

"Don't pay any attention to him," Joe said.

The Reverend Fairchild thrust the bucket forward, and Spike kicked it, strewing the hard white pieces of bread on the sand. The old man began picking them up and wiping them off.

"Please, Mr. Johnson," he said. "Let me talk to you seriously. You have an obligation to these boys who can't speak English and have only their heathen tongue. You have an obligation to yourself, to your own soul. Son, your soul is dangling over the fires of hell tonight. This minute. You are following Satan. Please! Let me tell you the gospel of salvation. We are all sinners."

Joe remembered suddenly that the soldier who had tried to make love to Lottie had been one who came to help the preacher in his church. He shouted, "Shut up! You have stuck your nose in the wrong thing, old man! Do you understand that?"

He began to plan their guard. They needed to get as much sleep as possible. They would remain awake one at a time, and each would have to guess when a quarter of the night was spent. He asked Bill Nappy, "Are you sleepy?"

Bill grinned. "No, I think I can make it now."

"Get your gun and watch this old buzzard. When your share of the night has passed or you get sleepy, wake up Slow Tom. All right?"

"All right. Could I use your gun?"

"Why? That Big Fifty is good. If he tries to escape you can blow his fool head off."

Spike said, "I think Bill has got something to tell you."

"What is it?"

It was something Spike was not happy about, but Bill was grinning.

"What is it?" he asked again.

"Hell, Joe, I couldn't get any shells."

"What?"

"I tried to. I just couldn't get any."

"I don't understand. You haven't got any shells for that Big Fifty?"

"No. I thought we might get some somewhere or some powder and lead or something."

Slow Tom said, "If we watch out, we might find some lying out on the prairie somewhere."

Joe said, "For the love of God, Bill! Why are you carrying the damned heavy thing along?"

"Well, I want a gun as much as anybody!"

It was unanswerable. He asked, "Has anyone else got any secrets? I'm the chief of this raid and I would like to know things. Slow Tom, have you got any shells in that twenty-two?"

"Yeah." He began to laugh and then all four of them laughed.

When Bill had settled before the preacher with the Winchester, the old man said, "Mr. Johnson, you don't need to guard me. I give you my word. My word is good."

"I don't want your word. Just don't try to run off."

The next morning the sky was still reddish brown and dust made a haze in the air. The wind still blew. They coughed up brown sputum. They left Slow Tom to guard the preacher while they rounded up the horse band, a task which took some two hours.

Joe thought about the trouble involved in keeping their prisoner. When they were finally strung out west, he rode alongside Slow Tom and said, "That old man is going to be too much trouble."

"Don't say that in front of Spike."

"No, I think he'd put an arrow through him and not bat an eye."

"Not that it's not true," Slow Tom said.

"What if we made him promise not to try to escape? Threaten him. Then we wouldn't need to guard him. Do you think he'd keep his word?"

"He's a queer man. A while ago he preached at me and read out of his Bible. I caught some of the words, but I just grunted at him. He knows he's seen me somewhere before."

"Do you think he'd keep his word?"

"I just about halfway think he might."

Joe rode over and stopped the buggy. "Reverend Fairchild, we won't guard you anymore. You must promise not to escape or we will kill you."

The old man's twisted smile was as much an enigma

as ever. His black suit looked dirty. "I don't want to escape, Mr. Johnson. I'm called of God to do his work. He sent me to you on purpose. I have a message of good news for you."

"Are you going to try to escape?"

"No. But you must hear me, Mr. Johnson. Please. You are headed for sorrow in this world and the next. You must give me an opportunity. One lost sheep is more precious than all of those safe in the fold."

"I don't know what you're talking about," he said. "If you try to escape, we'll catch you, and then it's going to be too bad."

As he rode away toward the horses, the preacher called, "I'll be praying for you!"

They had found no water the night before, and he could see no landmarks that he knew. The rolling plains looked desolate under the strange sky. Sometimes the dust swept along the ground so deep and thick that they could not see the horses' feet, and the earth looked eerie, unsubstantial. He felt certain that if they pressed due west they would find water in Elk Creek.

The band of horses kept trying to separate into small groups. Eight of the mules would stop together or wander to the side. It occurred to him that here was useless trouble. He talked to each of the other three about it and, agreeing, they let the mules go. The eight went of themselves; another one, which had been following the big paint and the Armstedt ponies, they had to drive away to join his own kind.

Sometimes the position of the sun could be seen, as if the clouds up through the red haze were patchy. It would show as a large glowing spot in the sky. Then at near midday it stood out as a clear round ball, as it sometimes looks at sunset.

He was thinking of stopping briefly for a drink of

water and a bit of food, wondering whether to offer the preacher water. Perhaps because they had released the mules on purpose, it occurred to him to ask himself: Why should we take the old man along? Make him promise to keep his mouth shut and turn him loose. He waved his three comrades in toward himself, and they left the horse band to drift. The buggy came up and stopped; the preacher sat in it looking forlorn. As the four of them untied their bundles, they discussed Joe's idea.

"Any white man will tell lies," Spike said.

"This one might not," Slow Tom said. "He's unusual."

Bill said, "We can't have any fun with him along. I don't like the way he looks at me."

"He'll go straight to the colonel," Spike said.

"Well, does he know where we are right now?" Joe asked. "I figure it would take him two days to get to Fort Sill and another two days to get back here. The cavalry boys are already a lot closer to us than that."

They agreed with him.

He walked over to the buggy carrying his horse-leg water bag. "Reverend Fairchild, we're going to turn you loose if you'll agree not to tell the soldiers anything."

"Son, it's not my place to confess your sins. It's—"

Anger flare in him. "Don't call me 'son'! I'll cut your guts out and spill them right here in this sand!" He did not know why he was suddenly furious. "Hand me that damned empty bucket," he ordered.

He splashed a quart of water out of his bag into the bucket. "Here! We're going to take these horses to Mexico. We don't have time to mess with you. Turn that worthless nag of yours around and go home."

The horse band was a quarter of a mile west, beginning to scatter. They retied their packs, mounted and raced on to bring them together again. The location of the sun in the sky was no longer apparent. The heavens looked a darker brown and the wind was veering to the north. The land ahead looked desolate.

When the horse band was moving in some order, he looked around to see whether the preacher was still in sight and was amazed. The hairy horse, the dusty black buggy, the man with the straggly flying beard was right behind them. Following.

What was the matter with the crazy fool? Surely he had made it clear enough. The thought came to him that old white men are more idiotic than old Indians even. If the old goat couldn't understand clear English, what could he understand?

He was torn between two ideas: a reluctance to repeat the order to turn around when he had already said it clearly, and a disgust at the man following. As he hesitated, he saw Spike turn back and ride toward the buggy in a lope. He turned his own horse.

Spike stopped the hairy gray with a jerk at the bridle, then dismounted and took out his brass tomahawk.

He yelled, "Wait, Spike!"

Spike began furiously hacking at the spokes in the left front wheel, then the rear wheel, yelling curses and threats. The Reverend Fairchild was talking at the same time. "Please, young man! Let me talk to you! Don't give way to your passions! Please, young man!" Neither of them was trying to understand the strange language of the other.

Chips and splinters flew. The spokes gave way and the buggy slanted deeply, nearly tumbling over. One free rim rolled across the prairie. The Reverend Fairchild clutched at his seat. The shafts cocked up on the horse as if to pull his harness off, and the beast began to prance clumsily, to rear up, to turn his head, trying to see past his blinders at what was behind him. Spike ran to the other side to work as fast and deliberately on the right-hand wheels. The skinny, nearly naked young man appeared to take great satisfaction in being angry and slashing at the thin wooden spokes and yelling.

The buggy dropped with a splintering jolt to settle level on the earth. The white-eyed horse stumbled and halfway sat down.

Spike was satisfied.

Joe had not dismounted. He said to the old man, "Can you understand now? Get on that ugly gray horse and go home! Turn him around and go home! Can you understand plain English?"

"Mr. Johnson, please let me talk to you. Give me a chance. Please listen seriously to what I have to say. You are not a vicious man. All I ask—"

"We are going to scalp you!" Joe told him. "Your talk doesn't mean anything!"

"You are lost, Mr. Johnson! Lost! Can't you see? Can't you understand? Please listen! You are lost!"

"We are going to stake you down over an anthill!"

The old man persisted in his preaching, sitting there in the ruins of his buggy. It was useless to try to say anything to him; at least it was impossible for him to repair his buggy. Joe wheeled his horse and rode with Spike back to their task.

A chill had come into the north wind. The brown sky was spotty. He could not guess how far west they had come because of the difficulty of driving the horses, but it seemed important to reach water before another black night. Sparse, small drops of rain began to fall, slanting in the wind. He thought that up above the dusty haze the sky must be rough with clouds. When a drop struck his forehead he felt that it was icy cold. He rubbed his hand on his forehead. Gritty. It was raining mud.

Spike had hunkered down over his horse. He alternated between riding wildly and yelling for a minute, then drawing down to ride quietly. Obviously he was cold. Joe had envied him his dress, or lack of it, but it was plain now that he had been right to tell them all to bring jackets or coats.

The brown haze had partly cleared. He could see what might be a yellow line of foliage ahead. Elk Creek. The horses could not smell it because of the north wind and were still hard to drive.

On impulse he looked around. He had almost known it before he saw. The Reverend Fairchild was coming on his buggy horse.

He was not as angry as he had been before. But determined. There must be an end to this. He turned his horse. Spike was going back too, but this time Joe would beat him to the old man.

The Reverend Fairchild reined up. He had taken all the harness off the hairy horse except for the work bridle and had shortened the lines. The two buckets, tied together with a strap, hung across the horse's withers.

"Get off the horse," Joe said.

"Mr. Johnson, please hear me."

"Get off, or I'll kill you."

The man's face, thin beard, straw hat, black coat were streaked with the muddy rain. His gaze was level but fearful. His long-lipped crooked mouth seemed to smile and tremble at once. "Mr. Johnson, are you afraid to listen to me?"

"You're the one who's afraid."

"Yes, I am. I believe you are going to kill me now. Or let your poor, cold friend do it."

"That's right. If you don't do what I say. Get down off the horse."

"I can't do it."

"Why not?"

"Because you won't listen to me."

Joe looked at Spike, who was crouched low on his horse, shivering, watching. He thought of the long cold walk that the preacher had ahead of him. He said, "I'll listen a minute after you get down. Take those buckets down too. I'll listen a minute and try to see your meaning."

The man, holding his Bible, struggled at dismounting, nearly falling, then took the two buckets down. He stood looking up as he spoke.

"You see, what you are doing is wrong. It's senseless. It's useless. But I don't really need to tell you. You know it yourself. If a man stops and looks at himself, he knows when he's sinning. But it's not my part to condemn you. God is more than justice, Mr. Johnson. Regardless of what you have done, no matter how black your sins, he wants to show you mercy. He is not willing for one poor soul to be lost. He knows when one sparrow falls. My message is not condemnation, but joy and forgiveness. Do you understand?"

"No, sir." He reached over and unbuckled the chin strap and pulled off the gray horse's bridle. "Reverend Fairchild, thank you for the message. But I think what I'm doing is not senseless and useless. Now, go home."

To Spike, he said, "We got us one more horse. Let's go."

As they were riding away, hazing the gray horse ahead of them, the old man shouted, "Jesus loves you, boys! Remember, Jesus loves you!"

When they had gone two hundred yards, he could still hear the voice, fainter: "Remember, boys, Jesus . . ." But when they had reached the horse band, he looked back and saw that the preacher had turned around and was walking east, carrying his Bible and his small supply of crackers and water in the buckets. They were free of him.

Between them they had brought three woolen blankets. Joe stopped Slow Tom and took one of the two blankets in his pack. Spike had not complained of the cold, but he took it gladly and gathered it around his shoulders.

A short time later they came to Elk Creek, a small stream winding down the plain with willows in it and scattered larger timber. A trickle of water ran in its sandy bed and pools lay in pockets where the stream turned. The horses splashed into it eagerly and drank. The four riders filled their water bags.

The rain had been light, but it had helped clear the air. They turned their backs to the wind and drove south along the course of the creek. At dark they camped and again built a fire in the lee of a bank, but this night turned out colder and cleaner. The moon came out and the stars, with the small, distant appearance of winter about them. The wind whistled through the half-bare tree branches above them.

Huddled in the three blankets near the fire, they laughed about the preacher and joked about the cavalry. When they had quieted, Joe felt again the elation he had felt the first night when they charged south with the horse band, which now seemed a month in the past. What a wonderful thing to be able to ride a good horse all day, the next day catch a fresh one and go on! An unlimited supply of first-class horses! The sand-storm and the cold—they had added to the challenge, made it more worth doing.

Slow Tom began snoring. Bill, mumbling in his sleep. He could feel one of Spike's sharp elbows in his back. A surge of appreciation for his comrades came through him and he thought of Mad Wolf's words: They were gods of the earth! He felt strangely jubilant and sad at the same time. The jubilation had no clear reason though it burned in his blood. It had something to do with the People—how they had dared to get horses and in the getting had set free their own spirit, as if they were Comanches only when they got the horses. Then they had pride and bravery and confidence. And now it seemed as if the four of them were living over this glorious song about the People.

As for the sadness, he understood it more clearly. Dust and cold had never stopped the white soldiers twenty years ago and would not stop them now. If he and his friends could just have one week more, or even just a day or two more.

I wonder if they know, he thought, that we can't have the horses. That when you have made a successful raid, you must take your horses and do as Iron Lance had said: Head for home country. And that there is no home country anymore. Do they understand? He thought Slow Tom did. Probably, in a way, the others did too.

15

THE FIGHT

THEY HAD GATHERED the horses early and pushed south. The sunshine felt good, for the plains land was in the grip of the first norther of winter. He sent Spike out to the side of their course to climb a lone point of rock and scout the terrain.

Spike came back toward him in a dead run, whipping his horse. The skinny young man's gray blanket, tied at his neck, flared out behind him.

"Soldiers!" he said. "Away back!"

"How far? Are they coming this way?"

"Going west. I could barely see them go over a rise."

"How many, Spike?"

"Maybe twelve. They're away back. About where we were yesterday at noon."

"See anything ahead?"

"No. I could see Tipi Mountain."

"Let's cut away from the creek and head that way."

The horses were frisky in the chill wind. The four men hazed them away from the small stream and into a lope across the prairie toward the southwest. He could not guess whether the cavalry had met the Reverend Fairchild, but he wanted to make a feint as if going through Texas toward Mexico.

Ahead of them rose Tipi Mountain and Soldier's Peak,

granite mountains along the North Fork of the Red. They did not stop at noon, but drove fast toward the landmarks ahead.

They were becoming acquainted with the horses, learning which were leaders and which followers, which stubborn and which docile, which lazy and which the kind that like to cavort and listen to the pounding of their own iron-shod feet.

Now in the cold wind they seemed to have inexhaustible energy. They were a charging wild force, like a thunderstorm, and the keen satisfaction of it was that they could be guided and controlled, but only with determination that matched their own. Joe found himself yelling, not so much to turn them as in response to their spirit. In the work of hard riding he forgot the chill. The dust of their hoofs blew low on the ground and they outran it, going south.

He felt that this band, in this hour, was somehow perfect. The horses were big and rangy, long-boned. Some were coarse. Others had clean lines and straight faces with veins showing beneath fine skin. But no delicate muzzles, no arched necks, no prancing gaits. These were large snorting beasts, feeling their freedom, suitable to the distances that stretched away all around them.

He noticed two in particular which were always trying to break out of the band, and which the others were willing to follow. One was a large horse who liked to toss his head, and he had one white-stocking front foot. The other, smaller, was a blood bay with strong black points, no white, agile and quick. He determined to ride one of them the next time they changed mounts.

They passed the rock point called Tipi Mountain and went on by rugged piles of granite until they could see the sweeping curves of the North Fork, a shallow stream of sand a stone's throw wide with a trickle of water in the middle. Here the cattlemen from the south had crossed their longhorn steers into the reservation in years past. The cattle trail had little use now, but it looked like a shallow stream bed leading over the low rise north. They pushed the horse band up to a water hole called Soldier Spring in the lee of a mountain.

He sent Bill Nappy to climb the rocks and take a look while the others of them built a fire and caught new mounts to stake out and have ready. Spike and Slow Tom had also been estimating the horses. They roped the big one he had thought of as Whitefoot and the quick one he had thought of as Red and two others and tied them by the spring.

Bill Nappy reported that he could see nothing. They found some warmth and comfort by the fire while they ate. It was late afternoon.

"This place is a good fort," Spike said.

"Too much fort," Slow Tom said. "Now, if you had five hundred warriors to put around on those rocks . . ."

Bill Nappy asked, "What do you say, Joe?"

"The soldiers know this place," he said. "They used to camp here."

"You think we've lost them?"

"No."

"We going to cross the river?"

"No . . . I think we'll go back north. This might be far enough south to fool them." He was thinking that they undoubtedly had Indian Police for trackers and that the soldiers themselves were smart trackers, but did not say it.

A short time before sunset he climbed a rocky point high enough to see to the north and east and south. It was cold in the wind. Below him the stolen horses grazed around the meadow formed below the spring. The two Armstedt ponies, the clumsy borrowed paint with the split ears, and the hairy gray buggy horse had wandered nearly a mile away toward the river. The running was hard on them, and they were deliberately separating themselves from the cavalry horses. He decided to leave them here.

The granite hills cast long shadows in the late sunlight. Far to the north and east the prairies looked yellow tan. He thought that the place where he stood would be a good point for a lookout, but cruelly cold without a fire through the night.

To the east a bow of the North Fork with its trees lay below him. Beyond, almost to the dim horizon, he thought he could detect the line of Elk Creek, more than five miles away. A tiny flash caught his eye.

He squinted and held his hand beside his face to shield it from the wind. He moved his eyes slowly back and forth across the distant sunlit plain. Another flash. Then for a moment he saw them, small, colorless, twelve riders, coming two by two. It seemed that he could almost read a thought in their minds: camp at Soldier Spring tonight, then scout for sign in the morning. It would be dark when they got here.

But he didn't want to underrate them. They might sleep tonight and they might not. They might have field glasses on him at this instant, but it was doubtful; they had the sun in their eyes. They might guess wrong and go south, or they might track by the moon and pursue relentlessly.

He bounded down over the rock outcrops which made up the hillside, and toward the fire, shouting at them, "Saddle up!"

They were throwing together their bundles as they questioned him. Slow Tom asked, "What did you see?"

"Spike's dozen soldiers. Headed this way."

"Where we going?" Spike asked.

"Straight north. Try to fool them."

Bill asked, "How far away?"

"An hour or more."

Nothing could be done about the fire. In a matter of minutes they mounted and swung around the grazing cavalry horses. The left the Armstedt ponies, the paint and the shaggy gray. As darkness began to close down upon the land, they drove north up the old cattle trail.

Facing the wind was hard. Their eyes watered, and these false tears blew back freezing cold onto their temples. At least the horses did not try to run away into it. They bowed their necks and bunched up, walking or trotting. Joe rode the blood bay and found him a quick and tireless mount, responsive to a firm rein.

What a fine night it would be, he was thinking, to sleep in a warm place! He found himself laughing, his body shaking with mirth and cold at the same time. We can sleep when we get old, Spike had said. How true! We can get warm when we get old.

He wished that there were more than twelve of them back there. But that was three to one. Good odds. He felt a measure of awe at his own confidence. Where was he going? Where was he leading his three magnificent comrades? He didn't know. But it was good. Boys sleep at night. Old men sleep at night. Comanches ride. Those twelve away back in the darkness, let them be as competent and sharp and lucky as they could, let them follow their orders and do their will—they would know, they already knew, that they were dealing with the same men who stole the horses from the gods.

At noon the next day they were up in Cheyenne-Arapaho country. Bill Nappy was asleep in his saddle. The cold wind still blew, but it was more bearable with the sun over them. The horses stumbled along, worn out. Joe had them dismount and walk a few minutes. But the walking wouldn't do it. Bill was asleep on his feet and the others little better.

They had turned out west of the cattle trail. He could see a great distance across the high rolling plains. Dusty clumps of sage dotted the land. He could see no trees, only a lone plum thicket in the distance. They would be a long time reaching any good camping place. He yelled at them, "Hold up! Four hours sleep!"

They loosened the saddle girths, took off the bridles and picketed the horses. The free horse band straggled ahead and stopped.

He took first watch. The others dropped on the ground and slept. He hunkered down with his back to the wind, gazing out toward the horizon. It was lonely. The horses slept, each with his rump cocked, resting one leg at a time. His pemmican had all been eaten and he judged that he should not search into the other men's packs. It seemed for a while that everything on the prairie was dead except the wind and himself. He considered the depth of his friends' sleep a moment, then eased his book from his back pocket and began to read, word by word, the story about the man and his son and their donkey. He read it carefully twice, sometimes looking up to check the empty plain behind them; then he replaced the book and woke Slow Tom. By the time his cheek had touched the blue canvas sleeve of his jacket, he was asleep.

As he awoke, he was conscious of the urgency in Bill Nappy's voice before he understood the words. "Joe! They're coming! Spike! Get up! Wake up! Joe! Slow Tom!"

It was midafternoon. He did not pause to study the low plume of dust to the southeast, but scrambled with the others after the saddled horses. The three of them who had been sleeping passed quickly from their state of confusion to one of excitement and awareness. When they had mounted and were whipping their horses ahead toward the drifting band, he turned in the saddle to look carefully. Their pursuers were clearly visible in cavalry blue, six pairs, coming in a deliberate lope. Maybe a mile and a half back.

They whooped and screamed at the horse band, slashing at the rumps of 'the laggard ones with rope ends. The band quickened into a trot and by degrees the excitement of the yelling men was transmitted to it until its lethargy was dispelled, and it charged ahead. The freedom of the individuals in it manifested itself; they ran wildly on a broad front.

If they could keep it up, they would not be caught. But they couldn't. Their own dust hid the land behind them.

They topped a rise and Joe saw out to their left a point like the eroded remnants of a mountain. The point was capped by broken boulders and a motte of head-high oaks. On the slopes around it, sage and small yucca grew thinly, and most of the ground, orange-tan and full of chalk-white gravel, was bare.

He got the other riders' attention and pointed. They crowded the horse band toward it.

Past the base of the point he could see more low oaks and he headed for them. The rocky point had no room to conceal horses. They slowed the band and eased them into the area of scrub trees. In the bottom of an eroded wash they staked the horses they had been riding, then seized their weapons and packs and water bags and ran back up the slopes toward the height. As he had thought, they could see a great distance from the top. Some rocks and sage marked the slopes, but there was no concealed way up to it.

Bill Nappy said, blowing from the climb, "We could hold off an army here."

Spike said, "Let them come."

At the peak a huge cap-rock boulder lay broken, guarding them waist high on three sides, and on the other side the trees clung to the edge of the point. They examined their fortress retreat with laughter and joking. It was perfect, except for a pile of dusty blue-green prickly pears spilling over the edge of opposite the trees.

Bill pointed to the cacti and said to Slow Tom, "That's your bed for tonight."

Slow Tom responded, "This is where we use our guns. If they storm the hill, maybe you can use yours for a club."

Two hours of sunlight remained as the soldiers galloped over the distant rise in their precise formation. They turned toward the point. Just out of long rifle range, they drew up and one of the tiny figures gave the other orders. They split and separated, passing on either side of the high place toward the scrub-oak forest on the other side.

In a short time Joe could see the free horse band being driven away and he had no doubt that their four saddled horses were being cautiously approached.

"The devils!" Spike said in disgust. "Why don't they come fight?"

As if in answer the voice of a Comanche policeman came from far down among the trees. "Surrender!"

Spike yelled at the top of his voice, "Go screw yourself!"

"Surrender!"

"You're not a Comanche!" Bill yelled. "You're a stinking Tonkawa woman!"

A rifle cracked and a slug ripped through the oak foliage near them.

In a few minutes they could see the soldiers afoot spreading out around their height, ducking and running from sage clump to boulder. Joe saw two fall on their bellies behind a flat rock that barely hid them. He took careful aim and squeezed off a shot. Sand spat from the stone where his bullet hit. They would think twice before coming closer.

Crouching, he went over and looked down the opposite slope. A soldier was snaking along flat in a washed-out depression. The man disappeared. He thought he could see a rifle barrel. He fired carefully at it and raised a splash of dirt. Maybe he had put dirt in a soldier's eyes.

Spike leaped into view a moment with his strung bow and quiver in his upthrust hand, shouting, "Come on and fight, you cowards!" The range was obviously long for a bow.

Bill Nappy sprang up with the Big Fifty held high and yelled, "Old women! Go home!"

Slow Tom had fired twice, calmly and deliberately. The smell of hot gunpowder hung about them in spite of the wind.

Spike, his blanket cast aside, evidently could bear his inactivity no longer. He drew an arrow back until its metal head came against his bow, aimed high and sent it arching down the slope with a meaningless shout.

Out below them all around little puffs of smoke flared out and wafted away on the wind. Sometimes a bullet whacked against one of the boulders and skipped away droning like a bee.

Bill Nappy laughed in a frenzy as he moved in the

fortress, mixing the laughter with screams toward the soldiers. "You dog eaters!" He exposed himself to the view of the enemy, flaunting the empty Big Fifty and yelled, "Fish eaters! Old women! Grandmothers! Old grandmothers!"

It was not so foolish as it might seem, Joe thought, if they would keep moving. They were giving an impression of a strongly defended fort without wasting shells. Also, he was caught by the spirit of it. He sprang to his feet, thrust the Winchester high in his right hand, filling his lungs, ready with a taunting shout.

He did not hear the shot. He was struck in the chest as if by a hard-thrown rock, and jerked back. His legs crumbled.

It was difficult to believe. His impulse was to rise, as if he had merely stumbled. He could not.

While waiting a second for his strength to come back, he moved his right hand to find the unseen rifle that must have fallen beside him. The movement made a raw pain amidst the numbness. Beneath him, the skin of his right shoulder blade must be torn. He raised his shaking left hand to the front of his jacket and knew that it had found the center of the numb spot. The bullet had struck him almost in the center of the chest. It had gone through.

His mind was clear. Not much pain. He breathed slowly, for, though it didn't hurt much, he could feel a bubbling in his chest. He could not lift either arm now. He discovered that he was bound by complete weakness.

They were shouting, "Joe! Joe!" a long distance above him. He could see their faces up there clearly, filled with consternation.

While their eyes were on him he thought in a calm, lonely way, So it has come to me; this was my day. Of all the days, this one was the single one that waited for me and ended my life. How curiously short life is! And confused! It's long when you remember back, but ridiculously short to get things straightened out. It's funny that it would be no more than this.

I must tell them, he thought, to tell my mother that I loved her. Not about the raid. She wouldn't like that. But she ought to know that I thought about her, and I could never really feel as harsh toward her as I have acted the past month.

And Lottie. They must promise to tell Lottie that he had been the chief of the raid.

When he was gone they would find the book in his pocket. Don't be too hard on me, my good comrades, he thought, about the book. Believe what Spike will say; maybe it was my medicine bundle.

Their eyes were filled with dread as they moved around above him. He heard Slow Tom say something about "stop the bleeding," and then give an order: "Build a fire! Stop sniveling! Build a damned fire!"

They were trying to take off his jacket and vest. He felt deathly sick and wanted to tell them to let him lie still, but another idea had fought to the center of his mind. He saw Slow Tom's face close and he whispered, using little breath, "Tell my mother all about Powell."

"Tell her what? About what?"

"Powell."

"What about him?"

"All."

"All right, buddy."

A gun was firing nearby, his own .44 rifle. He heard Slow Tom's loud, authoritative voice. "Stop wasting shells! Bill! Spike, put my gun down and help me!"

The sky was streaked faintly with high clouds and the light of sunset was on them. Mixed with the acrid scent of powder he could smell a distinctive odor: the burning of the flinty thorns of prickly pears.

In a moment, through the haze of his sickness, he knew that they were chewing up prickly pear leaves and stuffing them in the hole in his back. He was unconscious for a time. When he found himself, the sky was before his face, the sunset still on the clouds.

Then flitted along the passages of his mind as clumsy and as adroit as a yellow butterfly the thought: I would like to live.

He discovered that he had a small spot of breath, a tiny margin, where he could draw in air and send it out without the bubbling, without disturbing the great numbness on his right side. Shallow. Careful. Precious. He tested the limits of it cautiously and disciplined himself. For a long time he was aware only of his own breathing, for it seemed that in the manner of this act lay his chance for life.

It was dark. He lay on a blanket between two poles, and was being carried with difficulty downhill, across rough ground. They grunted and whispered urgently. Slow Tom's voice was calm. "Hold him level. Be quiet. Easy. Easy." He dozed, now and then aware of the movement and their effort. Once this comparison came to him: Mad Wolf picked up young Tabananica and carried him out of danger, and now my friends are carrying me out.

Later, Slow Tom was saying, "Joe, can you hear me? Joe? Joe?"

The faint light of dawn was on the prairie. He carefully saved his small quantity of breath to say, softly, "Yeah."

"Hang on, buddy! It's going to be all right."

The numbness was receding and pain coming in its

place. He felt the swaying of his stretcher, and saw first one then another of his companions the other side of his feet, hands on the poles, walking. He noted that it was cool and tried to think of other things to forget the pain.

Later they were sprinkling water on his face. "Joe?" Slow Tom said. "Here, take a little drink." He eased the water carefully down his throat. Bill offered a dribble of honey from his old tin canteen. They put water in the canteen, shook it and poured it slowly in his mouth. He drank as much as the interference with his breathing would allow, then closed his mouth. They wiped his face off with their hands.

They grinned at him. Slow Tom said, "I don't believe you can kill a man like Joe with a bullet."

Bill said, "Not unless you hit him straight in the head."

"Hell, it would bounce off his head."

They couldn't know how weak he felt. He thought he could be killed right now with a large blade of grass. He managed a smile and asked, "Where's Spike?"

"He's coming back now," Slow Tom said.

In a matter of minutes Spike was with them, breathless. He wore only his breechclout and had been running.

"They've gone," he said.

Slow Tom asked, "All twelve?"

"Yeah. I saw them up on the point. Then I saw them with our horses. They went back east."

After that they carried him through light and darkness for a time that seemed interminable, and he fought with pain all the way.

One morning he woke up and the pain was bearable. The little space in which he could breathe was larger. He lay on his back on the ground. Bill Nappy was snoring a few feet away.

Down in his vision a streak of green grass grew in a swale, as if along the tailings of a spring. Four horses grazed: the Armstedt ponies, the paint with the split ears and the gray buggy horse. Beyond he could see the sand of the North Fork. They were back at Soldier Spring. He felt of his chest; the bullet hole was bound over with prickly pear leaf. He could move his right arm, but it sent stabs of pain through his shoulder blade.

Six days after he was shot he sat up. The world swayed. He felt weak as a baby colt when it first rises on its thin legs. They had kept him wrapped in the blankets and now decided to try to dress him in his vest and jacket. Those two garments were as stiff as rawhide from the dried blood in them. Bill Nappy took them to the spring and washed them.

Joe could talk without much difficulty. He asked Slow Tom, "How in the world did you carry me back down here?"

Slow Tom laughed. "It wasn't real easy."

"Easy!" Spike said. "Man, you're as heavy as a big rock!"

"Every so often we would think you were dead," Slow Tom said, "but about that time you would groan."

"Say!" Spike said. "You know now's the time to insult old Joe or pick on him; he can't do a thing."

Joe picked up a pebble and flipped it at the nearly naked young man and said, "By the way, where's my Winchester?"

"Bill has adopted your Winchester. You may have to fight him for it."

In the past few days they had eaten half a dozen rabbits and most of one white-tailed deer. That evening sitting by the fire they finished the scraps of venison and gnawed the bones.

Bill Nappy was chewing on the end of a rib and spitting out bits of bone. He said, "You know what we need to eat?"

Not knowing whether he was serious, none of them answered.

"Buffalo meat," he said. "That's what. Some good buffalo meat would put old Joe back on his feet in two days."

It was an interesting thought. They discussed the richness and strength of the meat in question, what others had said about it, what they themselves remembered of it.

The following morning Slow Tom and Bill took the two guns to hunt upstream along the North Fork, where its broad curves wound below the granite hills. It was warm enough for comfort after the sun got up in the sky. Joe sat up and watched Spike scraping on the deerskin.

It was nearly midday when they heard the rifle shot, followed by the lighter crack of the .22, both echoing among the rocks above them.

"Another rabbit," Joe said.

Spike said, "Bill missed and Slow Tom had to get it with the twenty-two."

They were both surprised by a sudden resumption of the firing of both guns in a flurry, six or seven shots in all. Then finally a single shot from the .44.

"What could that be?" Joe asked.

"Sure wasting shells," Spike said. He was standing with his bow in one hand and his quiver in the other, hesitant.

"You better go see," Joe told him.

An hour later the three of them returned to camp.

Joe did not know what it was at first; it looked like a shaggy black animal with six legs. They carried on their shoulders a black bear larger than a man. When they tumbled it down onto the ground at his feet, the beast was still bleeding from several bullet holes, a ponderous, limp creature with a strong musty smell.

They were elated and filled with good humor. Bill and Slow Tom took turns telling their bear-hunting strategy, what the bear did and what they did; but they did not allow their high spirits to divert them from the main task at hand, which was to get some meat on the fire. That afternoon and night they gorged themselves on the dark, pungent, greasy meat.

In a week Joe could sit on a horse. They headed east early one morning when the frost was still on the dry grass.

Bill Nappy said, "I didn't think of it. But you know we started out with three horses and now we've got four."

"Forget it. That gray thing isn't a horse," Slow Tom said.

Well after dark they came into the camp on Blue Beaver, where Spike and Bill stopped. Sometime after midnight Slow Tom and Joe came into the area of East Cache below the fort. The hairy gray buggy horse they tied to the hitching rail in front of the Reverend Fairchild's white-painted church. Then the two of them rode the ponies down to the Armstedt place.

16

THE FALSE GHOST DANCE

FOR MORE than a week Joe and Slow Tom had seen no one except the Armstedt family. It was midmorning of a sunny, moderately cool day when the two of them walked up toward the large gathering of people in the open area north of the Red Store. Joe thought that the feast and field day, planned by the agent, was a kind of peace offering to the Indians and was also designed to demonstrate that no trouble existed on the reservation.

A large number of people were scattered over the flat land. Some had come the night before and camped out, sleeping in covered wagons or on the ground. Around the great clearing were parked buggies and wagons of every description as well as pack mules and an occasional horse standing patiently between travois poles.

Some of the Indians had a bundled, rounded appearance as they strolled about, their blankets wrapped tightly to their necks, but many of the women and girls, in bright blues and yellows and reds, disdained the cool air to show off their dresses. People gathered in knots to visit. Children scrambled after one another, laughing and crying out, or stood wide-eyed and bashful, looking at all the strangers. Far across the clearing near some trees smoke rose where the soldiers were cooking the beef in open pits and serving coffee to a few spectators. The faint smell of pecan wood burning drifted in the air.

Joe saw a family from the Iron Lance camp and wondered briefly whether he would see his mother. Or Mr. Powell. Or both of them. But Mr. Powell had been having harsh words with the army people and was not likely to attend.

Out past the Red Store the dance had started. Some twenty of the more forward and eager men and women had formed a circle around a newly planted cedar tree and were shuffling sideways as they sang a song. A short, agreeable Comanche in buckskin directed them and urged them on. The song, not loud, but pervasive, could be heard over the hum of other voices.

He-ee-yo!
He-yo Hah-nah Hah-ee-yo!
He-yo Hah-nah Hah-ee-yo!
The Sun's beams are running out—*He-ee-yo!*
The Sun's beams are running out—*He-ee-yo!*
The Sun's yellow rays are streaming out—*Awhi-ni-yo!*
The Sun's yellow rays are streaming out—*Awhi-ni-yo!*

As yet, more people watched the dance than took part in it, but the spectators were nodding their heads to the song. A short distance from the circle a buggy and an army ambulance were parked, in them officers and their wives and white visitors viewing the ceremony. Beside the ambulance a photographer, hunched under a black cloth, was trying to make a picture of the dance.

He and Slow Tom stood at the rear of the crowd.

Slow Tom laughed and asked, "You think the whites know it's a big fake?"

"I don't know," he said. "Surely some of them do."

One of the Longwater girls came up and persuaded Slow Tom to join the dance with her. It was not a dance for couples, but he went, grinning, oblivious or uncaring that he was the only participant wearing a felt hat.

Joe retreated a few steps and sat down on a wagon tongue. He could hardly feel his wound. He mulled over Slow Tom's question. How could the whites not know that the Ghost Dance was a mockery? That if the dancers meant it, it would be sacrilege to do it here for show?

But the dancers, who were they making fun of? The whites who claimed that a Messiah had come to them long ago and they killed him? The Arapaho and Cheyenne and Kiowa, who, believed the Messiah was coming again, and from whom the Comanches had audaciously stolen bits of the ceremony and song? Themselves, for their lack of faith? The white observers, who wanted two things, a safe, passionless dance, but a real one, so that they could say they saw the dreaded Ghost Dance? He thought of Mad Wolf's words: For what reason shall we dance?

But he was thinking too much. Probably a lot of them just enjoyed holding hands and singing and moving together. Certainly some of them felt generous and obliging—if the agent and the soldiers would give a feast and field day with horse races, foot races and a plowing contest and prizes, they would give a demonstration of the Ghost Dance.

He could not sit alone long without thinking of his mother, and the thought brought an aching in his chest older than his bullet wound. Sooner or later he must go to her and tell her everything he knew. He felt more confidence now than he had before in his ability to be near her without being dominated by her, but he saw no solution to the problem of the white woman who lived with Mr. Powell. If he could find no other answer, he would do whatever drastic thing he must to get it settled—force the three of them to confront each other and accept the truth and decide upon their loyalties.

He had heard that Mr. Powell now lived in the house which had once been the home of the carpentry teacher, east of the old agency headquarters. Evidently the man still had not received a permit or license to operate a store, but spent his time going around and talking against the division of the reservation. It was known that he often went over to West Cache to talk to Chief Quanah.

Joe had begun to feel detached from the scene that stretched out before him, with the color and bustle of several hundred people. Then with a thrill he heard his name called and saw Lottie coming toward him, Annie skipping before her.

"We're mad at you, Joe Cowbone," Annie said, "because you don't come to see us."

Lottie said, blushing, "Annie, I believe you're the naughtiest little snip that ever lived." She had on her bright-red dress and had yellow ribbons on her braids.

He rose laughing and asked her, "Are you mad at me?"

She laughed and seemed flustered. "If I am, I can tell you for myself."

"Well, I am," Annie said. "So I told him. Joe, I'm going to run in a race and I might win a shiny hunting knife. Are you going to bet on me?"

"Sure I am. You're half jackrabbit."

Lottie had two empty tin cups, which she thrust toward her little sister. "Go on and get your father some coffee."

"I want to talk to Joe Cowbone."

"Listen, young lady, you may not get to run any race if you're not nice. Now, don't spill them. Put in plenty of sugar."

The younger one took the cups and ran away. Lottie stood near him and in a moment she said, "I thought you would come to see us. I thought everything was all right."

"I've had a lot of things to do."

"But I thought you meant to. It's been so long." She briefly searched his face, a slight frown on her brow. "Is something wrong with you, Joe? You don't look the same."

"Not much."

"What is it?"

He grinned at her. "Don't worry about it."

"All right." She seemed as if determined to be friendly and obey his suggestion. "If you'll join the dance, I will."

"It's not supposed to be for couples. It's a religious dance."

"Reverend Fairchild says it comes from Satan instead of from good religion."

"Are you still listening to him?"

"No, I didn't mean to say that. I just said it to have something to say." She took his arm lightly. "Come on. It's real simple. Maybe it's fun."

"No, I can't."

"Why not?"

"I just can't."

"I guess you want me to go away and stop bothering you."

He laughed. "No. Did I tell you? You look real pretty today." He had realized that he had been giving the wrong impression. She was as appealing to him as she had ever been, or more so.

"Joe, sure enough! Have you been sick or something? You look changed."

"I feel pretty good, thank you."

"You look older."

"I guess I get older every day." It sounded flippant to him as he said it and, seeing that she fell quiet for a moment, he searched for more agreeable things to say to her.

She said, making conversation, "I guess you've heard all the stories about the big horse raid?"

"I heard some of it. What did you hear? Who did it?"

"Oh, goodness! They say it was the Pawnees. Then they say it was Texans dressed up like Indians. Some say it wasn't Texans, but Kiowas and they took the horses to Texas and sold them; or others say they took them to Mexico and sold them. Old Chief Tabananica told my father that he wished he had done it himself."

"Who do you think did it?"

"I don't know. A Chickasaw freighter was telling some people in Trader's Store, and he swore he knew what really happened. He said the men who stole the horses went up to a high rocky mountain fortress. The soldiers killed all of them, but when they climbed up to the fortress, the bodies vanished into thin air."

"Do you believe that?" he asked.

"I'm not sure," she said.

"Why do people say it was Pawnees or Kiowas when the greatest horse thieves that ever lived are around here on this reservation?"

Her eyes brightened and she said, "Let's start a rumor it was Comanches."

He was thinking that he would surely tell her someday. She had become silent and he saw that she was studying his face. He thought she would again say something about his having changed, but when she finally spoke, she said, "At Reverend Fairchild's church, if a white soldier comes ... well, if my father isn't there, I leave and go home."

"Why? Do they speak to you?"

"No. I want to ... I do it because I thought you wanted me to."

"Do you," he said, grinning, "think very often about me and what I might want?" It occurred to him that it seemed years since the last time he had been with her.

"Yes." She looked at his face and said, "Please don't tease me, Joe. I feel silly standing here. ... And you won't dance."

He said, "I'd much rather talk to you than do that silly dance."

"Is everything all right? About us?"

"Yes," he said. "I think so."

"Are you going to tell me why you won't dance and why you look different?"

"Not right now. One thing, that dance is partly just a show for white people."

"But they're having fun too. Don't you think? Look, there's Spike Chanakut and that Nappy boy from Blue Beaver. It's a big circle now."

They watched the dancers moving to their own songs without a drum. Sometimes the leader sang a meaningless song borrowed from the Arapaho or Cheyenne, and when they had heard it through twice the dancers would take it up and sing it as if the words were clear Comanche. People joined the circle or left it at will. The spectators laughed or talked in low voices, but when one joined the circle he invariably became drawn into serious concentration.

Lottie said she had better go hunt up her little sister. She asked, "Will you eat with us? We have plates. Our wagon is right down there."

He told her that he would. As he watched her walk away he wondered at his own changing attitude toward her. For a long time they had been as free and easy as children with one another. Then slowly the trouble had come between them, having something to do with marriage. He had grown irritated and frustrated, even in some way fearful of her influence. But now, for no reason that he could name, they seemed to be moving back toward that free and easy time. But not exactly. How wise she was to be so simple! He had not understood it until she said it: he was older. Not because he was weak; in fact he was stronger. Maybe a man's heart becomes stronger when a bullet passes close by it.

He sat back down on the wagon tongue. His eyes were drawn to the figure of a man kneeling on the dusty turf out a distance from the dance circle. A white man in a black suit. Both his knees were on the ground, one hand to his forehead, the other out in front as if asking help or begging. Praying. He seemed familiar, but it was only when he lowered his hand and his long, straggly beard came in view that Joe recognized him.

The Reverend Fairchild rose and came in his direction. He could not believe that the man had seen him, yet he was coming straight to him. If he got up from the wagon tongue, he would only call attention to himself. The man came on, and it was too late to avoid him at all except by running away like a child, which he determined not to do.

"Mr. Johnson," the man said, seemingly not surprised to see him, "I must have a word with you."

Joe looked at him a moment. The man looked exactly as he had away in the sagebrush country except that his clothes were cleaner. He rose and said, "My name is Joe Cowbone."

"Yes, I wondered if you had given me the wrong name. You see, it really doesn't matter so much. We have only one name in God's book. He knows our right name. He enters our deeds against our right name and never makes an error. And, Mr. Cowbone, a lie in words is not so bad as a lie in deeds."

"What are you going to do?" he asked.

"You must go to the officers and tell them what you've done. It's the only way you can find peace. Every living human being has a soul, Mr. Cowbone. You have one. I have one. Everyone has one. Inside it is a still, small voice that we call a conscience, and it speaks to us. I tried to explain this to you before, for I believe that everyone will do right and wants to do right, and it's only from the lack of understanding of the truth that we do wrong."

"Are you going to tell the army officers?"

"Please don't cause me to do that, Mr. Cowbone. It's not my place to confess your sins. And you lose the blessings of knowing that you are doing right on your own and according to the dictates of your own conscience. I ask you to think about it very carefully and prayerfully and you will understand that we must do it for your own sake. Not for mine. For your own sake. Look into your own soul. God is speaking to you."

"If I don't confess, are you going to tell them?"

"Please don't force me to do that, Mr. Cowbone. It is for your own peace of mind that you must do it. You have a still small voice telling you that you must go and make this matter right with those you have wronged. You don't have to take my word for it. Listen. It's the voice of your own conscience speaking to you. You cannot run away from it. It's inside you. God, in his wisdom, put it in every human breast. You can never have any ease until you obey it."

Some things about the man made him want to laugh, but the man's intense sincerity made laughter impossible. He thought of Old Duncan Bull and that man's wild eyes and desperate certainty. But there was a difference. This one would not fall down and foam at the mouth, for he had a kind of support from the countless numbers of white people. And it might even be possible that the man was saying something true, and the only trouble was that the man didn't see how difficult it was to understand or that the words seemed meaningless.

He asked, "If I tell the army people I stole the horses, will you leave my friends alone?"

"But you see, that isn't the issue, Mr. Cowbone. You must confess for the sake of your immortal soul. Get right with your fellow man; it's the first step toward getting right with God. How can you find peace burdened with this guilt? It eats at your insides like a canker! And your friends, you see, you have a special obligation to them. Consider this: they are confined within the limits of their tongue as if they were locked in a prison. The gospel message comes in the English language. How fortunate you are to understand it! What a wonderful opportunity you have to bring the message to them! You can reach them so much better than I ever could."

He was becoming exasperated. "Then if I tell the army people, you will leave my friends alone?"

"Mr. Cowbone, if you will carefully search your own conscience and if this leads you to go and confess, as you know is right, then I will leave your three friends to you. And my prayers will be with you in your efforts...."

The man went on talking but Joe said, "I'm sorry, I have to go," and walked away.

As he went out across the field he watched the old man from the side of his eye. The Reverend Fairchild knelt there a moment with his hand to his head, then walked out to the dusty road and down it toward his church.

They were holding races now on a staked-out course, alternating horse races and foot races. These had drawn two strings of cheering spectators, and occasionally the crack of the starting gun sounded over the hum of continuous noise, but straggling knots of people still did nothing but stand and talk. The Ghost Dance circle swelled and ebbed as Indians joined it or left it for some other attraction.

He could distinguish the words of their song if he listened carefully. They were singing:

> *Ya-ni Tsi-ni Hah-waw-na!*
> *Ya-ni Tsi-ni Hah-waw-na!*
> We shall live again.
> We shall live again.

He found Slow Tom and Pearl Longwater and stood with them awhile near the racetrack. He scanned the field of people to try to see Lottie or any of the Manybirds, but could not. Someone told him that the foot races for girls were to be run late in the afternoon.

The chanting song from the dancers stopped. It seemed to leave a vacant place in the air. The circle had stopped moving and had broken in places.

They saw Bill Nappy running and started across the field toward him. He saw them and came toward them, yelling as he ran, "Come help me! Spike's dying!"

Joe asked, "What is it? What's the matter with him?"

"I don't know. He just went all to pieces."

They hurried toward the dance area, Joe, Slow Tom and the Longwater girl trailing Bill.

Slow Tom asked, "Is he drunk?"

"No, but I think he's dying."

Two women and Spike Chanakut lay rigid on the ground where they had fallen out of the circle. People were bending over the women, beginning to lift them. Spike's blanket had dropped from him and he lay spread-eagled dressed only in breechclout and moccasins. His face was contorted. Shudders passed through his bony frame.

Joe said, "Spike? What is it? Spike? This is Joe."

Bill took hold of one arm as if to set him up. Spike wrenched free. "He won't let me touch him," he said. "Spike? Please, Spike! What's the matter?"

Joe slapped him lightly on the cheek. "Wake up, Spike! it's Joe and Bill and Slow Tom."

"Let's get him out of here before some fool steps on him," Slow Tom said.

They began to lift him as he struggled against them. Slow Tom said to Joe, "Turn loose: we can handle him," but Joe continued to aid in the effort. His wound was not hurting and it seemed important to help carry the distressed young man.

Spike moaned and begged, "Leave me alone! Leave me alone!"

The dance circle closed up behind them and the stumpy, agreeable Comanche was trying to get the ceremony going again.

They laid their skinny comrade down beside a wagon and spread his blanket over him, though the day had become warm. He writhed as if in pain.

Joe gently held his shoulders down and said, "Spike? It's all right. Everything's going to be all right, man."

Spike said, as if speaking through a mouth that was hard to move and control, "I saw the mist . . . and the buffalo coming back."

Bill said, "No, Spike, it's a joke. You didn't really see it. It's all just a joke."

Spike moaned and his eyes seemed to look through them without seeing them. He did not wish to be held down and kept saying, almost incoherently, "Leave me alone."

"Take it easy, man," Joe said. "Take deep breaths."

Slow Tom said, "Somebody get some water. Hey, Spike, you want a drink of water? I'll go get some water. If he won't drink maybe we can wash his face or something."

Bill said, "You just got carried away, Spike. Lie still. It's all right."

The skinny young man shook as if he were cold and said with effort, "I saw Jesus with buffalo horns . . . leading the People back."

"No, you didn't, buddy. It's a fake. See? There's no buffalo here."

"Leave me alone."

"It's all just for fun," Bill assured him. "It's a show, Spike! It's a joke, see?"

He would not respond anymore. They continued to speak to him reassuringly. They wiped his face with water and poured a small amount from a cup into his mouth. His breathing became regular and he slowly relaxed and apparently slept.

As soon as he opened his eyes, he sat up and said, "Where have you fellows been?"

They got to laughing at him.

He would not admit that he had experienced any difficulty and finally asserted that he would rejoin the circle to prove that he was not affected by the Ghost Dance.

"Like hell you will," Slow Tom said.

Joe ate with Lottie. They sat under the trees at the edge of the busy field. When they had finished, she took the utensils to their wagon and returned to him. He wondered that she did not seem worried about her family's missing her. He asked her about it.

"Didn't I tell you?" she said. "My father won the plowing contest. He's so tickled he doesn't know what's going on."

They walked among the trees. He considered her question about his not dancing and, as she had said, looking different—this along with the strongly implied threat from the Reverend Fairchild. The someday when he would tell her would need to be soon.

"I said I'd tell you something," he said.

"Yes, you did."

"I'll show you." His jacket was open. He unbuttoned his vest and bared his chest.

She stared, frowning at the round blue scar, then touched his skin lightly with her fingers.

"Here." He slipped out of his jacket and vest and turned to show his back, where a large scab still clung to his shoulder blade. When he turned to see her face, he saw that she was aware that a bullet had passed through his body.

"Joe, what if you had been killed?"

"Some fellow told me it proved that a bullet couldn't kill me."

Her lips trembled and when she spoke it was like a whisper. "You were one of them, weren't you?"

"Yes." He added quietly, bragging a little, "I was their chief."

"How did you get off the mountaintop? When you were away up in the fortress? They said they killed all of you and your bodies vanished into thin air."

He laughed. "That's a good story."

"But how did you get away?"

"Got to keep a few secrets."

"From me?"

"Yes. I want you to believe I have strong medicine."

She clung to him a moment, then said, "Let me see your back again. This needs a bandage on it. We have some white cloth at home. Let me fix it."

He put on his jacket and vest, and they walked toward the Manybirds place, staying off the road, holding hands, like two children.

She said, "Joe, I don't believe you want to get married in the white man's way. I thought you didn't. Anyway, I have an idea maybe you would want to hear."

He told her that he did.

"I have a mare. You know, the filly my mother used to ride? Well, she's mine now. I could say I traded her off or gave her away, only I would really give her to you. She'll foal in the spring, so she should be worth something, shouldn't she?"

"What would I do with her?"

"You could take her to the Caddoes or somewhere and trade her for another horse, then bring that one and give it to my father."

He laughed and teased her about it. She saw the humor in it and did not mind.

"It would be a good joke on him," he said.

"Don't you think it would work?"

"I don't know. But you're worth more than one horse. I'll tell you what—if you'll trust me, I'll get horses."

"All right." Suddenly she stopped and said, "But no

more dangerous things. I trust your strong medicine only so far."

"All right."

She tied a bandage over his wound and in the back. They lay on the small low bed where she always slept and made love gently. For a long time they lay silent in each other's arms. The languor of it made the troubles that stood ahead of him seem distant. He felt that he was storing up strength and memories for times when he would need them.

Lying beside her, he said, "Have you thought that your family might come home?"

"I've decided to leave it up to you to worry about my reputation," she said.

Late in the afternoon he took her back toward the crowd in the clearing in front of the Red Store. They saw Slow Tom Armstedt's sister, and Lottie went ahead by herself to join her.

That night he slept on a gravel bar. The next morning he walked up the rise to the granite buildings of Fort Sill.

17

PRISON

THE BUFFALO SOLDIER stiffened and began to stare straight ahead as he approached.

He asked, "Can I see the colonel?"

"Go on away. Man, can't you see I'm on guard duty?"

"I need to see the colonel or somebody."

"Go on away. You going to get me in trouble."

"I need to see the colonel about some stolen horses."

"Colonel! Man, you can't see no colonel. You don't go on away, I'm going to turn you in."

"That's what I wanted you to do. I stole some horses. I think they want me."

Fifteen minutes later they took him in to see a captain who sat behind a desk. The man was heavyset, pink of face, with thin, carefully combed blond hair. He stared a minute, then asked, "What's his name?"

"My name is Joe Cowbone," he said.

"You say you stole the horses?"

"Yes, sir."

The captain said to the guards, "You can take your hands off of him. Did he have any weapons?"

One of the guards said, "Just this here pocket knife and this book."

The captain took them. "Can you read, Mr. Cowbone?"

"I can read one story and part of another."

"Where did you get this book?"

"A man gave it to me. But he had nothing to do with the horses."

"Who was your leader when you stole the horses?"

"I was the chief."

"How many men did you have with you?"

"I don't want to confess their sins."

"I see. Did the Reverend Fairchild send you up here?"

"He talked to me. I came by myself."

"I see. Now, Mr. Cowbone, how many horses did you take?"

"Fifty-two bay geldings. Nine pack mules."

The captain jerked his eyes up and stared at him, his mouth hanging slightly open. Then he seemed to become more thoughtful. "When you had the horses, where did you stop at night? What places?"

"On a branch of Rainy Mountain Creek. On Elk Creek. At Soldier Spring. Up west of the cattle trail."

"Well, Mr. Cowbone, I'll say one thing. You certainly know a lot about it. It was thought that one of the thieves was badly wounded. Did he die?"

"No, sir." He unbuttoned his vest and showed the round blue scar. The captain stood up, leaned forward and peered at it.

"Amazing. Where did it exit?"

Joe slipped out of his jacket and vest, but when the captain saw the bandage he said, "That's all right. I believe you. Amazing. Is it healing satisfactorily?"

"Yes, sir."

"Of course you understand that you have admitted a serious offense, Mr. Cowbone. We'll have to hold you." The man handed his book back to him.

"Yes, sir."

They took him outside and to another stone building.

Inside it they stopped in front of a wooden door with iron straps across it. A guard took both hands to pull it open. The granite wall through which the door led was three feet thick. They pushed him lightly on his back and he went in. They closed the ponderous door. He heard the clink of iron as they fastened it.

He stood in the dark. The only light came through a small square window in the door with three bars across it. In a moment he could see dimly that he was in a small room. Half the space was taken up by a cot with a blanket on it. On the slab stone floor sat a bucket. The place smelled like rocks and mold. He sensed the weight of thick wood and iron and stone all around him.

He stood awhile with his arms folded, feeling the smallness of the place. He thought that he was like an animal in a den deep inside a mountain. It was a bad place for a man. The sense of heaviness and nearness of stone did not decrease as he waited. His legs became tired from standing still and he began to wonder how long he had been there. Too long. He sat down.

Then began a passage of days which were the most difficult of his life. He could distinguish day from night, not from the dimness of his cell, but because sometimes white daylight filtered through the small square window and other times yellow lantern light. Each day seemed longer than a week.

The food was good. They brought him three or four different things to eat on a plate at each meal, besides coffee. They would set it on the floor; then, when they had pulled the door to, he would stand and hold the plate near the window so that he could see what he ate. They brought it regularly, three times a day. But the hours in between and the nights seemed to drag on forever. He sat. He stood. Nothing happened. The crude confines of his cell looked just the same as they had looked a long minute before, a long hour before, a long day before. He waited, watching the dimness, smelling the damp stone and the sharp scent of his urine in the bucket.

Through the window he could see nothing but the empty outer room, sometimes the lantern hanging on a hook. The smell of its oil-oaked wick penetrated faintly through the bars. Often he held his book in his hands, wishing for enough light to study it.

He realized that time passed slowly because he did not know the end of it. Could it be possible that he must exist here the rest of his life? It would have been better to have died from the bullet out there in the wide land under the open sky. He had never known before how precious are the sights of sky and distant terrain. The man had said it was a serious offense. When would they tell him his punishment? If he must stay here forever, would they tell him or merely let him understand it as the years passed? He would prefer to be shot. But they hanged people instead of shooting them. He could imagine the captain saying, Of course, you will be sent to Washington; the President will hang you. But that wouldn't be it. Fort Smith would be more like it. Of course, you will be sent to Fort Smith, and Hanging Judge Parker will take care of you. Or Jacksboro, where they sent the Kiowas long ago. The trouble was that he had no way at all to know what the captain actually meant by "serious" or what might seem like proper punishment to white army men.

When he had endured seven days in the cell, the guards took him back before the captain. One of them stepped near the man, made his back bow in, struck his shoes together, saluted and said, "Captain, sir, this here is that Indian prisoner, Joe Cowbone."

The man's desktop was covered with papers, over

which he had been working. He frowned and checked from one paper to another, then said, "Mr. Cowbone, one army saddle is missing. What did you do with it?"

"Where we turned off the north agency road . . . about two miles . . . We stopped there and threw the saddle in some bushes by a draw."

The captain wrote it down. "Now, Mr. Cowbone, you crossed over into the Cheyenne-Arapaho reservation, it seems. Do you have any statement to make about that?"

"No, sir."

"The question has been raised as to whether you left this reservation. It has to do with the jurisdiction. Now, there is an old Comanche-Cheyenne treaty, at least the question has been raised, but the United States was not a party and possibly wouldn't recognize the legality of it. Would you say . . . did you have any arguments to make about whether you took the horses off the reservation?"

"No, sir."

"I don't blame you. It's a bunch of nonsense. All this red tape!" The man turned, frowned out the window and slowly smoothed the hair on the back of his head "You're lucky, Mr. Cowbone, that Major Truax has been relieved of active duty while he waits for the Court of Inquiry. You've ruined his career. Burned a great amount of government property under his charge. Left his command afoot in the field. Very serious. Are you prepared to give us the names of the other men who took part in it?"

"No, sir. I don't want to confess their sins."

The captain wrote it down and asked, "Do you have anything else to say?"

"No, sir."

"We'll have to hold you. That's all."

The guards took him out. He got a few breaths of the

cold free air before he was again shut up in his cell.

As he waited through the limited and dreary hours, he searched for things to ponder, to mull over. But one day an idea sprang into his mind on its own: Why in the hell did I come up here and confess to the army just because old Fairchild told me all that crap? Why? Partly it was so that he would leave the others alone. But that wasn't all of it. He might as well admit it. Knowing how crazy and muddled up old men were, knowing the confused nonsense they spouted, he still expected them to tell him something. He could give excuses, but the truth was that beneath his cynicism he wanted something from them. What was it? From old red men or old white men he expected something. It was maddening, also true. Also sad. At last, in a detached way, he saw that it was also humorous.

He thought that it might be a natural impulse to hope for wisdom from old men, but he would never let the desire put him in a prison cell again. If he ever got out. What he should have done was threaten to cut old Fairchild's throat if he didn't keep his mouth shut.

Day followed monotonous day. Time moved like a dry-land terrapin crawling along the prairie and at times it seemed to draw into its shell and not move at all. The dim cell felt like a weight pressing in on all sides of him.

After another slow seven days, the guards took him out again. He greedily sucked in the cold air and stared at the sunlit details of the army post as they marched him to the captain.

After the guards went through the blank-faced, stiff motions before the officer, they went back out the door and closed it. He immediately wondered how far away they were going—whether they waited beyond the door.

The captain was looking him over. It was hard to see the man clearly because he was framed in the window, but Joe knew from past visits that the captain was a fit man. His arms almost filled the olive-drab sleeves of his shirt and his shirt collar was tight on his pink neck. Sometimes such a heavy man is active and fast. The estimation was important, for a daring possibility had come into his mind as soon as he realized the guards were going out the door.

The man said, "You speak English rather well, Mr. Cowbone."

"Yes, sir."

"Do you think you speak it well . . . or . . . That is, do you understand clearly all the words . . . or nearly all the words, at least enough to grasp what is said?"

"I believe I do." If he sprang for the door, would he be able to get it open and get out before the man could rise and catch him? There would be the moment at the door as he pulled on it. What if, as he pulled it open, he turned and shoved the approaching captain as hard as he could, then jerked the door closed after him?

"What I'm trying to get at is this," the captain said. "Suppose you have a conversation with someone in the English language. Suppose after this exchange of views you think about the matter. Do you feel, at that time, that you have grasped the point of view and the meaning of the other person?"

He was interested in the question, or interested in the captain's concern with the question, but he was not through with the idea of running. Would he find the guards out there? Would he be lucky enough to find a door to the outside which was open? And where outside might he run into soldiers standing with guns ready? If they yelled "Halt!" and raised their guns, he must run in a zigzag path, ducking low. But the captain's question seemed to postpone for a moment any decision about running.

"Do you understand my question?"

"Yes, sir."

"Well . . . uh . . . pardon me for asking this, but would you repeat my question? You see, Mr. Cowbone, I know that a lot of misunderstandings arise."

"If I speak with someone in English. Then I go away. Do I know what was in the other person's mind?"

"Yes!" The captain was pleased. "Yes, that's the idea. Now, are you able to answer 'yes' to that question?"

He thought about all the ways in which one person might mislead another, intentionally or not; and, when two people talk, how it is that all the unthought-of memories in one mind help determine what the person thinks about their talk. He said, "I don't know."

The man appeared to be frowning mildly, "Well, let's pass on. Would you sit down, please? Right there."

He sat down. He could see the captain's pink face more clearly. The man's thin blond hair was carefully combed, as he had noted before.

"You are very fortunate, Mr. Cowbone, to speak English. I have often thought what an advantage it would be to me in my work if I spoke the Indian tongue.

"Mr. Cowbone, I have an important duty placed on my shoulders by the agent and the Indian Court and my superior officers. It seems somewhat out of place. I want you to understand that I don't assume the duty on my own initative, but, having been given the duty, I take it seriously. The duty is serious. Its successful implementation has no tangible immediate results, and thus it may be passed over or forgotten or ignored or handled superficially. This is done, but it should not be done."

What in the world could the man be talking about?

If it was his duty to hang him, why didn't he say so? At least he did seem sincere.

"Do you know what a lecture is, Mr. Cowbone?"

"No, sir, I don't think so."

"Well, we might say that it's an explanation or a complete exposition. . . . It ought to be complete and to be a sincere attempt to get to the heart of the matter. Let me just . . . Well, suppose I begin by asking this question: Do you care to tell me why you stole the horses?"

What a peculiar question! How could he possibly explain it? He could say that he had wanted some good horses to give to Frank Manybirds as a part of a marriage. But suppose he said that and the captain laughed? Or more likely, suppose the captain pointed out that he could work and get money or wait for his share of grass, then buy horses?

"Mr. Cowbone, I'm very anxious that you understand. I'm not taking this down, you see. Nor trying to get you to convict yourself, or anything. I'm trying to find an opening, you might say. That's the heart of our problem. It's crucial that we find some kind of mutual understanding. Now, do you care to give me any kind of answer to the question: Why did you steal the horses?"

"No, sir."

"Well, I think I really haven't explained very well about a lecture, the purpose of it. It's not understood by many people. It's not to express displeasure or to threaten. Or to warn. It ought to be explanatory. The result of it ought to be a better understanding of the entire problem, in its essential elements, and from it ought to come a sense of agreement that would result in willing compliance. It's my duty, you see." He touched his chest, then pointed. "But it's for you. I wish

I could explain it better. We will talk, see, but it's for you. The benefits are for you. I don't have any selfish reason for the lecture, except in so far as doing my duty is a source of satisfaction, but I would sincerely like to say somethings that might be of value to you. So that's my problem, you see, to find those things. Do you understand?"

He answered, "Yes, sir." Behind the man's words was an honest intention and the man knew it was difficult. He was interested but suspicious. He thought, Why is this man trying to make me believe that he has something precious to tell me? I'm not the fool I was when I went to Duncan Bull. He wanted to watch carefully and be ready to decide quickly what to do and act quickly.

"I might mention some incidental facts, Mr. Cowbone, general facts. You took the horses west, which would be a rather logical direction in some sense. You really didn't take them very far. There is some question as to whether you took them off the reservation. I wonder, do you know the boundaries of the reservation?"

"I believe I do," he said.

"I wonder if you know the land beyond. I'm thinking that the logical course, in some sense, would have been to go farther west. Your ancestors knew that land well. The question rises: Why didn't you go on farther? Some would have done it. Of course, they would have been acting more sensibly in some immediate sense, but, of course, they would have been in error also. Out there, depending on the route, you would come to Mobeetie, Tascosa, Santa Fe, or maybe Dodge City, Denver, Salt Lake City. I suppose further along this line I should mention the great numbers of United States soldiers and their mobility all over the land, but your people have known this for a long time. Please don't misunderstand me; actually all of this is incidental, not really central to my lecture at all; you might even say that I'm trying to designate the kind of thing that my lecture should not deal with. But out of these considerations comes one point that perhaps is more than incidental, the futility of your action. It's not so much that I'm telling you of the futility as it is that you surely knew of it already and yet you went ahead. I can't see where that would lead us. It's . . . it's not simple. I wish I could find some . . . key . . . or follow that thought out in some manner. I don't suppose . . . You didn't care to answer the question as to why you stole the horses. I don't guess you would care to comment on this question: Why did you steal the horses in the face of the futility of it?"

He could not think of anything to say except, "I don't believe so." He was watching the words, suspicious of it all. He searched the names of the white man's places, Denver, Santa Fe, for a clue to his fate; if it were to be prison forever or death, they might send him somewhere. But in the face of these dark possibilities, the manner and words of the captain affected him. He asked himself, Why does he act so sincere? He won't catch me with it. I've outgrown long-winded old goats like Fairchild. These protests did not subdue a peculiar breathless hoping that was rising in him.

"I'm really not satisfied, Mr. Cowbone, with my ability to explain. All I can do is assure you that I am attempting to find a way to say some things that might be of value to you."

He sat silently, divided as if he were two people. One part was calm, experienced, suspicious; and it observed the other part, a youthful spirit which wanted to believe the impossible. This latter part, a memory as much as a fact, a weak, unsubstantial ghost of youthful spirit, was crying out: Please! Captain, I understand a little bit of what is in your mind. Behind your words. You would like to tell me something. You really would. Try to tell me, man! Don't give up. What is it? What is it? Even though it's only a little important to you, try to find a way to tell me. What is behind your pink face, behind those pale eyes with the little frown about them, underneath that thin combed blond hair? Try to tell me, man! Find a way! Tell me the things Mad Wolf told me, in your words and from the world you know. Do you have things in common with Mad Wolf? Why is one white man better than another? How do you know? How do you measure? Try to give me a clue to the pride you sometimes must feel, and try to tell the glory that is possible on your road. Where is the entrance, out of the chaos? How does one come stumbling out of all the white scattered bones on the prairie and put his foot on the road? Surely you didn't destroy it for nothing! If it was great, you wouldn't! If it was not great, still it was a way to live and a man knew what to think and what to do. You wouldn't destroy it for nothing. Tell me! By the Earth Mother! Try to tell me!

But the calm, experienced part of him was dominant. He said none of it.

"I think I might try to explain the idea of private property to you," the captain said. "I don't know how exactly to start. That is, I will doubtless oversimplify and overexplain, but it's better, I think, to go too far in that direction than to leave things uncertain. Private property is a thing that is owned by a person. Let's take an example. Say we have several men here and they each own a shirt. Each one has a shirt that fits himself and suits him in regard to color or other qualities. He can wash the shirt and take care of it, for he knows that it's his and if it is clean he will have the benefit of its cleanliness. Also, he won't tear it or burn holes in it; it's his."

The youthful part of him examined the words eagerly as they came from the sincere captain's mouth.

"Now, there's an agreement in this, Mr. Cowbone. Each of the men looks at the other and says, 'That's your shirt and this one is mine. It's your property.' You see, they agree. I think property and its benefits depend upon the element of agreement. For, of course, it is a benefit to all men that we have property and agree on it. If the men take off their shirts for bathing, it's not necessary for them to have a big fight and tear the shirts to pieces. Each man goes willingly to his own shirt. He puts it on. It fits. He is satisfied. They agree among themselves, you see, that this is best and most profitable for everyone concerned. Do you understand my meaning?"

He didn't know, but he said, "Yes, sir, I think I do." The youthful spirit in him found its blaze of hope spluttering as it searched among the words; in their simplicity seemed a suggestion that the man might yet say something.

"Well, this classification extends to every kind of article, of anything if you can say of it, 'I own it. It's mine.' If there is a benefit to most people that a certain kind of thing will be more useful as private property, then they will divide it up and own it as individuals. One of the benefits is that a man can own the particular property he wants; one might want two shirts; one might want one shirt and a hat. So a man takes his money and exchanges it or trades it for the particular property that suits him. Well, where does he get the money? He gets it from working or selling some property he owns. There is a kind of chain of property and work and money; any of them may be exchanged for another if both of the parties are willing.

"But I think that the crucial point is the agreement between men that things shall be as I have described them. People must agree on it or it won't work. No one can afford to spend his time constantly defending what is his. He would have no time for constructive work. Also, if a man was weak he would wind up with little property, for the strong would always take it from him, even though he had worked hard for it, and that does not seem just. Therefore, the agreement is made. But what happens if it is broken? There is no end to it. If a man takes your shirt, you are inclined to take his hat. Anarchy. Everyone comes out with torn clothing and clothing that doesn't fit and property he doesn't want, while someone else has his property, which he wants, and no one is happy. In addition to which, he cannot leave anything he owns without a guard, lest someone make off with it. That's the result of breaking the agreement. Confusion. And that is why men frown on those who break it and take action against them. Do you understand my general meaning, Mr. Cowbone?"

"I think so," he said.

"Well, to break this agreement is called 'stealing.' I think you understand that. Of course, it may be more serious at one time than another, depending on the property that is taken. On principle, stealing is stealing, but in practice one instance is more serious than another, more likely to lead to anarchy. If a thief takes a pumpkin or an ear of corn out of another man's field, it might be called 'petty theft.' It's wrong, but not too serious."

The foolish youthful spirit gave up its hope. No precious message was coming. He was no longer divided.

"Horse stealing is something else again, Mr. Cowbone. Horses are considered of considerable value in this country. In the west, you know, distances are long, and people travel great distances on horseback. Sometimes, for instance, in dry country a man's very life may depend on his horse; he wouldn't be able to get to the next water hole without him. If the horse is taken, it might be a question of life or death. In any case, we place great dependence on the horse and value him highly, perhaps more highly, relative to his actual monetary value, than any other single thing. In other words, we look beyond the utilitarian value because of pride in ownership of this particular property.

"To sum up what I'm trying to say, and I guess this is the point of my lecture: horse stealing is serious. It's wrong. It must not be done."

The man sat silent for a moment, then rose and walked slowly back and forth behind his desk. He was holding one elbow cupped in the opposite hand and was biting the inside of his under lip. If he turns his back on me completely, Joe thought, I'm going to run for it.

"Well," the man said, "perhaps if you had some question or some statement to make . . . Did you?"

"No, sir."

"Maybe you would have something to say about my lecture or . . . or something along that line?"

"No, sir."

The man looked out the window a minute, then sat back down. "I'm not well satisfied with what I've said, Mr. Cowbone, but I can't think of anything else. Or . . . any other way to state my meaning.

"Now, in regard to the disposition of the case, no charges have been brought. Or they have been dropped. In fact, there is a difference of opinion as to whether they have been dropped or have not been brought, and there is a disagreement about the jurisdiction. To be frank, there doesn't seem to be agreement about any of it, as to whether you might have left the reservation without a pass or as to whether it was a rebellion rather than a felony. One opinion even has it that yours was an act of war and therefore you are guilty of nothing more than any soldier, which would lead to the foolish conclusion, I suppose, that we should sign a peace treaty with you; but the official position is that there is no war and not even any trouble on this reservation. The Indian Court doesn't wish to try the case because the military is involved as the owner of the horses, and the agent insists that only he can impose the penalty of withholding rations. So that's the status. My orders are twofold: number one, lecture you, which I have done to the best of my ability. Number two, release you. I guess that's all."

He thought he understood what the man had said, and could not believe it possible.

"Here's your pocket knife, Mr. Cowbone."

He took it, trying to look as calm and composed as he could. The man smiled and Joe grinned at him. He felt awkward. It was not that he doubted his own understanding of English; rather it was the question raised earlier by the captain about knowing what is in another man's mind, which may have in it unknown principles that contradict words. The whole thing seemed too important to be so simply ended, and he dreaded to presume what seemed clear, only to have it said to him: We don't mean that.

The man was looking out the window again. A lieutenant had come in and was talking to him in a low, excited voice. Joe vaguely recognized the young man as one he had seen before down at the cow camp, but it was only an interruption. He wanted to say, Thank you, Captain, or for the man to say something else that would affirm his freedom.

He heard the lieutenant say something about a "brawl" and the words "wagon teams stampeded over them."

The door was open, but he did not want to sneak out, or even run out if it was not necessary. He wanted to go calmly and deliberately.

He heard from the lieutenant the words, "that drunk Great Eagle," and, "They say the other one's name is White Buffalo."

The sense of the outdoors seemed to seep through the open door toward him. He thought that he would speak up, interrupt them, say that he would go now, but the captain had put on a belt with a pistol in it. The captain was heading for the door. "Have they dispersed?"

"Yes, sir. The surgeon went down to help the agency doctor."

They went out the door. The captain had forgotten him.

He walked out of the building, forcing himself to move naturally, unhurriedly. As he passed between the buildings, in his mind he was running. Every step away from the stone cell seemed like a leap. He went toward the timber, toward where Medicine Bluff Creek empties into East Cache. When he was among the trees, out of their sight, he began to run, not out of fear, but gorging himself upon his freedom and the distance around him.

He turned down the stream and ran until he was panting. It occurred to him that though he was breathing as deeply as he could, he could not feel his wound at all.

His time in the cell had been so oppressive and his release so affective that his mind did not settle upon the words he had heard about the fight until he saw the small procession coming toward him. A boy led a brown horse, beside which walked a woman holding a burden across the horse's back. At the rear came two girls, half grown. Each of them wore blankets against the cold. He recognized the boy as the one he had seen that time at Great Eagle's aborted feast.

The burden was the limp form of a man, bloody and dirty. The arms and legs and the head, with its half-length hair hanging down, all flopped awkwardly to the plodding movement of the horse. There was no doubt that Great Eagle was dead. The procession passed by within twenty steps of him, but none of them looked at him. They went on toward Caddo Crossing.

I should not hate the dead, he thought, looking at their dull, clumsy movements.

He remembered the fire that night at the macabre feast, the still air, the true column of smoke rising from a burned sheep to touch a little bit of the last sunlight. It had stuck strongly in his mind. It seemed now that he could see Great Eagle on the fire instead of the sheep, making smoke, trying to send a message or a plea with the agony of the recent years of his life. An unwilling sheep. An untidy, inept messenger, almost a joke, like the false Ghost Dance. But as piercing as a man screaming from a mountaintop: "Help us! We can't stand it! Help us! Help us!"

18

TWO WIVES

HE COULD FEEL his mother's nervous reluctance as he
was reaching out with his fist toward the door. It had
been that way all during the journey from the Iron
Lance camp, and he had managed to get her here only
by the constant assertion of his will. He gripped her
upper arm as firmly as he could without hurting her.
Any hesitation on his part and she would be offering a
dozen protests: Wait a day or two; I have to dress up
better; you go alone. He pounded loudly.

The minute he waited seemed much longer. The white
woman pulled the door in until a small chain stopped it.
He could have seen her better in the twilight had it not
been for the yellow lamplight behind her. But he saw
her harried face full of suspicion and her eyes squinting
to identify him. While he was saying, "Please, Mrs.
Powell . . ." she gasped a meaningless sound.

She tried to close the door. He put his hand on it to
prevent her. She was succeeding in her jerky pushing
until he threw his shoulder into it, tearing out the chain,
smashing it open.

She stumbled back and said, "Get out! You . . ."

He said as calmly as he could, "Mrs. Powell, I don't
mean to hurt anyone."

It seemed as if his good English and calm words agitated her. She screamed, "No! Get out!"

His mother was pulling back, and he retreated a step or two with her to restrain her as gently as possible. The white woman looked from side to side in indecision, like a cornered animal, then sprang through the door, brushed past them on the low porch, and out into the evening light toward the agency.

He had no time to lose. He gripped his mother, his face close to hers, and said fiercely, "Stay here! If you leave, I swear I'll drag you back by the hair!"

He rushed after the running white woman. Once she tripped, but had hardly touched the ground before she scrambled up to flee onward. Except for the light-colored dress she wore he would have lost her in the mixture of trees and shadows. He could see faintly ahead the square yellow windows of the agency building, almost within yelling distance, and pushed himself with a desperate effort to come up to her. She was crashing through a patch of tall dry grass when he caught her shoulder with one hand. Then she fell. He got hold of her threshing figure in the grass, pinned her, clamped his hand over her mouth as she gathered herself to scream.

He felt her relax. He paused, panting. It was as if they agreed on a truce in order to get air. When he could speak, he said, "Mrs. Powell, I don't mean to hurt you. But we are going back. I want to have a thing settled. Tonight. I've waited as long—"

She bit his hand and twisted her head free, but her attempted scream was muffled against the ground. Out of her cramped position she mouthed, "You savage heathen! How dare you!"

Fighting her, he said, "Mr. Powell is going to choose tonight."

He pulled her out of the crushed grass and dragged her back in the direction they had come. It was a hard struggle, pushing and jerking her, holding her, tugging, anticipating when she was going to try to yell in order to choke it off.

"You filthy Indian! . . . Take your hands off me! . . . Help! . . . You are going to murder us! . . . You brute! . . . You animal!"

"I'm not going to hurt anyone," he told her, "unless talking will hurt. . . . Mr. Powell is going to choose his wife tonight."

She did not seem to hear anything he said.

"You savages have already half killed him! . . . Isn't that enough? You ignorant—"

"I'm through with lies and not knowing," he said. "We've waited . . . long enough. . . . Mrs. Powell, I'm going to break your arm if you don't go. . . . I'm going to choke you if you don't stop trying to yell. . . . I may break every bone in your body . . . but you are going to stand beside my mother in front of that man tonight."

She tried to scream and he hit her in the neck. She wrenched free and he scrambled after her. She was like a cat, showing surprising strength and always the twisting agility that made it impossible to handle her gently. He was not certain that he would be able to control her. It was just as well that she did not know about his recent wound. Who would have guessed that a slight, pale-faced woman could so oppose him?

"You are going to kill us!"

"Mrs. Powell, I don't mean to hurt anyone . . . if you'll go on quietly. . . ."

"You are going to murder us! . . . He's half dead already! . . . You dirty Indian! . . . You bloody . . ."

The distance they had covered in a minute of running required half an hour as he took her back. He saw the huddled form of his mother still on the porch, her hands covering her face and eyes. "Go inside!" he ordered her.

She went in and he pushed the white woman after her. The house contained two rooms with a large opening between them. Outside it had grown dark, but the inside was well lighted by three lamps, one of them on a bedside table at the rear. The man in the bed was covered to the arms with a quilt. His legs appeared to be swollen or wrapped heavily, and his posture made it seem as if he were anchored by his legs. His right arm, wrapped, stuck out stiff and useless. With his left elbow he propped himself shakily off his pillow. A bandage around his head covered both eyes and one ear. Blood, now dry, had seeped through it. "Who is it?" he asked. "What's the matter?"

"Tell them to get out!" the woman urged. "He's going to murder us!"

He overrode her voice with his own. "It's all right, Mr. Powell, she's frightened, that's all. I had to bring her back."

"Who is it?" the man asked. "What's all the trouble about?"

"It's Joe Cowbone, Mr. Powell. It's all right. I don't mean to hurt anyone."

"This is what happens!" the woman said. "I told you we should never come to this place! They're savages! They've crippled you and blinded you and they're not satisfied to let you go!"

"What's this all about? Who is it? Is it Joe Cowbone?" The man was in an awkward position, straining on one elbow.

"Yes, sir. And my mother."

"Who are these people?" the woman demanded, almost hysterical. "Who are they? Tell them to get out! I won't have them! Who do they think they are! I told you a hundred times we shouldn't have come to this place!"

"Mr. Powell, the story I told you that day is true."

The man held up on his shaking elbow, straining. It seemed that at any moment he must surely lie back and ease himself. It was painful to see him suspended in such a way, as if he balanced himself with a strength that was not equal to the task.

The woman screamed and he allowed her to do it, only watching that she did not escape again. Three times she screamed in frenzy and fury, then she subsided into a broken audible breathing.

He said deliberately, "Your wife is here, Mr. Powell. She's over there by the door."

The man tottered on his straining elbow. Listening. His steel-gray hair was a rumpled shock over the bandage. The suntan of his lower face seemed like a film over a whiteness underneath. He said, in the Comanche language, "Is anybody there?" The expression of his voice was so simple as to be childlike.

The sound of his voice seemed to set off the white woman again. "Don't speak their language! Tell them to get out! I won't have it! I told you! Don't speak their dirty words!"

He asked again in Comanche, "Is someone there?"

"Speak to him!" he ordered his mother. "Come over here! say something!"

The white woman began screaming again, with words, "If you speak their language, I'll leave you! I won't have it! If you don't make them leave . . . Don't talk to them! I'll leave you! I won't be treated like an Indian!"

When it grew quiet again, his mother came halfway to the bed. At the screaming and yelling she had been holding her hands over her ears. Tears glistened down her brown rounded face. Now she said softly, *"Tosakura?"*

"Who is it?"

The white woman persistently poured out her frantic protest. She seemed ready to pounce upon the broken man in the bed. In the intervals of relative quiet the other two spoke in the Comanche language.

"It's me, *Tosakura*."

"Is it Little Brown Girl?"

"Yes."

"Is it really you?"

"Yes."

The man's straining body relaxed and he laid his head back onto the pillow.

He remembered that day when he and his mother had listened to the gay voices of the women coming into the house by the new trading store, and how, outside the meanings of the words, the sounds carried their own indisputable meaning. Here in this different way it was true again. They were two people meeting who had known each other long ago. Their voices said that they had been lovers.

"Why did you run away from me, Little Brown Girl?"

Among the strains of the night, the clashes of stubbornness, the screams, the pity, his observations of his own willingness to violence, nothing had shaken him like this question. Knowing it, that it must have been she who had left and knowing less consciously that he did not want to examine his own motives, he had put it out of his mind to sustain his fierce righteous determination.

"I was scared of Saint Louis."

He was not sorry for his action—elation still grew in him—but with the question and his mother's answer he knew that he could push none of it further.

The white woman bolted, and he made no move to stop her. She jerked the door wide and escaped through it. He could hear her crying out as she ran.

"She's going to the agency," he said. "We have to leave. We don't want any trouble."

His mother went to the bed, took the man's left hand and held it a moment. She was too much overcome to say anything more.

Then the two of them walked out the open door. He was conscious that they were not running in the darkness, but walking deliberately. Two hundred steps from the house, as if by plan or spoken agreement, they stopped and waited in silence. It seemed as well that he could not see her face and that there was no need for talk between them.

Finally the buggy came down the road, clopping and jangling in the darkness, and stopped at the porch. They could see clearly the two who entered, the doctor with his bag and a nurse in a white dress.

His mother said slowly, "She didn't come back."

"It's time for us to go home," he said.

19

OLD BULLS LIE DOWN

HE WENT to work for a rancher down on Red River, breaking and training horses. When he proved adept at it, he was offered top wages of forty dollars a month, besides his grub; but he chose to take his wage in horses. It was good work, but could not be permanent, for he had a knot of bone on his right shoulder blade, which gave him trouble during the days of jolting riding. He worked four months and earned three good horses.

He gave two as a present to Frank Manybirds. The old man was pleased and satisfied and by his manner made it clear that he had forgotten any objection he may have had in the past. But for the sake of Lottie, for the sake of any feeling she might have that he did not understand, for the satisfaction of anyone else whose business it might be—he was becoming more aware that the world is a complicated place and the business of human beings is involved—he took her to the Reverend Fairchild, who married them by the white man's laws and religious words.

When he got the letter from Saint Louis he tried for two days to read it, comparing the handwriting with the words in his book. Some of the words he could guess and others he could not. He could make out the name Powell. It was from his father.

He would want to tell his mother what it said anyway—she still lived at the Iron Lance camp up in the northern edge of the mountains—so he rode up to get Freddy Bull to read it to him. The letter said this:

Dear Joe,

Am still crippled up a good bit. I don't know why I let them bring me here to these fancy doctors. One doctor says they will have to saw my leg off, but I don't aim to let them take it. My eye is all right. I figure to be good as ever in a few months.

From all I can find out they are going to cut up the reservation, and nothing to be done about it. They say it's already decided. I guess they will have a run of settlers on it.

Well, I have got some land east of Kansas City, and also have got a quarter interest in a store here that is doing business, and what I want to do is get my money out and come out there and put it in land joining yours. There is settlers that will do anything to get a piece of land, but soon find out they don't know what to do with it, so I could buy some. If they have allotments and you get to choose, ask your mother for you and her to get land joining.

Tell your mother I am coming back as soon as I can get loose.

Your friend,
Joseph W. Powell

He had Freddy Bull read it three times, then he took t and was able to read it to his mother. She said, "He'll lo it. He'll come back as soon as he can get loose. I hope they don't cut his leg off. He was always such an active man, you know."

She had traded rations for two deer hides, which she was tanning with great care and patience. She explained that she was going to make Mr. Powell a fancy buckskin jacket with pockets and with fringe in front and on the shoulders and on the bottom. He would be very pleased with it.

The army officers wanted to bring the Apache prisoners, one of them Geronimo, to live on the reservation. It was debated at the agency, during the issue gatherings, in the camps, in the deteriorating councils; and finally those who were considered or considered themselves Kiowa and Comanche chiefs gave their reluctant consent.

It was a more important concession than the white soldiers knew. The Apaches were one of the great enemies, as the Pawnees or the Utes had been at one time and another, or as the Cheyennes had been before the Bents. The Comanches had met the Apaches in a thousand skirmishes, had raided and been raided, had feared and suspected them, challenged them, exchanged cruel revenge, had guided their lives on the enmity through long generations. They had hated Apaches, reviled them, defied them, threatened them, and had understood their strength. The word had been: "Let the stinking Apaches go back to the dry mountains where they belong! If we want anything out of them, we'll go after it! Let those filthy creatures stay in their own country!"

In the latter years of turmoil, as their world was coming to pieces, some few Comanches had found themselves fighting beside remnants of eastern Apaches; but they had expected deceit and had practiced it and had accepted any brief alliance only as a necessity.

Their attitudes and assumptions lay not only in memories, but in stories, some so old that they were legend. In the dim reaches of legend was one tale with forgotten parts and added parts and varied parts that might be substituted for others, concerning a time not long after the Comanches got the god-dogs, when the Apaches stood in a line along a river and the buffalo stood in a huge circle around them. The Comanches rode through the circle and against the line, and the battle raged up and down and across the river day after day with fury and determination, while the circle of buffaloes solemnly watched. The Apache line broke on the ninth day, and those who could travel fled south and west. Among the vague parts of the tale was a vague judgment of it, that it was the most important battle they had ever fought in all their past, that every Comanche man who had achieved greatness since had had an ancestor at the river battle, and that the victory was the beginning of their era of magnificence.

Now they did not refer much to the legends and tales. For one reason, they had grown dubious and cynical about them. Then, also, it seemed unfitting to analyze too deeply their own feelings. They said things like, "Well, you know how those Apaches are, but, after all, it's only a small bunch." They knew when the strangers would arrive, for it had been in the newspapers and in talk of the soldiers and civilian whites.

Joe Cowbone had driven up in a wagon that day to take a look at the unused house and store his father built. People had been tearing them down and taking the lumber, and he needed to decide whether to wreck them to save the lumber. He took Lottie and his mother along for the ride. Lottie was expecting a baby, and his mother was visiting them. She refused to consider it other than a visit, for she said she would live alone until her husband came back. She had been sick the winter before, but had continued to live by herself. When the three of them were driving back, as they came near the fort they met a straggling crowd going out along Beef Creek, going to see the Apaches who were arriving.

He turned and followed them. Two or three people climbed into his wagon to ride, and Slow Tom Armstedt, now a member of the Indian Police, rode alongside. They were all mostly curious, and some intended to joke or tease the Apaches a little, perhaps ask them how they enjoyed being prisoners.

The wagon train bringing the strangers from the railhead had stopped on a small rise of ground. The new Indians were getting out, for this was to be the location of their camp.

They were a sorry-looking lot, skinny, even sickly. Their clothes were thin and torn and they seemed to have hardly any baggage in the army wagons they had come in. They had no horses, nor mules, nor cows, nor sheep, not even a dog. They huddled together and looked at each other, stealing glances at the Comanches and Kiowas, then looking back at the ground, stealing glances at the countryside, then back at their own feet.

They spoke Comanche to them, and Kiowa, and bits of Caddo and Cheyenne, to no avail. They tried hand talk, but the Apaches obviously did not understand.

Joe saw among them a boy, nearly grown, whose hair was cut like that of a white man. On a hunch, he yelled in English, "Hey, Carlisle! Don't your people talk with the hands?"

The boy brightened and said, "No, they don't understand it."

"You have been in Florida, haven't you?"

"Yes, and in Alabama."

"Hey, Joe, ask them how they liked Florida."

"What did your people think of Florida?"

"They didn't like it. Too much water."

"He says they didn't like it. Too much water."

"Ask him did they like Alabama."

"What did your people think about Alabama?"

"They didn't like it. Too many trees."

"He says no good. Too many trees."

"How long have they been prisoners?"

"How long have your people been prisoners?"

"Seven years now."

Then the Apache boy ventured a question: "We have been wondering if any cactus grow here."

"Yes, a few prickly pears and catclaw. Also a little chaparral and Spanish dagger and mesquite."

"Hey, Joe, ask him which one is Geronimo."

"Which one of you is Geronimo?"

The boy pointed, and they were surprised, for Geronimo was as poorly dressed and as skinny as any of them.

"Hey, Joe, ask them if they intend to fight us anymore."

It was such a ridiculous question that he wondered whether he should ask it or whether he could find a way out to put it so that it would not sound sarcastic. But while he was undecided, a softhearted Comanche woman suddenly began to cry. Then an Apache woman who held a naked baby on her hip began to cry.

Someone said, "Tell them it's all right, Joe. This is a pretty good place to live. It's all right."

Joe's mother wore a knitted blue shawl. She went forward and took it off and gave it to the Apache woman with the baby and patted the woman on the shoulder. A friendly spirit came over them. They called back and forth and laughed at each other because they could not understand. They found that they had some Spanish words in common and they yelled these, mostly, *"Bueno! Muy buneo!"* They petted the women who had cried and laughed at them.

And so, while the Apaches were not exactly welcomed, neither were they rejected.

There was historical basis for the tale about the river battle. It had taken place somewhat less than two hundred years before, a long time for a people who have no written language, and enough time for the rise and fall of a civilization. During that time the two peoples had never faced each other so far north; this time it was the Apache who came from somewhere else into the heart of Comanche country. As they faced each other on this October day, a circle stood around them like the legendary circle of buffaloes, as invisible, as intangible, as real, made of white men.

The implications of it were not in their minds, but in their hearts. Some of them wept a little. The others, by their manners, said, "It's all right. This is a pretty good place to live."

Whenever Mr. Powell wrote, he always said that he was coming back. One of his letters read thus:

DEAR JOE,

I'm very proud and happy to hear the news, and I would like to see my grandson. I know that he is quite a boy.

I have had a little more trouble with my leg. After they took off the first part, it got worse, and finally they had to have another go at it. But it is doing better now. They say I'll be able to get around fine on a wooden leg, and I know I will.

I've been thinking about the boy, and I want to ask you a favor. Why shouldn't he have the last name of Powell? I would sure appreciate it. That goes for you too, because it's really your right name by the white way of naming. This is all up to you. Whatever you say. But I would sure appreciate it. I don't know how your mother is signed up, but it ought to be by the name of Powell. Tell her I think that would be right.

Tell her I'm coming back, by next spring at the latest.

Your friend,
JOSEPH W. POWELL

They were sick with influenza all over the reservation that winter. The doctor got some of them to come to the agency and others were put in the military hospital, but some of the older ones stayed in their camps to lie on their beds in canvas tipis and be treated by the medicine men.

Mary Little Brown Girl Cowbone Powell died of influenza. It was bitterly cold. Joe alternately walked and rode through the cutting wind with Freddy Bull, who had come with the sad news, back to the Iron Lance camp. He made the women unwrap her face so that he could see her once more. As he stared at the set features, he knew that a part of himself was gone as surely as if it had been cut away with a knife. Not only had she brought him into the world, but most of the care and love and concern that he had ever known had come from her. He realized that she had passed through, in her own mind and heart, the same era of violence and uncertainty and fear that he had known; and if he could be half as much a man as she had been a woman, it would be enough. He marveled at her strength, how she could have been so patient and persevering, so gentle and human.

They had come to accept burial in the ground. He chose her resting place on the rough rise south of camp. Oak trees grew thickly, but there was no grass, only broken chunks of granite littering the ground. It seemed bleak, but private. He took satisfaction in doing the hard labor of digging alone; then he let them take her and put her in the earth.

Back in her lodge, one of the women showed him the new buckskin jacket with fringe, also four new pairs of moccasins. His mother's message had been: "Joe will know who they're for." There was no mistaking the moccasins; one was for a baby when he is first taken off the cradle board, one for a young woman, two for men. He held the fringed jacket in his hands and wept and said to himself, "He shall not have it. Why should he have it? She waited for him twenty-five years and he wouldn't come back." But her presence was strong in her lodge with him and he could almost hear her voice saying, "Joe will know who they're for," and finally he whispered, "All right."

He gave her saddle to Freddy Bull. Each of her other possessions—her saddle, her rope, her blankets and clothes, her boxes and pans, her dwelling—he gave one by one to the neighbors, men and women. He took south with him only the buckskin jacket and moccasins.

The following spring Mr. Powell came back to live with Joe and Lottie. He walked very well on his wooden leg, and he spent most of his time playing with his grandson. As the boy grew old enough to be interested, Mr. Powell told him wild stories about the early days, which might or might not have been true. They played cowboys and Indians and never argued about who should be which, for the old man always wanted to be an Indian and the boy always wanted to be a cowboy.

One other activity occupied the old man. He went to see the Comanche men he had been acquainted with forty years before, to sit around with them and talk. They accepted him into their peyote sessions and called him White Buffalo. They had ceased to fight over the land division; in those days they were beginning to think carefully and discuss calmly what they might save that could never be taken away.

The Powells put the boy in a day school at the mission. On some days Joe took him on horseback; other days his grandfather took him in a hack. One of them went after him each day. Every evening Joe went over his lessons with him, then after the boy was asleep, studied ahead in the schoolbooks. On occasion he read him a story out of his book by a man named Aesop. Mr. Powell also helped the boy. Sometimes the three of them would work together on a lesson, all huddled over the oilcloth-covered kitchen table under the light of the kerosene lamp. Lottie laughed at them and accused the men of taking the boy to school only so that he would bring book learning home to them.

The white man's century turned over, and not long afterward each of the people was required to select his allotment of land. The government agents would not recognize Mr. Powell as a Comanche. Several chiefs swore that he had been born with them and had been with them all his life—that he was a full blood. He was white-haired now, had aged greatly, had become childish and sometimes wrongheaded; possibly he believed himself that he was a full-blood Comanche. But it was to no avail. The government agents would not give him an Indian allotment.

His buckskin jacket with fringe on it had become as molded to his form as if it had grown on him. He was never seen without it.

What he could not do, Lottie did. A week before the deadline she gave birth to a baby girl, and Joe selected the fourth piece of land to fill out a square mile for his family.

Then the reservation was gone. The settlers drew lots and came in, swarmed in. They built a town below the south agency, another up on the Washita at the north agency, another out in the Kiowa country beyond the mountains. They built roads and railroads. Every Comanche family came to have white neighbors.

As Mad Wolf had said, the older ones, the long-time warriors, lay down one by one, like old feeble bulls that are deserted by the herd. Mad Wolf himself went willingly to the Other Side during the winter after his long talk with Joe Cowbone. His granddaughter and the young couple sent a good traveling horse and a good war-horse along with him.

Old Yellow Bear had died in the Pickwick Hotel in Fort Worth while on a visit to the Fat Stock Show. When he was ready for bed he blew out the gas light and went to sleep.

Iron Lance had died in the same influenza epidemic that took Little Brown Girl. His brother, Duncan Bull, who lost every flu patient he treated, lived on to receive his 160 acres and to finally pass away of old age.

Chief Tabananica, the Voice of the Sunrise, was overcome with heart failure, caused by his running to catch a train at Anadarko, the new town at the north agency.

But Mad Wolf had also suggested that the others of them might go on alone. Whatever strengths in their blood had made them once lords of a great land were in them still. No people in all the history of mankind had faced a more difficult and painful dilemma. They wavered in anguish in a void between two worlds. Their frustration and sadness and hope were beyond the comprehension of those who had not faced it. Then one by one they packed their dearest treasures from out of the past, made bundles of them, took these bundles upon their backs and set out for the journey on what they called the white man's road.

431